Praise for the Novels
of Season Vining

"Season Vining has incredible taste in men. This quirky target and overly serious bounty hunter make an incredible duo. Things quickly heat up between the two with each turn of the page, and the undeniable physical attraction will make you beg for more." —*RT Book Reviews* on *Held Against You*

"If you love a good romantic suspense, then you will enjoy *Held Against You*. It kept my imagination piqued and the plot had many twists and turns that made this a very entertaining read." —*Cocktails and Books*

"I devoured this suspenseful sexy tale of the bounty hunter falling for his target. A sexy, heartwarming story." —*The Book Hookup* on *Held Against You*

"Heightened emotions, broken hearts, futures on the line, and running out of places to hide are all a perfect recipe for adventure. The romance is the cherry on top!" —*BiblioJunkiesm* on *Held Against You*

"I LOVED *Held Against You*! It was witty, entertaining, adventurous, gritty, and a very sexy read. Read this book! It will not disappoint!" —*Smut Book Junkie Book Reviews*

"Tristan is a hottie, [a] tattooed man who loves to read. Does it get any better than that?!" . —*Girls with Books*

"I never expected this book to grab a piece of my heart and not let go! I am still going through each of the characters and reliving

ALSO BY
SEASON VINING

BEAUTIFUL ADDICTIONS
HELD AGAINST YOU

PERFECT
Betrayal

SEASON VINING

ST. MARTIN'S GRIFFIN ≈ NEW YORK

PERFECT BETRAYAL. Copyright © 2015 by Season Vining. All rights reserved. Printed in the United States of America. For information, address St. Martin's Press, 175 Fifth Avenue, New York, N.Y. 10010.

www.stmartins.com

Designed by Anna Gorovoy

Title spread background image by Evelyn Flint/Texture Time

Library of Congress Cataloging-in-Publication Data

Vining, Season.
   Perfect betrayal / Season Vining. — First edition.
      pages ; cm
   ISBN 978-1-250-04880-6 (trade paperback)
   ISBN 978-1-4668-4987-7 (e-book)
 I. Title.
   PS3622.I57P47 2015
   813'.6—dc23

               2015016938

St. Martin's Griffin books may be purchased for educational, business, or promotional use. For information on bulk purchases, please contact the Macmillan Corporate and Premium Sales Department at 1-800-221-7945, extension 5442, or write to specialmarkets@macmillan.com.

First Edition: August 2015

10 9 8 7 6 5 4 3 2 1

THIS BOOK IS DEDICATED TO
EVERY DREAMER AND EVERY DOER.

(SORRY, DAD, THERE'S JUST TOO MUCH SEX AND
ILLEGAL ACTIVITY IN THIS BOOK TO DEDICATE IT TO YOU.
THANKS FOR ALL THE LOVE AND SUPPORT, THOUGH.)

acknowledgments

Thanks to the usual suspects, Bridget, Vanessa, and Lindsey, who read this in the early stages and offered up their brains to me when mine was spent. All my love to the Fuckery Book Club. They keep me together on days when there is no sanity left. A special thank-you to the hipsters on the N train (and New York City in general) for your inspiration and for providing phrases to look up on Urban Dictionary.

Rainbows and butterflies to Rose, who takes my hot mess mass of words and transforms it into a pretty, pretty princess. Crazy love to Rachel, who is the wind beneath my wings, the Sword of Gryffindor, and the sprinkles on my sundae.

To those who have known love worth fighting for, felt rejection that hurt like death, and still have hope, thank you for sharing your wisdom and strength.

1. fistfights and tomorrows

"Whoa. You chasing something away, honey?"

Levi set down his nearly empty beer bottle and looked over to find a pretty brunette perched at the bar next to him. She was an older woman, but attractive and well aware of it. Levi's gaze dropped to her cleavage before snapping to her eyes again.

"It's okay. You can look," she said, leaning over just a bit. "These babies cost so much, everyone should get a peek."

He chuckled and shook his head. Levi's knee bounced up and down, rattling the barstool. It was the only outward sign of the buzzing excitement inside his head. He downed the rest of his cold beer and waved at the bartender for another. When it was delivered, he swallowed half of it in one long pull.

"Definitely chasing some demons," the woman offered.

"Hell is empty, and all the devils are here," he said.

The woman placed her hand on Levi's forearm, her red nails tracing the lines of ink. "Let me know if I can help in any way." Her smile was infectious. Before he knew what he was doing, Levi was smiling back.

"What the hell is this?"

Levi looked over his shoulder to find a giant of a man glaring at them, his eyes focused on where the woman was touching Levi.

"We're just talking," she said, removing her hand and sliding two seats away. "Calm down, Gary."

"Don't tell me to be calm, Maggie." The man's chest heaved with deep breaths while his fingers stretched and curled into fists. Levi recognized the habits of a violent man. He grinned.

"You should listen to your old lady before you have a stroke or something." Levi finished his beer and swung around on his barstool to face the man now. Though Gary was only a little taller, he had about fifty pounds on Levi.

"Mind your business," Gary shouted. He turned to Maggie. "I work a double, come in here to grab a beer, and find you cuddled up with some piece of trash?"

Levi was on his feet in a flash. Blood pumping, adrenaline singeing his already frayed nerves.

"What the fuck did you call me?" Levi growled.

"A punk kid piece of trash that doesn't know when to shut his mouth."

It wasn't a conscious decision to throw the first punch. It never was with Levi. His temper was short, and once the fuse was lit, there was no stopping him. The cracking sound was heard even above the conversations and music of the bar. Levi wasn't sure if it was his hand or the guy's face.

"You son of a—" Gary roared, but he didn't finish his thought as he swung.

Levi was too fast for the big, slow beast. He dodged the man's effort and threw his right hand forward again, this time landing in Gary's gut.

"Oomph," was all the man could get out as he folded over in pain.

Levi felt the euphoria wash over him, the physical manifestation of everything churning inside him. The bar had gone silent now, and as he checked on the lady who started all this, he missed the telltale sign of Gary's retaliation.

The blow hit Levi's mouth, snapping his head back. Blood coated his tongue and he spit it onto the floor between them. He brought his thumb to his bottom lip and swiped away the crimson there. Gary was waiting, fists raised. Levi smiled, a dark and sinister kind of grin.

"Out! The both of you!" the bartender shouted. "I'll call the cops!"

Gary grunted and shoved his way out the door, giving up easily, while Levi reached for his wallet.

"Get out!" the bartender repeated.

"I'm just paying my tab."

Levi threw a twenty down and tucked his wallet away. He then turned to Maggie, who was still sitting at the bar, wearing a guilty look.

"Thanks. I really needed that." He shot her a wink. The bartender glared. "I'm going," he said, raising his hands in surrender.

As Levi stepped out into the cool night air, he felt empowered. He took in the boarded-up buildings covered in graffiti and the dark streets and knew that he would always belong here. In this impoverished neighborhood, Levi had always earned an honest living. He didn't have much, but what he had, he had worked for. He used to think there was honor in that. There were only two places to go from here, over to greener pastures or upstate to prison. Either way, Levi was determined to leave behind this life and start new.

Sometimes opportunities come along that call to your most basic desires—to be better, to take control. They are too tempting, too promising to pass up. Tomorrow would bring that opportunity.

Taylor moved around the edges of the room, the fruity drink growing warm in her glass. She wasn't interested in getting drunk tonight—though, the longer she stayed here, the more she wanted to drink. Bodies huddled in the middle of the room, dancing and grinding away their inhibitions, surrounded by antique furniture and priceless artwork. Each face she passed gave her a practiced smile, all wanting a piece of her.

"This party is so lame," Reese said as she leaned against the wall and stared out over the crowd.

"It is," Taylor agreed.

"So why are we still here?"

Taylor sighed and set her drink down on a nearby table. "It's our last party with these people. The end of an era."

"Thank God," Reese said. "High school is over. I'm going to get another drink. You want?"

Taylor shook her head. "No. I'll be out of here soon."

Beau spotted the girls from across the room. The crowd parted as he moved toward Taylor and her friend. By the time he reached them, Reese was gone.

"Where'd your BBF go?" he asked, his sandy blond hair standing up in all directions.

"It's BFF, Beau."

"Not with her. Bitch Best Friend. BBF."

Taylor rolled her eyes. "I'm ready to go."

"Already?" he asked.

People passed by, slapping Beau on the shoulder or offering a fist to bump. The girls looked at him with stars in their eyes, lovesick and completely docile.

"Aren't you tired of all this?" Taylor asked.

He leaned one hand against the wall and tipped back his drink. The permasmile and glassy eyes meant she'd be driving tonight.

"Tired of what exactly? Being loved by everyone? Being captain of the soccer team?" He lowered his voice and brought his lips to her ear. "Being able to land any girl I want?"

"And who do you want?" Taylor asked. She knew his answer. It was always her. And in this moment, she would take advantage of that.

"Let's get out of here," he said, like it was his idea.

Taylor nodded and turned toward the front door. The house was so crowded now, it was hard to navigate their way through. Mentally, she said good-bye to each person she passed, knowing that—with any luck—she would never see them again. Nameless faces who knew way too much about her passed in a blur. Good-bye, girl who copied Taylor's haircut. Good-bye, guy who always had gum. So long, chick who slept with teachers.

Once they made it outside, Beau led them through a maze of high-end cars until finally locating his. Taylor grabbed the keys from his pocket, unlocked the doors, and they both climbed in.

"No one drives my car," Beau said from the passenger seat.

"I'm not 'no one,'" Taylor clarified. "And you're drunk."

She rolled down the windows and backed out of the space. Just when Taylor put the car in drive, a group of boys blocked their exit.

"You're leaving? Dude!" one of them shouted.

"Beau, you can't go yet!" another said dramatically, throwing himself on the hood of the car.

Beau laughed at their antics while Taylor revved the engine.

"Move," she said through gritted teeth.

"But how can we party without the Party Master?"

Taylor honked the horn.

"Fine, fine. Just go!" a blond guy, still wearing his graduation cap, yelled.

They moved out of the way and Taylor floored it, leaving them all behind.

"How can you be tired of that?" Beau asked, a satisfied grin on his face.

Taylor shook her head and kept quiet. She didn't want any of it. She was exhausted from being this girl, playing this role. With their adolescence behind them, Taylor was holding out for something bigger and more meaningful. She was ready. With summer officially here, tomorrow would be different.

2. the look and the inside man

Monday morning, Levi used the provided four-digit code and waited as the large iron gate slid open. It creaked and groaned like an eerie warning of what lay beyond. The camera perched above the entrance looked down on him, and he felt judged. Levi kept his eyes averted, a nervous tell in this poker game he was anteing up to. He drove his poor excuse for a truck down the driveway and parked behind the garage as he was instructed to do. Before him was an enormous house surrounded by a perfectly manicured lawn, a tennis court, and a pool with accompanying pool house.

"All right, Levi. Can you hear me?"

Levi pressed the tiny earpiece farther into his ear, securing its place. He tapped the hidden mic beneath the collar of his shirt. "Yeah. Sound is good. You getting me?"

"Loud and clear," Kyle answered.

"What about visual?" Levi asked. He studied his reflection in the rearview mirror, smiling as the adrenaline worked over his nerves.

"Affirmative, hat camera is functioning. You ready to do this?" Kyle asked. Levi nodded, knowing his friend could see it. "You look like a fucking janitor, dude."

"I look like your fucking dad, dude," Levi replied.

"Hey! You leave that dirty bastard out of this."

Levi laughed and exited the truck, slamming the door behind him. He adjusted his hat and straightened his posture as he readied himself to start his first day as head of maintenance at the Hudson residence.

Henry Hudson III had a lot of money—a shit ton, actually. The Boss got the inside scoop from Hudson's ex–financial adviser that Henry was overly paranoid. Against the advice of his accountant, he kept more than $15 million in cash inside the home. Rumor was that more than anything he feared a financial collapse and refused to risk his family's wealth by keeping all their funds tied up in the market. Some people called him crazy, some thought he was the smartest bastard alive. Either way, when they were done with him, he'd be $15 million lighter.

Growing up, Levi knew they were poor. Their home was old and in disrepair, but always clean. He almost never had anything new—his clothes, his toys, and even school supplies were often from thrift stores or yard sales. Still, Levi realized that their life wasn't so bad. He was kept safe, fed hot meals, and always made to feel he was loved. There was constant music and happiness in the home, even when his mother had gotten sick. To him if felt like he had everything he ever needed.

Levi made his way around to the front of the house. The words of a familiar song floated through his head as he followed the immaculate limestone path to the front door. This was his crutch, his calming device. The habit was Levi's anchor to calm, passed down from his father along with an inherited black lacquer 1939 Gibson acoustic. Melodies, poetry, any kind of rhythm kept his head cool and his focus sharp.

He rang the bell and wiped his palms on his green uniform pants while waiting. When the ostentatious door swung open, he was shocked to find a pretty girl smiling back at him. Her long brown hair was pulled into a braid that hung over one shoulder. She wore a uniform similar to his, and while it was much more flattering on her, it still looked like they worked in a prison.

"Hi! You must be Levi," she said excitedly, holding out her hand. He took it and shook once before dropping it.

"I am."

"Welcome to the Hudson compound," she said, waving her arm in a sweeping motion. "I'm Amanda, housekeeping."

"Nice to meet you, Amanda Housekeeping." Levi hit her with his most charming smile, the one he'd perfected in sixth grade. She actually giggled. "Wow. You have to wear the same uniform as me?"

"Minus the hat," she said. "I think it's a requirement of Mrs. Hudson, something about not being a temptation. Come on in." Levi followed her inside. "You can call me Mandy. I just loved your uncle Zach. He was the sweetest man and could fix just about anything. Oh, look at me talking like he's dead or something. I'm sorry."

"He was ready to retire. I'm lucky I got to take his place," Levi said, having a look around the large space. The foyer floor was marble with an intricate pattern centered below a chandelier. Everything was pristine and looked brand-new.

Mandy led them into the kitchen and motioned for him to have a seat at the island.

"Good Lord, her ass is fantastic," Kyle said in his ear. Levi tilted his head, startled by the sudden commentary. "How does an ass look that good in janitor pants?"

"I'd show you around myself, but I'm right in the middle of cleaning out the fridge." She gestured to a row of condiments lined up on the counter. "Let me page Curtis."

She approached a panel on the wall and dialed a three-digit extension. There were two sharp beeps and then a male voice came over the speaker.

"Yeah?" he said.

"Curtis, Levi is here."

"Great, send him back."

Mandy gave him directions to a shed at the back of the property, where Curtis, the head groundskeeper worked. Curtis turned out to be a nice guy and gave Levi the lowdown on what to expect from his job. Levi smiled and nodded like he'd never heard it before. His uncle Zach had worked here for almost twenty years. Anything Levi needed to know, he already knew.

"We got a picnic table out back," Curtis said while motioning over his shoulder. "Me and my helper have lunch there on nice days. Feel free to join us. Any tools or supplies you need will be here in this shed or in the garage. Nice lip, by the way. You get any hits in?"

Levi smirked, his fingers rubbing his battle wound. It was a little swollen and the cut was sensitive.

"A couple."

Curtis grinned and told him where to find his list of jobs each day and sent him on his way with a slap on the back and a mumbled bid of luck.

"That guy seemed sketchy," Kyle said. Levi's shoulders jumped, startled again by the comment.

"No, he didn't. And I don't think I'll ever get used to having you in my ear all day."

"What about that big scar down the side of his face? Looks gang related to me."

"We did background checks on all employees here. We know more about them than their own mothers do. Are you insinuating that a man is sketchy just because he has a scar?" Levi asked.

"Seems legit to me."

"And how would you know if his is gang related or not?"

"I don't trust him."

"Okay, well, I'm going to get to work on my job list while you get your paranoia in check," Levi said, making his way back to the house.

"Copy that. I'll be here if you need me."

As he walked, Levi thought about the real reason he was here. When his uncle's plan to retire was announced, the Boss had approached him. Levi was wanted for a scheme to rob one of the richest men in Southern California. Since he was a child, Levi had heard his uncle's complaints about working for the Hudson family. According to Zach, they were terribly selfish people who treated their employees like dirt. They used their money and privilege to live above everyone else. His whole life, Levi had wanted to punish people like the Hudsons. This was his opportunity.

Soon, Levi had persuaded his closest friends, Kyle and Crystal, to join in, and instantly they formed their own merry band of misfits. The three of them had known each other since high school, bonding over the course of a Saturday detention their freshman year. All had endured pain and loss in their home life. On top of that, the trio were all from the same neighborhood—where crime was rampant and money was not. They had what they considered a poor man's kinship.

For the last six months, the team had worked together, prepping for this job. They knew the house would be mostly empty all summer except for the daughter, Taylor. Their research had shown that she'd just graduated from high school and would be moving to the East Coast for college. She was valedictorian of her class and was active in several clubs. Other than that, they had no idea how much she'd be around the house or what kind of interference she could cause. Levi dismissed the kid, not worried about her presence one bit.

He reached the laundry room door and entered, wiping his feet on the mat. Pinned to the corkboard next to the sink was Levi's list of duties for the day. Curtis informed him that the list was made by other members of the staff and, when they were around, the Hudson family. He read over the list and the attached grounds map, then grabbed his newly appointed toolbox and headed outside.

The first thing on the list was a broken sprinkler head. Levi hummed a beat that matched his footsteps as he followed the diagram and set his tools down in the grass.

"This sucks, get to the good stuff," Kyle said, yawning in his ear.

"It might help solidify my position as a maintenance man if I actually maintain some shit first."

"Yeah, the Boss will be pissed if we screw this up before finding that safe. Carry on."

Now that high school was over, Taylor Hudson knew that she'd never again be a big fish in a small pond. She was okay with that. There was something refreshing about starting over, being a no one, anonymous.

The graduation party had been the same old scene with the same old people. Taylor felt no love for those lemmings who, for the past four years, desperately tried to befriend her because of money and status. She wasn't stupid, she knew that her status meant nothing out in the real world, but her money meant everything. It was a tedious job running that school, and she was more than happy to pass the ruling torch down to the next rich brat in line.

Taylor heard a snore and looked over to find Beau Upton on the other side of her enormous bed. Her eyes became slits as she stared at his sleeping form tucked beneath her down comforter. Among all the white fluff, the only thing exposed was one of his tan arms draped over a pillow. Beau let out another snore and Taylor rolled her eyes. He knew better than to sleep here. It was a self-imposed rule to keep him from smothering her. Also, Taylor's father would kill them both if he ever discovered that she was sleeping with the enemy.

Rolling out of bed, she trudged to the bathroom, passing her discarded cardinal red cap and gown on the way. She entered the shower and scrubbed away all the sweat, sex, and alcohol from the night before. As Taylor wrapped the soft cotton towel around her body and inhaled the steam into her lungs, she searched deep down for the transformation she'd been expecting since middle school. She always assumed that graduation meant she'd spin a cocoon between her and all immature, girlish things and emerge the next morning as a woman.

Taylor swiped the condensation from the bathroom mirror to study her reflection. She turned her head left and then right, lifted her chin and dropped it to her chest, but there was no physical difference. She didn't feel different at all, still the same rich girl in the same empty house with the same absent parents.

Throwing her blond hair up into a messy bun, she pulled on some yoga pants and a tank and stepped back into her room. She crawled into bed with Beau and checked her phone. Thirty-seven text messages, nine voice mails, and fourteen missed calls waited for her. She huffed and tossed the phone away, not wanting to deal with any of it.

"Mmmmmm." The moan came from the other side of her bed, a low growling sound from beneath the covers.

"Beau! Get up!"

He raised his head to glare at her, a patch of bed head and two deep blue eyes appearing over a mound of pillows.

"You're such a bitch in the morning," he growled, throwing a pillow at her head.

"Correction, I'm a bitch all the time. Now get going before Suzanne finds you. I swear I can't tolerate her I'm-disappointed-in-you look one more time."

"Aww, Suzy loves me. She just needs to get laid or something and she might lighten up."

Taylor crawled across the bed and straddled his naked body. Beau still had a round childlike face, but everything else about him was muscled and hard. He was the all-American, soccer-playing wealthy boy next door. He was intelligent—salutatorian of their class, just behind Taylor—and owned a smile that could outshine even Prince Charming. He was everything any girl could ever want. Any girl but Taylor.

"Can we not talk about Suzanne's sex life?" she asked while raking her nails lightly down his bare chest.

"Whatever you say. I'm much more interested in your sex life anyway," he answered, lifting his hips to show her just how interested he was.

"Beau, you are my sex life," Taylor said simply. He smiled and rolled her over, pinning her beneath his warm body.

"Yeah, until you leave me in August." He placed feather-light kisses on her neck as she opened her thighs and wrapped her legs around his hips.

"I'm leaving for college. Not everything is about you."

Beau straightened his arms and held his body above hers.

"Lies! Lies!" he yelled.

"Shhhh!"

Beau laughed and rolled them back over so that Taylor was stretched out on top of him. The way his arms held her, the way he looked at her, told Taylor that he was in this far deeper than she was. But the selfish side of her just couldn't let go. Even though she didn't love him, she couldn't deny how amazing it was to feel wanted by someone who truly knew her.

He peeled her clothes off piece by piece, kissing each new bit of flesh until she was a wanton mess. Over the next hour, they consumed each other lazily. When her third orgasm hit, Taylor felt drugged and euphoric. Beau fell beside her, his heaving breaths painting her shoulder with warmth. When the feeling in her legs returned, she untangled herself from the sheets and cleaned up in the bathroom. She threw on some new clothes and returned to find him still lounging in bed.

"Henry would flip if he found you here," Taylor said.

"Your dad can't really expect us to stop seeing each other just because of a business deal gone bad."

Beau pulled his jeans on and buttoned the fly while watching Taylor closely.

"We're not seeing each other."

"I see you now," Beau insisted, his voice a bit too wistful for Taylor's liking.

She had never developed feelings for the boy. They had been friends since they were toddlers. He was just a familiar place to find comfort and satisfaction. Beau was one of the few people she trusted. These things, along with the fact that he was forbidden fruit, made him all the more appealing.

"You've really got to go," Taylor insisted.

He frowned at her, but she dismissed him with a wave of her hand. It was the same routine every time. She pretended not to see the hurt in his eyes and he pretended that it didn't bother him, each of them perfecting the lie. For some torturous reason, he always came back for more.

When the door closed behind him, Taylor stepped out onto her balcony overlooking the pool and back lawn. The sun was shining and there was not one cloud dotting the Southern California sky. She smiled and lit a joint, knowing that it was going to be a good day. Of course, any day that began with three orgasms was promising.

Taylor settled into a chair and pulled the smoke into her lungs, letting it burn for a while before releasing it. It was punishment for her behavior toward Beau, something she both relished and loathed.

Summer had officially arrived, and while most of her classmates would head off to other countries before college, Taylor was stuck at home. Her mother, Virginia, wanted them to tour Europe together, but the thought made Taylor want to gouge her eyes out. There was nothing desirable about flitting from country to country with her drunk mother who tried to seduce men in every language. So she lied and said she wanted to stay home this summer to plan her first semester at Harvard.

Even with her absentee parents, Taylor didn't complain. They paid her credit card bills and kept her well equipped to live the lifestyle to which she'd grown accustomed. From the outside looking in, they seemed perfect, a loving little unit.

It had been this way as long as Taylor could remember. Her parents had never reprimanded or disciplined, hugged or congratulated their daughter. Her entire life had been run like a business account, an investment of sorts. She was constantly told to be the brightest, look the prettiest, pay attention, and do better. It wasn't because they wanted what was best for her; it was all about appearances.

Taylor crushed the last bit of her joint into the ashtray and blew out a lungful of smoke. The door to her bedroom flew open, and she turned to see Suzanne come barreling in. The tiny woman ran around Taylor's room, mumbling to herself while picking up clothes and stuffing them into a basket she carried. She tore the sheets from the bed and threw those on top of the clothes before stepping onto the balcony.

Suzanne stood, with her hands on her hips and hit Taylor with the Look. It held all her disappointment and worry for the girl. Although it was fierce, Taylor had seen it far too many times for it to be effective.

"What on earth are you wearing?" Taylor asked, containing a giggle.

Suzanne looked down and pulled the hem of her oversize top away from her. Its bright mosaic pattern made Taylor dizzy.

"What? You don't like it?"

"It's tragic, Suzanne. And three sizes too big."

"Well, I don't like my clothes to touch me."

Taylor let out a laugh and leaned back in her chair. "What does that even mean?"

Suzanne shrugged and propped herself against the balcony railing. A few tendrils of hair escaped from her bun and whipped around in the breeze.

"Thanks for attending my graduation ceremony," Taylor said. "And for clapping and whistling when my name was called like you were at a Justin Bieber concert."

"Don't be silly, I would never go to a Justin Bieber concert. You know I wouldn't have missed it for anything, sweetheart." Taylor nodded and looked up at the sky. "I'm sorry your parents couldn't make it. I'm sure they're very proud of you, Taylor."

"At least they're consistent, right? Why should they start taking an interest in me now? It doesn't matter anyway," she answered, shrugging. Suzanne ran her fingers through Taylor's hair and placed a kiss on her forehead. It did matter, but she tried to convince herself otherwise.

"That boy was here again."

"His name is Beau," Taylor replied, chewing on her thumbnail.

"I don't care if his name is George freakin' Clooney. Well, I might care a little. You know how I feel about that salt-and-pepper-biscuit of a man. But that's not the point, you know Beau can't be here."

Taylor looked up at her, feeling a tiny bit guilty. "Suzanne, Henry is never home. He leaves before sunrise and that's if he even comes home at all." She sighed and sank back into her chair. "Work keeps him tied up, and so does his sassy little personal assistant. So unless you're going to report to my father who I've been sleeping with, I think we're safe."

"And what about Virginia? You think your mother would approve?"

"I think my mother doesn't care much about anything other than her next procedure. Honestly, Suzy, you were hired to look after me when I was still in the woman's womb. Even then she knew how inadequate she'd be as a parent."

The exasperated woman threw her hands up and stomped back into the room.

"Maybe next time Beau leaves he could bring down your sheets with him. Save me the trip," Suzanne called out.

"And miss the chance to see your beautiful face? I don't think so."

Taylor stood and watched as a man dressed in the Hudson green uniform strolled across the back lawn. She couldn't see much with his hat pulled down low over his eyes, but his wide shoulders and confident walk certainly got her attention. He stopped at a spot, knelt down, and opened a toolbox. Taylor eyed the half tattoo sleeve peeking out from his uniform shirt on his right arm.

"I thought the maintenance guy quit?" she yelled to Suzanne, who was busy in Taylor's closet.

"Zach didn't quit. He retired."

"So who's that in the yard?" Taylor asked.

Suzanne made her way to the balcony and stood at the railing. At four eleven, Suzanne didn't have the same vantage point as Taylor. She strained her neck to look.

"I can't remember his name. Calvin? No, that's not right. Jean? I don't know. It's some kind of clothing. I didn't realize he'd be starting so soon. Anyway, that's the new guy."

Taylor's eyes slid over him. While the hideous uniform did little to show off his body, she couldn't help but wonder what that tattoo led to under there.

Suzanne pursed her lips and cut Taylor a suspicious look. "Taylor, why the sudden interest in the maintenance man?"

"I always take an interest in the goings-on of the house," she said without looking away. "I have no idea what you're talking about."

Suzanne rolled her eyes and returned to Taylor's room. There was no response, and a few seconds later her bedroom door slammed shut. The sound echoed through the room and across the lawn. New guy whipped his head toward the *bang* and caught her watching, then returned to his work.

Taylor leaned over the railing, putting her chest on display while pulling her hair down and dragging her fingers through it. She kept her eyes on him, willing him to look her way again. Minutes went by while her stare burned into his skin. Finally, he closed his toolbox and stood, dusting off his knees. Taylor tipped over a bit more and wet her lips, anticipating his attention.

He walked toward the garage, crossing the lawn in front of her. Just when she thought he was going to ignore her completely, he looked up. Taylor held her breath as his shadowed eyes connected with hers. There was an instant pulsing tension in her body when one side of his mouth lifted up into a lazy smile. He shook his head and released her from his gaze.

Taylor flopped into the lounge chair thinking maybe this summer might not be a total loss after all.

3. the new guy and introductions

"This is boring," Kyle said through the earpiece.

Levi set down the boxes containing new lights to line the front walk and scratched his chin. "Would you shut up?" he said. "You're sitting at your house, probably in your underwear, watching me work. Yes, it sounds so painful for you to endure."

"You know me so well."

"I know you like long walks on the beach, romantic comedies, and the soulful sounds of Kenny G," Levi answered.

Kyle was a tech geek. If it was electronics, he knew it inside and out—computers, gadgets, devices, anything he could get his hands on. He never talked about his home life, only his Internet girl-friends and latest downloads. He was intelligent to the point of being socially awkward and easily became the brains of the operation.

"Shut it, you two," Crystal chimed in. "I've hacked into the Hudsons' video surveillance system. I'm rerouting the outgoing feed to come to me before going to the security company. It was too easy. There are cameras everywhere but in the bedrooms and bathrooms. So watch yourself. We need a heads-up before you do recon."

Crystal was a tall, fiery redhead who had been labeled as the Bully Whisperer in school, saving geeks from beatings on a daily basis. Her sweet face often misled people, and they weren't prepared for her sharp wit and quick thinking. She was a no-bullshit kind of girl who had the ability to insult you in a way that had you thanking her for doing so. Inside she was a sensitive introvert who loved rap music and reading the articles in *Playboy*. She served as the heart of the heist.

Levi was the inside man. He was supposed to go in and lull everyone into a false sense of security before pulling the $15 million rug from under them. He had been working since he was sixteen years old, holding various jobs from mechanic to salesman, each one contributing to his experience for the position here. The Boss trusted him to get the intel needed to make this heist a success.

"All our prepping comes down to this," Levi said into the mic.

"Who are you talking to?" a female voice asked from behind him.

Levi spun to find a gorgeous girl staring at him. She was pretty, but in a money kind of way. Wild, curly hair framed large brown eyes and a pouty mouth that frowned at him. Barely there shorts and high heels made her legs look endless. His eyes took in every inch of her flawless cocoa skin.

"Uh. Myself. I said I've got to take a piss," he answered, though it sounded more like a question.

"Nice," she said, raising one perfectly arched eyebrow. The girl made her way past him and entered the front door without knocking.

"Who was that?" he asked Kyle.

"I'll find out and get back to you. We don't need any surprises. But, damn, this place is like Hot Babe Wonderland."

"How eloquent, Kyle. Any other observations you'd like to share?" Levi asked.

"Bite me, Reference Desk."

Chuckling, Levi got to work installing the solar-powered lights along the edge of the front walk. As the sun climbed higher in the sky, it started to warm up. He used a red rag from his back pocket to wipe the sweat from his neck and forehead before tucking it back in place. This rag wasn't issued as part of his uniform. It had belonged to his father many years ago. Levi's earliest memories of the man consisted of him bent over the hood of their crap car in the driveway with a red rag hanging from his shirt pocket like a mechanic's boutonniere.

"Okay, Levi. Beyoncé's mini-me is Reese Sutherland. She graduated with Taylor Hudson. Apparently, they are BFFs," Kyle said, imitating a girl's voice.

"How the hell do you know that?"

"I have their yearbook. She was voted Most Likely to Be Famous, was active in the Gay Straight Alliance, and was captain of the dance team."

Reese and Taylor emerged, both wearing oversize sunglasses and toting logo-emblazoned purses. Wavy blond hair fell to the middle of Taylor's back, just where her waist pulled in. Levi's eyes slid around her curves and up to her face, getting distracted by the movement of full pink lips as she spoke to her friend.

"Please tell me Taylor Hudson is eighteen," Levi said into his mic.

"Yeah," Kyle answered. "As of January. Why? You thinking of mixing business and pleasure?"

"No. Just feeling guilty for my thoughts. Damn."

"Who wears shoes like that in the middle of the day?" Kyle asked.

"Shoes? I can't get past those legs," Levi mumbled.

Both girls passed him without a second glance, and he was thankful for it. It was best to remain undetected and off their radar.

"Fantastic ass," Kyle said.

"Which one?" Levi asked.

"Excuse me?" Taylor said, stopping and turning to face Levi.

"Uh, I said this is *no fun*. I'm struggling with these lights," Levi answered from his spot on the ground. He gestured to the mess of light fixtures.

Taylor turned toward him slowly. There was nothing timid or apprehensive in the way her body moved, and it wiped out all efforts to look away. She placed a hand on her hip and leaned over so that their faces were at the same level.

"Don't worry, New Guy. You'll get it." She smiled at him and headed for the driveway with a lot more sway to her hips. *Temptation is the fire that brings up the scum of the heart.*

Levi breathed a sigh of relief and sat back on his heels. His pulse was thunderous, and he knew it was from more than the summer heat.

"I told you he was hot. Did you see his tats?" Taylor said to her friend.

"Are you serious?" Reese shot back. "Taylor, he's the help. And he is so weird. He probably got those in prison, you know." Both girls climbed into Reese's car and buckled up.

"Mmm. I would lick the skin off that man."

"And probably catch some kind of disease," Reese said, rolling her eyes.

"How old do you think he is?" Taylor asked.

"Does it matter?"

"No," she answered. "He's fuckhot."

"First, that's not a real word," Reese said as she turned the car around and headed down the driveway. "Second, you're delusional and have no standards. He's the handyman, for Christ's sake."

"Like your standards are any better. At least the guys I want are born in the same decade as me."

"Hey! I can't help it if I find older men attractive. Besides, they're good to practice on until I find my trophy husband."

"There are older men and then there are fossils. Gross."

"Mature, desperate men with bottomless pockets are not gross. Your maintenance man is gross. What will you do after you guys hook up? It might get a little awkward when he comes to change a lightbulb or unclog your drain."

"Girl, he can unclog my drain anytime," Taylor answered.

"Be serious!" Reese said. "Not to mention your father would fucking die."

"Oh, that's reason enough for me." Both girls laughed, but it felt empty.

Taylor's phone buzzed and she fished it out of her purse, checking the screen.

"Yes?" she answered, already annoyed.

"Hi, Taylor. It's Nadine." The woman's voice was too sweet, sickening.

"And what message would my father like to relay through his personal assistant today?"

Nadine huffed before continuing, her cheerful attitude unchanged. "Mr. Hudson wanted me to remind you of the museum gala tomorrow night."

"Right." Taylor's grip tightened on her phone as she remembered another social event she'd be forced to attend in her mother's absence.

"It's at seven o'clock at the Four Seasons, downtown. He'll be working late, so I'll have a car pick you up."

"Of course he's working late. Is that all?" Taylor asked, throwing an annoyed glance at Reese.

"Yes. Have a great day, sweetie."

She rolled her eyes and threw her phone back into her purse after ending the call.

"Nadine the Slut Machine?" Reese asked, using the nickname invented during a drunken night of girl bonding. Taylor nodded.

Taylor wasn't sure where all the hostility for her father's number-one employee came from. Henry always had some young girl around, sticking it to her at the office or in some four-star hotel. However, this woman bothered Taylor more than any of the previous ones. Maybe it was her tiresome positive attitude or her bargain knockoff shoes. Whatever it was, the mere mention of the woman's name irritated her.

Taylor's therapist said that she was unjustly misdirecting her anger. He pointed out that Taylor was disappointed with her father for being absent from her life and for constantly cheating on her mother. He insisted that she was taking out her frustrations on that poor innocent woman. Nadine made her whore bed. As far as Taylor was concerned, she could lie in it.

"So, Beau was totally wasted last night?" Reese asked.

"Yeah. Don't worry, I took care of him."

"I bet you did."

Taylor sighed and closed her eyes. The kind of relationship they had was supposed to be simple. It was all about pleasure and no emotions. On her end, anyway. She couldn't help but wonder if she could ever learn to love him, or if there was something more out there just waiting to grab hold of her.

"I'm kind of tired of playing this game with him. Maybe I should find a new man."

"You'd cheat on Beau?"

"You can't cheat on someone you're not dating, Reese. He's my friend, and my father hates his father. What we have is a purely physical relationship."

"I don't get you, Taylor. You could have any guy. Why do you string him along?" Reese turned onto the highway and pointed them toward South Coast Plaza.

"I don't. He knows how things are."

Taylor laid her head against the seat and pushed down the guilt that tried to take hold. She knew what Beau wanted. He wanted a commitment from her, but it wasn't something she was willing to give. And even though she was happy to keep him to herself for now, a small piece of her worried about her lifelong friend. Their relationship was too off balance, and eventually he would get hurt. The thought alone created a lump in her throat. Though she didn't love him like he did her, she didn't want to cause him pain.

She pondered the idea of being with just one person for the rest of her life. The notion left her feeling smothered and miserable. With no real role models, Taylor never saw the appeal of monogamous relationships. Even before she was having sex, she had two or three boys waiting around to carry her books or ask her to the dance. She never made promises to any of them, always honest about her intentions. Those guys all wanted a piece of her and were willing to get it on her terms.

After puberty hit, Taylor's awkward, skinny body filled out. Her sharp angles became curves, and every boy seemed to take notice.

It was then she learned she could use her body to get anything she wanted. Boys were easy. A touch here or a smile there, and they were putty in her hands.

"All right, Kyle. I'm finished with the lights, and the Hudson girl is out of the house. Want to work on some layout?"

"Sounds good. Give me a minute to pull up this software and let Crystal know to loop the current video on all cameras."

With the next item on his list being a broken fixture in the master bathroom, Levi finally had an excuse to work inside. He cleaned up his mess before making his way to the front door.

"I'm heading in. Are we go?" Levi asked as he opened the door.

"Crystal, here. Video is a go. I took a few seconds of feed from the empty rooms and will loop them until you are finished searching."

"Use the digital laser measurer to get the size and then a sweeping visual with the hat camera," Kyle said.

"Copy that."

Stepping into the foyer, Levi sighed as the cool air hit him. He wiped his face with the red rag and tucked it back into his pocket. Spinning in place, Levi tried to decide where to start in the massive space. They had acquired a set of blueprints for the house but later found out that major renovations and additions had been done since. The team assumed that was when the safe was installed.

The furniture here set the feel for the rest of the house. It was expensive and modern, completely pretentious as far as he was concerned. Levi would take his Goodwill sofa and lawn chairs over this stuffy shit any day.

Not seeing any other employees about, he made quick work of the bottom floor of the house. He crept from the dining room to Suzanne's bedroom, giving Kyle the size, cataloging the layout and possible hiding places. Levi noted that her room was the only place in the whole house that felt comfortable. There were photos of Taylor scattered around, along with well-used furniture and an antique mirror. The urge to check behind every piece of art and look under every rug gnawed at him, but the Boss insisted on surveying the entire layout before beginning the search.

His pace was fast and thorough until he reached the study. As soon as he entered the room, his breath abandoned him along with every thought of the job. Two entire walls were covered in shelf after shelf of books, with the back wall being completely glass. New books, old books, reference books, and first editions flew by as his fingertips slid along their spines. He smiled and his eyes shone as he was transported back to his childhood. The smell of ink and paper returned Levi to a time when he sat tucked into a leather chair at the public library where his father worked.

After his mother died, the school bus would drop Levi off directly in front of the library. His father worked until closing, so he would have to stay until all the books were put away and the building cleared. There were always ladies around to help him with his homework or keep an eye on him. That place became his second home. Levi had spent many evenings there, combing the aisles until something caught his eye.

When he was eight years old, he found a nice secluded corner on the third floor, and that was where he read until his father came to fetch him. Levi had allowed reading to give him an escape from his own troubles, letting stories transport him to a different life. Then something happened and he grew out of reading, more interested in girls and video games.

"No," his father's voice echoed in his memory. "Put this finger here and your middle finger there. That's right."

Levi fumbled to get his hand in the right position and then

strummed the strings. He smiled when the G chord sounded perfect.

"Sweet. When are you going to teach me a song?" he asked. "I want to learn 'Here Without You' so I can play it for Michelle Coleman at the talent show."

"Michelle Coleman, huh? Is she pretty?" his father teased. Levi blushed. "You know you have to learn the basics first. It's all about breaking down the chords. You learn how to play. Not how to play a song."

His dad left him at the kitchen table, still practicing the two chords, and went to stir whatever boxed dinner they were having that night. Levi's brow dipped low as he concentrated on finger placement and moving back and forth between the two chords seamlessly.

"Good job," his father said. He wiped his hands on a dish towel and leaned against the counter. "You haven't been by the library in a while. The girls at work keep asking about you."

"Dad, please. I spent enough time there to last me a lifetime. Plus, I think I read every book in there."

His father threw the dish towel at him and frowned. "I doubt you read every book in the library. I bet you never read any poetry."

Levi made a face and threw the towel back. "You mean that girly stuff about love and flowers? No thanks."

"It's not girly. If you think that playing a song for Michelle Coleman would impress her, you should try some poetry." Levi's eyes widened, his attention captured. "We are Italian men, Levi. We come from a long line of wooers. Poetry has a cadence all its own. It can tell stories, declare confessions, and seduce lovers. Just like music."

"Poetry can do all that?" Levi asked, placing his guitar to the side.

"How do you think I married your mother?" His father winked

and returned his attention to the stove. Meanwhile, the seed had been planted, and Levi would never be the same.

Levi envied the way poets thought and their ability to express complicated emotions in such short, simple prose. Stanzas could always be molded to fit certain notes or chords. He'd spent many nights trying to translate the feel of a classic piece of poetry onto the strings of his guitar.

"Earth to Levi. Are you geeking out?" Kyle said.

"Absofuckinglutely," Levi answered, not embarrassed one bit.

A few minutes of silence ticked by as he stood in the middle of the room, taking it all in.

"Okay, you're on the clock here," Kyle reminded him.

Levi tore his eyes from the spine of what looked like a first edition of Poe's *Tales of the Grotesque and Arabesque* and stepped to the farthest wall. They got their measurements and moved on.

Walking into the sprawling kitchen, he found Mandy wiping down the countertops with earbuds tucked into her ears, the faint smell of lemon-scented cleaner in the air. The music was so loud he could hear the simple beat from where he stood across the room. Light from the window above the sink poured in, bathing half her body in gold. He smirked and recited the words to Mandy's rhythm as she shimmied and shook her ass while cleaning. It made him think of "I cannot dance upon my Toes" by Emily Dickinson.

I cannot dance upon my Toes—
No Man instructed me—
But oftentimes, among my mind,
A Glee possesseth me

"Wow, I could watch this all day," Kyle said.

"You need to get laid," Levi replied.

"You think sex with someone would make me appreciate a show like this any less? If that were the case, married men wouldn't have a need for strip clubs or porn."

"You're naïve if you think married men get laid," Levi pointed out.

"Then what's the point? I'm good with my Victoria's Secret lotion and subscription to kink.com."

Mandy didn't see Levi there, so he was able to sneak to one corner and provide the measurements and layout before trying to sneak away.

"Levi! Hi!" she yelled. She looked embarrassed and pulled the earbuds from her ears. "You startled me," she continued, lowering her voice. "Did you need something?"

"I came to ask where the master bath is."

"Oh, you didn't get a tour? I guess I was supposed to do that," she said, frowning. "It's a big place, but you'll learn it in no time. Go up the stairs, turn left. It's at the end of the hall, through the double doors."

"Thanks."

"Have you eaten lunch yet?"

Levi stopped. He hadn't thought about food, but now that Mandy brought it up, he realized he was starving.

"Nope."

"Have a seat. I'll make you a sandwich," she offered. His eyes darted to the stairs and back to her smiling face. "No worries. You're allowed a break."

Levi took a seat while Mandy disappeared into the pantry and emerged with a loaf of rye bread.

"Looks like you've got a fan," Kyle said.

"You sound jealous," Levi replied quietly.

"What?" Mandy asked, sticking her head around the refrigerator door.

"I said *I like lettuce*."

"Oh, good."

Kyle's laughter echoed in his ear as Levi grinned down at the countertop. A few minutes later, a sandwich on a pristine white plate slid in front of him and his mouth watered at the sight. Mandy leaned on the counter, resting her chin on her hand.

"Are you going to watch me eat?" he asked.

Her eyes widened as she snapped up straight, a pink blush crept into her cheeks.

"Uh, no. I'll just . . ." Her words trailed off as she pointed to another room and scurried away.

Levi practically inhaled the food, which he admitted was pretty damn tasty. How unfair that rich people even had better sandwiches, he thought. He dropped his plate in the sink and headed up the elaborate staircase to the second floor. Once up there, Levi spotted another housekeeper milling about, so he decided to do the layout later. He moved to the end of the hall and entered through the double doors.

"Holy shit! Now, that's what I call a bed," Kyle said.

In the middle of the largest wall sat an enormous four-poster bed covered in gold and white pillows. It was a large, bulky piece of furniture, masculine and overbearing. Levi thought it felt odd in the space of the room.

"Why would anyone need all those pillows?"

"They're decorative, Levi, not functional," Kyle answered, sounding bored.

"Thanks, Martha Stewart. Do you have a delicious recipe for goat cheese tarts you'd like to share as well?"

"No, but I can fold a napkin to look like a vagina."

Levi chuckled and shook his head. "You're special."

"Thanks for noticing, big guy," Kyle answered in a light and flirty voice. "Now get back to work."

After they got the layout and measurements of the room, Levi couldn't help himself as he checked behind portraits and mirrors. They knew that Henry Hudson would want to keep his money as close as possible. Though when he came up empty, he was not surprised. They all knew it would never be that easy.

"I'm going to work on this fixture. Take a break for now," Levi said.

"Copy that," Kyle answered.

He found the new fixture waiting for him on the bathroom counter. For a few seconds, Levi took a seat on the edge of the lake-size tub and absorbed his surroundings. Everything was marble and glass, sleek and clean with sharp edges and no privacy. This room alone was bigger than his entire apartment. He ran his calloused fingers along the smooth edge of the bathtub, and for the first time without bitterness he wondered what it was like to live this kind of life. Levi grinned at his reflection in the mirror and knew when they succeeded, he wouldn't have to wonder anymore.

After installing the new fixture and trashing the old one, Levi made his way outside. The next item on his list was a stuck garage door. As soon as he stepped outside, the heat engulfed him. He felt smothered in his stiff uniform and glanced at the pool, wanting to throw himself in the cool water.

"Don't even think about it," Kyle said in his ear. "You'd probably get electrocuted you've got so much gear on."

"Good to know you're back. Next time, a little warning, dick."

After blowing a few thousand dollars on summer dresses and handbags, Reese and Taylor stopped for a quick lunch at their favorite sidewalk café. Nothing like an $18 salad to round out an exhausting morning of shopping.

When they arrived back at Taylor's house, Reese pulled right up to the garage. The maintenance man was bent over inside. He did not acknowledge their arrival. With one foot, he stepped on a long metal bar to hold it in place and used all his strength to bend it. Taylor adored the look of concentration on his face, so serious and hard. Her eyes swept over the muscles of his arms, straining and pulled tight beneath those tattoos.

"You're drooling," Reese said as she parked the car.

"Huh? Oh," Taylor said, checking her reflection in the visor mirror before hopping out. She glanced in the backseat, spotting a mountain of bags just for her, and a plan formed. "Hey!" she shouted toward the garage. "Hey, New Guy!" His head turned toward her, eyebrows raised. "Could you help me with these?"

He stood and wiped his hands on his pants. "Me?" he asked, pointing to his chest.

When he stood in front of her, Taylor was overwhelmed by his rugged handsomeness. Cool hazel eyes looked down at her, framed by thick dark lashes. They were an icy mix of blue and gray with flecks of gold around the iris. His jaw was sharp and square, covered in a day's growth. He was much taller than she first thought, his wide shoulders hit right at her nose. Taylor was breathless as she drank him in. Reese honked the horn and both of them jumped.

"Uh, I couldn't possibly carry all these by myself. Could you help me get them inside?" she asked, brushing her bangs from her eyes.

"I don't know. I'm really busy with—"

"I'm sure you could make time for me, right?"

He looked at the house and back to the car. Taylor stepped out of the way as he grabbed most of the bags.

"Where to?"

She smiled victoriously and retrieved the last three bags. "Later, Reese. Follow me, New Guy."

Taylor moved smoothly and seductively, hoping he noticed the show as she led him upstairs into her room. She dropped her bags and threw herself onto her bed, kicking off her wedges.

"Where do you want them, Miss Hudson?" he asked, his voice wavering as he watched her stretch out on top of the white duvet.

"Next to the closet is fine, thanks," Taylor said, pointing to the door beside her bathroom. "And don't call me Miss Hudson."

As he walked over and placed the bags on the floor, Taylor hopped up from her bed and followed him. She imagined running her hands over his shoulders and what his salty skin tasted like. She wanted to feel that prickling stubble against her cheek and those hard hands touching all her softest spots. He spun to find her blocking his exit from the room.

"What should I call you?" he asked. His voice was softer now, deeper. It resonated with the craving inside her.

"Taylor," she answered, though it was barely a whisper.

He leaned closer, his head bent, lips near her ear. His warm breath ghosted over the skin of her neck and shoulder. The heat from his body penetrated her thin shirt. Taylor noticed her pulse surge at his proximity. She suddenly felt nervous and way out of her league.

"I'm Levi, not New Guy. And if you keep looking at me like that, it's going to be a long, disappointing summer, sweetheart."

In an instant, he was gone, and Taylor found herself clutching the wall and staring at the empty space where the manly scent of aftershave and physical labor lingered.

4. open mics and polyester blend

"To your first day on the job!" Kyle toasted. He ran a hand through his dark curly hair and clinked his beer bottle against Levi's.

Crystal joined in and raised her own bottle. "To the job," she and Levi replied.

They took long pulls from their drinks and leaned back in a corner booth of his favorite bar, Mavericks. The woman on stage sat at the edge of her chair, her long flowing skirt dusting the floor. She wore too many layers of clothes, scarves, and jewelry, but it seemed to work for her. The music she played floated around them. With one hand, Levi tapped out the notes on the thigh of his jeans.

The soft and smooth lyrics and amateur guitar playing brought the energetic mood down.

"So this is where you spend all your time, huh?" Crystal asked Levi.

"Haven't been in here in the last couple weeks. But yeah, it's the only place I haven't been kicked out of."

"Yet," Kyle chimed in.

"It's a cool place. I dig it," Crystal said. "Better than Cheney's. That place was getting skimpy with their drinks. I gave them the best drinking years of my life, and they gave me cheap alcohol hangovers."

"Let's get down to business," Kyle said. "So, we already have a complete layout for the first floor. Not bad for day one. We just need to get the second floor and then I'll start marking the most likely locations for the safe."

"Don't forget the attic and basement spaces," Levi said. "There are other buildings on the property, too."

"Right. I'll keep transferring the footage and measurements into the house schematics and rerouting the security camera feed while Levi keeps fucking around all day," Crystal said before taking another sip of her beer.

"What? I'm the only one doing actual physical labor," Levi defended.

"I don't know about labor, but I know you'd like to get physical with Taylor Hudson. Am I right?" Crystal said, wiggling her eyebrows. Levi blew out a breath and kicked Crystal's shin.

"I'm not getting physical with her. I'm stealing her father's money."

"Uh-huh," Kyle said. "I bet you nail her before the week's done."

"Are you assholes questioning my ability to remain professional?"

"No, we're questioning your ability to repeatedly turn down that hot eighteen-year-old piece of ass," Kyle teased. "Don't feel bad. I don't think I would have the strength. She's a legit ten on the hotness scale, man."

"Yeah, well that's because your last online girlfriend turned out to be a middle-aged mother of five from Wisconsin," Crystal said.

"Fuck off. Let's play pool."

"I can't," Levi said. "I'm up next." He nodded toward the stage. "I'm going to grab another beer. You guys need one?"

Both friends shook their heads. Levi slid onto a barstool and waited to get the attention of his favorite bartender.

"Wassup, Levi?" Gregory greeted. "Be there in a sec, man."

Levi watched as the bartender filled a drink order, offered his best smile and a little bit of flirting for his tip. Gregory leaned over the bar, flexing his biceps for the girl. He was pretty new to the gig but had this down to an art.

"I'll take another," Levi ordered, holding up his empty bottle as Gregory approached. He nodded, grabbed a beer from the cooler, and popped the top off for Levi. "Thanks."

"Haven't seen you around in a while. Where you been?" Gregory asked, leaning on the counter behind him.

"Been busy with a new job."

"Finally got a record deal? Signin' contracts. Gonna make that paper?"

Levi laughed and sipped his beer. Though he loved music, he never imagined that kind of success.

"Nope. You're looking at the new head of maintenance."

Gregory raised one eyebrow and lowered his chin toward the floor. "Where at?"

Levi shook his head. "Some rich family in Newport Beach."

"Ohhhhhh," Gregory said. "Well, glad you could come back here and slum it with these middle-class folks."

"I like the haircut. Barely recognized you without the braids."

"Yeah, well, that shit was childish. Figure if I want to catch a honey, they need to understand that I'm grown folk."

Levi laughed and looked to the stage. "Well, I'm up."

"Go do your thing, man," Gregory said.

Levi grabbed his father's guitar and stepped onto the stage. He took a seat on the stool and felt held in place by the white-hot spotlight. He strummed his guitar and adjusted the strings until each note was in tune. As always, he kept his eyes down, focused on his fingers and not the audience. The nervous energy that swelled in his chest dissipated as soon as the first words left his lips. Behind the mic, Levi could let go and give himself over to the music, the lyrics, and their rhythm. Here, in his element, he shined.

The alarm clock screamed at Levi to get up. He groaned and slapped the button to quiet it. After a shower and some black coffee, he grabbed his keys and left for the Hudson house. Just as he pulled into the driveway, his phone rang. He checked the screen and prepared himself.

"Boss," he answered.

"How did the first day go?" The voice was no-nonsense and sharp. There was never any small talk or casual greetings. The Boss always kept it professional.

"Good. We got the first-floor layout done. I'll try to finish the second floor today, after that, the basement, attic space, and outlying buildings on the property."

"Excellent. And the Hudson girl?"

"She won't be a problem," Levi insisted. "I've got this under control."

"I'm counting on it, Levi."

The call ended and he couldn't help but feel the threat in those parting words. The Boss had a lot of faith in this team, especially

Levi. While he believed in his own abilities, it was hard not to let doubt creep in. So much of the job's success depended on him, the pressure sometimes felt like clammy hands around his throat.

After he arrived at the house and checked in with Mandy, Levi spent the entire morning ignoring his job list and mapping out the second floor. There were two offices and four bedrooms total, with the two extra rooms looking as though they'd been uninhabited for a long time. Nevertheless, each one was decorated in the same expensive furniture as the rest of the house.

In Taylor's room, he tried not to think about her splayed across that bed. He tried, but was not successful. Now that he could take a closer look at the space, he found it odd for an eighteen-year-old girl's room. There was nothing personal about the space, no posters on the walls, only one photo on the dresser. It was a candid shot of a petite, middle-aged woman and a young Taylor in a dance costume. Her smile was different, genuinely innocent, but the same blue eyes stared back at him.

Taylor's bed was massive, and instead of being pushed up against a wall, it stood directly in the middle of the room, a centerpiece of sorts. When he finished, Levi left with one more parting glance at that bed.

There was a room on the second floor with a keypad next to the door. Levi tried the handle and found it locked.

"I can't get in," he huffed. Levi heard clicking in his earpiece. "What are you doing?"

"Flipping through the video feeds. Ah, yep. There it is. Looks like it's probably Henry's personal office. Huge desk, filing cabinets, and bookshelves. We'll have to figure it out later."

For now, they ignored the room and moved on. Levi followed the narrow staircase to the attic. As soon as he opened the door, the smell of stale air and dust overtook him. He could tell that the same dedication and care that was shown to the rest of the house was not carried out here. He stepped into the space and closed the door behind him.

There were a couple of attic vents that let slivers of light in, enough for him to make his way around. Boxes were neatly stacked in the corners, each labeled with a family name—Henry II and Eleanor Hudson. Antique furniture littered the space, most of it draped in white cloths turning gray from the dust.

"Well, this place is creepy," Kyle said.

"Yeah," Levi agreed while lines of Poe's *The Raven* raced through his head.

> *Deep into that darkness peering, long I stood there wondering, fearing,*
> *Doubting, dreaming dreams no mortals ever dared to dream before;*
> *But the silence was unbroken, and the stillness gave no token . . .*

"Let's get what we need and get out. I doubt a safe big enough to hold fifteen million would be in the attic anyway."

Levi stepped to the nearest wall and placed his laser measurer against it and watched the red beam appear across the room. He called out the number for Kyle to record and made his way around a large stack of boxes, repeating the process on that wall.

"Done here," Levi announced. "I'm heading back downstairs."

"Copy that."

When he turned to go, Levi's shoe caught on something and he fell on all fours.

"Damn."

The movement kicked up a swirling mess of dust and he choked on it. After coughing a few times to clear his lungs, Levi looked back to see what he'd tripped on.

He pulled the cloth away and found a child's wooden rocking horse. It was elaborately decorated with a lifelike mane and tail and glass eyes. There was even a saddle carved into the piece. It was painted pink with flowers along the edge and the name JULIA on the seat.

"Kyle, you still there?"

There was a long beat of silence before Kyle answered. "Yeah. What's up?"

"In all our research on this family, do you remember the name Julia?"

"Julia . . . Julia . . . no, I don't."

"Huh." Levi ran his fingers over the name before covering the rocking horse back up and getting to his feet. "I'm going to grab some lunch and get started on my work list."

"Okay, I'll check in with you later," Kyle said before signing off.

Downstairs, Levi crossed the main room. From there he could see Taylor laid out next to the pool. The plate-glass window ran along the length of the room, making it feel like he was standing outside instead of in.

She lay facedown on a lounge chair, the strings to her top undone and hanging to the ground. Her long golden hair was pulled to the side, hiding her face. Levi's eyes followed the curve of her back, over her round ass, and stopped at her toes.

"Do you often spend your time staring at teenage girls?"

Levi turned to find the woman from the photo in Taylor's room staring through the glass next to him. Her face was kind and attractive, with her brown hair pulled into a tight bun at the nape of her neck. The way she watched Taylor, Levi could tell she cared about the girl.

"Uh, no. I was just, uh . . ."

"I'm only kidding. She almost looks sweet and innocent when she's asleep, doesn't she?"

He turned and extended a hand to her. "Hi. I'm Levi, head of maintenance."

She slid her hand into Levi's and shook it. "Suzanne, head of Taylor."

Levi laughed, leaned against the glass, and tucked his hands in his pants pockets. "I didn't think anyone took responsibility for that," he said.

"Yes, well, it has been my job for the past eighteen years. Some days it's rewarding. Other days, I think I should have just gotten a Pomeranian. It's always been an adventure, though. After this summer, she'll be on her own." Levi felt the sadness in Suzanne's statement. "We'll have to say a prayer for the residents of Massachusetts when she attends Harvard in the fall."

"She's a bit old for a nanny."

"Henry tried to let me go when Taylor was twelve years old. She threw the biggest fit. So there was a compromise made. They changed my title to house manager. Ever since then, my salary has come out of Taylor's trust fund. She thinks I don't know."

"Wow," Levi said, looking back at the girl sunbathing. "You must be important to her, then."

Suzanne gave him a smile and nodded. "We're important to each other."

"I was going to grab some lunch. Have you seen Mandy around?"

"She's in the kitchen. Been waiting to see you all day," Suzanne teased. He sighed and leaned his head against the glass. "Don't worry, Levi. Mandy is harmless. But that?" Suzanne said, gesturing toward Taylor. "That's the one you need to worry about."

Levi held up both hands, palms toward her. "Hey, I'm just here to do my job."

Suzanne nodded but kept her eyes on Taylor. Levi left her standing at the window and made his way to the kitchen. Mandy stood over a pot, stirring.

"Hi, Levi." Her enthusiasm was off-putting, but the smell of whatever she was cooking made him sit down. She spooned something onto a plate and slid it in front of him. "Here. I made you lunch. Eat," she commanded.

After a few bites, he looked up to find her staring. "This is great. What is it?"

"Beef Stroganoff. It's my mom's recipe," she answered proudly.

"Wow. I've only ever had the Hamburger Helper version." Levi shoved another bite into his mouth. "This is much better."

"Well, I would hope so."

When the last bite was gone, he pushed the empty plate toward her and mumbled a thank-you before making a quick escape.

Taylor's skin felt like it was on fire. She lifted her sunglasses, wiped the sweat from her face, and lowered them back over her eyes. Even in her tiny bikini, the heat was too much to bear. She retied the strings around her neck before standing and stretching her hands high above her head. The burn and pull in her muscles reminded her to have Suzanne set up yoga sessions again.

She stepped to the edge of the pool and eyed the aqua water. Its surface was slick and reflective, showing a squatty distorted version of her against the sky. Taylor dipped her toe in and kicked at the water, making that Taylor disappear. Diving in, she relished the instant cooling effect the water offered. She swam to the other side of the pool, holding her breath until her lungs burned.

When she surfaced, she leaned her head against the edge and saw Levi's junky truck parked behind the garage. She smiled as she thought about his sexy smile and that vibrant ink covering one arm. Taylor hadn't seen him since their introduction the day before in her bedroom. As wrong as it might be, she wanted him.

And for the first time in her privileged life, she knew she was going to have to work for it.

She lay back in the water and floated, letting her limbs sway weightlessly. The sun heated her skin again, while the cool water beneath her made Taylor feel like a two-sided coin. One Taylor used cutting words to distance those around her. Not trusting anyone, she secretly wanted people to dislike her. It kept them from getting too close.

The other side of Taylor liked cheesy romantic movies, dancing around in her pajamas, and genuine smiles. She wanted everything to be simple and honest. Above all, she wished for happiness and for people to see past her surface. But her biggest fear was that, someday, someone might do exactly that.

Suddenly, her sun disappeared and she opened one eye to find Levi standing at the side of the pool. He didn't hide his appraisal of her body as she dropped her legs and stood in the waist-deep water.

"You're blocking my sun," she said.

"I'm supposed to clean the pool today."

"Well, don't let me stop you."

Taylor used the steps to remove herself from the pool, dried off, and took a seat on her lounge. She sat back, untied the strings from around her neck, and tucked them into the cups of her bikini top. Throwing on her sunglasses, she pretended to take a nap and not watch him work.

Levi moved around the pool, using a net to scoop out leaves and trash until he was back to where he started. He squatted down to check something, letting Taylor get an up-close view of his ass. An involuntary sigh escaped her lips. Levi turned at the sound as Taylor quickly closed her eyes, trying to seem uninterested.

"Do you enjoy watching people work?" he asked over his shoulder.

"Nope. Just you. You'd make a fantastic cabana boy, you know."

He faced her and crossed his muscled arms, the material of his shirt pulling tight against his biceps. "Cabana boy? Like one of those idiots parading around in a Speedo and having an affair with the housewife?"

"Or daughter," Taylor said, smirking. "Aren't you hot in all that polyester blend? Surely, you'd be more comfortable shirtless, in some board shorts?"

"This is my uniform."

"That's a shame. I'll have to talk to Henry about that." She raised her sunglasses and looked him over thoroughly. "Even that hat?"

"Especially the hat," Levi answered, tugging on the brim.

He grabbed the net and tucked it away in a supply closet before heading back toward the house.

"Leaving so soon?" Taylor asked, suddenly upset at his dismissal of her.

"Yes, Miss Hudson. I don't get paid to stand around all day and flirt with the boss's daughter."

"Flirting? Is that what you think we're doing? And I told you to call me Taylor."

Levi tilted his head. "What exactly are we doing, then, Taylor?"

"Foreplay."

His brows knitted together and his mouth pulled down into a bothered frown. He turned and disappeared into the house without a response. Taylor replaced her sunglasses, satisfied that even if he wasn't going to act on it, he was going to think about having sex with her.

Taylor sat stock-still in front of a mirror while her stylist, Robye, worked her over. Her reflection looked like a classic painting surrounded by a gilt frame and hung in a museum somewhere. When her makeup was flawless, Robye curled her hair, creating soft waves down her back, and pinned one side up with an antique comb.

"What is wrong with you? You seem tense. It's fucking up my chi. And, girl, I just got centered."

Taylor shook her head. "I just don't want to go to this thing tonight. Henry parades me around the room, introducing me to a bunch of stuffy old guys talking about their investment portfolios and what's happening in professional golf. Not to mention the married ones who hit on me while their wives are in the bathroom. It's like they're all part of the Asshole Club for Men and Henry is the president."

"Well, you are legal now. They'll be circling like vultures," Robye said. "You want to borrow my Taser?"

"No, I'll be okay." Taylor grinned. "I can't wait until I'm on the East Coast and don't have to deal with any of this. I'll be free from the Hudson name and legacy. I'll just be Taylor, that freshman in honors classes with the killer rack."

Robye laughed and eyed her chest. "The girls are pretty stellar. Not that I'm an expert. You know I like my chests hard and waxed. Anyway, don't take shit from anybody tonight. Not even dear old daddy."

He left her with a kiss on the cheek and a little gift of her favorite Chanel lipstick.

Taylor slid out of her robe and pulled the evening gown from her closet, laying it on her bed. It was a deep blue one-shoulder gown with a beaded belt. Taylor chose it because of its timeless look and the way it made her eyes shine.

"Want some help?" Suzanne asked from the doorway. "You'd have to be a contortionist to reach that zipper on your own."

"Sure."

Suzanne started pulling the gown out of the bag. "Wouldn't

that be neat? To be a contortionist, I mean. I'd love to be able to fit into a tiny little box. Imagine how easy it would be to paint your toenails."

"Just imagine," Taylor deadpanned.

She slipped into the gown and strapped on her heels before standing in front of the full-length mirror. Suzanne stepped next to her and admired their reflection.

"You look so grown up, so beautiful. Just like an after picture."

Her affectionate smile warmed Taylor yet made her uncomfortable.

"An after picture? Have you been watching *Extreme Makeover* again?"

"You know I love that show. If I could just get in on the ground level with one of those ugly ducklings before the makeover, I'd have me a hottie by the end."

"Dream big, Suzy."

"Always, sweetheart."

Suzanne patted her shoulder and disappeared from Taylor's side. Taylor slid her hands over her flat belly, enjoying the way the fabric hugged her body. The silk against her skin felt like cool breaths of air. The heels gave her a four-inch lift, elongating her already shapely legs. She thought about Suzanne's words. She did look older, more mature, like the woman she wished to be.

"What about these?" Suzanne said, holding her open palm toward Taylor.

"My grandmother's diamonds?"

Suzanne nodded.

"Perfect," Taylor said.

She put the earrings on and was immediately reminded of the afternoon she received them from her granny. Suzanne had taken Taylor to visit her grandmother at Henry's request. Back then he liked to pretend that family was important.

Taylor closed her eyes and remembered how the entire house

always smelled of baked bread and flowers. She envisioned her granny's dark green sofa covered in lace doilies and stacked with satin throw pillows. There were priceless vases and artwork scattered around the room. It always felt stuffy and at odds with her granny's sweet personality.

That day they'd spent the entire afternoon going through trunks in her granny's attic. Taylor remembered squealing as treasure after treasure was discovered. Vintage dresses with matching hats lay strewn across the floor as she pulled out shoes and handbags.

She slid on a small coat and spun around giggling as her granny looked on.

"Where's Grandad?" Taylor asked.

"He's at work, sweetie. Always at work," her granny answered with a sigh.

Taylor stuck her hands in the pockets of the coat and cocked her hip, giving a proper model pose. Granny smiled.

"You look lovely," she said.

Taylor's fingers wrapped around something in the pocket and she pulled it out. It was a gold locket necklace with an engraved *H* on each side. She pried the pieces open and looked inside, finding a black-and-white photo of a toddler with curls.

"What's that, dear?" Granny asked.

She showed her the photo and her grandmother gasped, her shaking fingers covering her mouth instantly. She took the locket from Taylor's hand and stared at it for a few minutes with watery eyes.

"Who is that, Granny?"

"Her name is Julia." Granny did not meet Taylor's smiling face.

"She's pretty," Taylor said excitedly. "Does she like tea? We could invite her over for our tea party!"

Her grandmother just shook her head and wiped a tear from

her cheek. Taylor didn't understand the sadness that seemed to weigh on her grandmother.

"What's in this one?" Taylor asked, distracted by another wardrobe locked and labeled.

"I don't know," her grandmother replied. "Let's open it and see."

"Can't you read it, Granny?" Taylor pointed to the sticker on the side of the wardrobe.

"Yes, but it's hard. Grandmother has trouble with words. Sometimes they just look like a jumbled-up heap of lines to me." Taylor was confused by that. She was only in second grade and she could read lots of words.

Her grandmother twisted the locks on each end of the wardrobe and began to pull it open. Her voice was soft, almost wistful. "I was raised to be seen and not heard, to be a wife to my husband and a mother to my children."

"Oh! I love this one!" Taylor yelled, distracted by a pink dress with a ruffled skirt.

Taylor slipped out of the coat and stepped into the dress. Her grandmother helped her pull on some short gloves and placed a hat on her head.

"Do I look beautiful?"

"Almost perfect," Granny replied.

"Almost?" Taylor frowned.

"You're missing something. But what could it be?" Taylor straightened the hat and tried to smooth the wrinkles in her dress. "Ah! I've got it." Granny removed the diamond earrings from her own ears and placed them in Taylor's. "Now, you're perfect."

Taylor smiled, her fingers tracing the diamonds adorning her ears. She leaned forward and traced the locket in her grandmother's lap, wanting so badly to try it on.

"You like the locket, sweetie?"

Taylor bit her lip and nodded. Granny draped it around Taylor's neck and clasped it. She ran her fingers along the chain and gently pressed the locket into Taylor's chest. "Then it's yours. But it has to be our secret. You can't tell anyone."

Taylor's tiny hand wrapped around the locket and she looked up at her grandmother.

"Not even Suzanne?"

"Not even Suzanne," Granny confirmed. "It'll be our little secret, just between the Hudson girls."

Taylor remembered how she felt that day, perfect and loved, part of a family. That was the last time she ever saw her grandmother alive. Over the years, Taylor had proudly worn her grandmother's earrings, but the secret locket still remained tucked away.

Looking at her reflection again, Taylor didn't feel any of the things she did then. She felt alone in this family, abandoned by people who should love her the most. She saw someone caught between who she was and who she wanted to be, someone constantly surrounded by the buzz and hum of the world but locked away in a tower.

"You better get going. The car is here," Suzanne said.

Taylor nodded and followed her to the stairs. Halfway down, she stopped in her tracks. "Shit! I need to grab a clutch."

She hurried back up the stairs and down the hall into her parents' room. Taylor flung her mother's closet door open and found Levi on his knees in the back of the closet. Already out of breath, she gasped and placed her hand over her heart to calm the furious beating.

"What are you doing in here?" she asked, her tone accusatory.

"I'm repairing this broken shelf," Levi said, holding a piece of wood that clearly belonged in the shelving unit.

He turned back toward the wall as Taylor started searching through her mother's things, throwing everything on the floor. Finally, she spotted her mother's Gucci clutch and held it up in victory.

"Found it!"

Taylor turned to find Levi's eyes on her. His gaze traveled down her body, and it felt like warm, rough hands on her skin.

"Like what you see?" she asked.

She cocked her hip and slipped her foot forward, letting her bare leg show through the thigh-high slit. He shrugged his shoulders and turned away, seemingly unaffected by her flirting.

"Just wondering who's going to pick up that mess you're making," he said, his voice laced with disgust.

"Someone who gets paid to." Taylor turned and stomped her way downstairs, where Suzanne rushed her into the waiting car.

5. louboutin and nurse taylor

On the drive home, Levi tried to drown out his thoughts with rock music so loud it rattled the windows. Even though the hard-hitting beat and guitar riffs soothed him, he soon realized it was no use. The thorough search of the master suite had gone great until they were interrupted by Taylor. Levi thought he was going to have a heart attack when he heard footsteps approaching. Needing an excuse to be there, he grabbed the shelf and yanked hard, ripping it from its brackets. Quick thinking saved him this time, but would it be enough next time?

Remembering the sight of Taylor in that blue gown, Levi

groaned and threw his head back against the seat. He cursed his reaction to the girl and vowed to get that shit under control. Taylor's attitude took away from her beauty and made him realize that she represented everything he hated about the rich: thoughtless and self-centered.

Levi had met Henry Hudson III only once, but it was enough to learn all he needed to know about the man. His interview for this job had been trying, to say the least. It had been in the middle of the day, in a secured building in downtown Burbank.

"Go on in and take a seat," the woman at the front desk directed. "He's expecting you."

Levi entered without knocking and looked around the sterile, unembellished space. He approached one of the leather chairs opposite Henry's desk and went to sit down. Henry frowned and shook his head.

"Don't bother sitting," he said before going back to his phone conversation.

Levi straightened his posture and waited. Henry continued to ignore him as he typed on his keyboard and frowned at the large flat-screen monitor. He finally ended his call, but continued to ignore Levi's presence.

Levi shifted from foot to foot, eyeing the two empty chairs before him. He crossed his arms and stared out the wall of windows to keep his temper under control. Emily Dickinson's "I had no time to Hate" became a repeating anthem in his mind.

I had no time to hate—
Because
The Grave would hinder Me—
And Life was not so
Ample I
Could finish—Enmity

Another few minutes ticked by before Levi cleared his throat and glared at the man in the expensive suit.

"You're Levi Russo?" Henry finally asked without looking away from his computer. Levi let his arms drop to his sides and stood up taller.

"Yes, sir."

Finally, Henry tented his fingers on his desk and turned toward Levi. The man's gray eyes barely glanced his way before dropping down to read a paper on his desk.

"You look young. How are you related to Zachary?"

"He's my uncle. My mother's brother." A long minute of uncomfortable silence sat between them. Levi knew it was Henry's way of retaining power, controlling the conversation. "You can call my previous employer if you need a reference, sir. I assure you, I can do the job."

Henry's eyes snapped to Levi, a menacing grin on his lips.

"And I assure you, I have already contacted your previous employer. I also completed a criminal background check. I don't take this lightly, Mr. Russo. I'm entrusting you with full access to my home, this includes my family. I expect you to remain professional at all times. Anything you see or hear at my home will remain confidential."

"Of course, sir," Levi said in his most controlled voice.

"My daughter, Taylor, will be home this summer. If she gives you any trouble, let me know immediately." Levi nodded, unsure what to think of that warning. "We're set, then. You're only getting this opportunity because of your uncle. I don't usually consider"— Henry paused, and this time his eyes settled over Levi in the most invasive way—"people like you. See Nadine on your way out. She'll give you all the details."

"The dark-haired lady out front?"

"The one that looks like she's begging for it? Yes, that's the one," Henry said, grinning. "She'll take care of you. She's *very* thorough."

Levi pulled into his parking space and killed the lights. Henry Hudson deserved to be taken down a notch or two. Levi would love to be the one to do it. If he could stay away from Taylor, they might be able to pull this off.

Just as Levi settled down on his couch with a cold beer and a microwave dinner, his phone rang. The familiar number displayed on his screen made his insides twist.

"Boss," he greeted.

"Levi. I hear you had a close call today."

The voice made him sit up taller and square his shoulders, an unconscious response to authority. Levi tilted his head back and stared at the ceiling with the phone pressed to his ear.

"Yeah, Taylor found me in her mother's closet," he said. "Crystal had already rerouted video feed in that room. And I invented a reason to be there. Covered myself. She wasn't suspicious."

"Good. See that it stays that way."

The call disconnected, and Levi stared down at his unappetizing food. He had no idea the Boss would be keeping such a close eye on their day-to-day operation. For some reason, it unnerved him. Though he tried to make it seem like it wasn't a big deal, being caught in that closet had nearly been his undoing.

Even with the scare, he had been unable to ignore the sight of Taylor in that dress. She looked like a vintage Hollywood movie star—all blond hair, blue eyes, and a body wrapped in fabric that looked edible. When her long leg parted the thigh-high slit, he had forced himself to turn away.

It was then that Levi realized Taylor Hudson might be a bigger problem than they first thought. She was tempting and off-limits, and that made her dangerous.

The next morning, Levi's alarm failed to go off and he was an hour late for work. He called and spoke to Mandy, who told him to take his time. It looked like it might be a good thing having an admirer on the inside.

When he made it to the house, he found Mandy and Suzanne having coffee in the kitchen.

"Make mine a double," he said as Mandy poured him a cup. She giggled and handed over the brew. "So, how long have you guys worked here?"

"I've been here six years," Mandy said.

"Do you like it?" Levi asked, sipping his coffee.

"I mean, most of the time it's pretty easy, especially with Taylor being the only one in the house. She doesn't bother us much. Not like when Virginia's around." Mandy rolled her eyes. "Geez, that woman is a tyrant."

"Aw, Virginia's not so bad, as long as you keep a martini in her hand." Suzanne laughed. "I've been here eighteen years, since Taylor was born. Feels like a lifetime."

"Wow," Levi said, looking her over. "And you don't look a day over twenty-five."

Suzanne put her mug in the sink and laid a hand on his shoulder.

"Flattery will get you everywhere, young man. If I was thirty pounds lighter and twenty years younger, you'd only kick me out of bed to do it on the floor," she said with a wink.

"Good morning, sunshine," Reese said, barging into Taylor's room. "Look who I found at Starbucks this morning."

Taylor closed her laptop and swiveled in her chair.

Adrienne Cavill followed Reese into the room. She had been part of their trio since they were eight years old. Though she'd grown a bit distant in the last few years. Reese said it was because Adrienne *thought* she was better than them. Taylor said it was because Adrienne *was* better than them. She gave Taylor a wave.

"We come bearing gifts," Adrienne said, dropping off a large vanilla latte on Taylor's desk.

"What's up, ladies? Ade, I thought you were delivering meals to kids in Africa or something this summer."

Adrienne squished up her face and shook her head. Her jet-black ponytail swayed against her back. "I was going to volunteer with Doctors Without Borders in Guatemala. It fell through. Now I've got nothing significant to show for this summer. Might as well hang out with you hags."

"Please tell me you're here to rescue me from boredom," Taylor whined.

"Ta daaaaaa," Reese sang, producing a bag with six rolled joints. "I brought herb, so you better be pleased to see us."

The three girls made themselves comfortable on Taylor's bed and lit a joint, passing it back and forth until it was finished. Adrienne and Taylor discussed big plans for when they attended Harvard in the fall and decided they should definitely get a dorm room together. An easy silence fell around them and Taylor was thankful for the high.

"You know, psychoactive chemicals are currently running through our bloodstream they're changing the chemical balance in our brains while releasing dopamine creating the euphoric feeling of being high."

"Thank you, Dr. Cavill," Taylor said. "But I think that was a run-on sentence."

"The Discovery Channel has helped prepare me for Harvard premed, not sentence structure."

"Sorry you didn't get to hook up with any hot doctors this summer," Reese said, patting Adrienne on the shoulder.

"That wasn't exactly the point of volunteering."

Taylor rolled over toward her friends. "What exactly is the point of volunteering?" she asked.

"I've been doing it since eighth grade." Adrienne shrugged. "It's rewarding. If you find something you're passionate about, then it's even better. Plus, it looks stellar on a college application."

"The only thing stellar on my college application was Henry's generous donation check to the Harvard Alumni Association."

"Remember in Beta Club when we had to volunteer at that youth center in Santa Ana?" Adrienne asked. Taylor nodded. "You seemed to enjoy that. You should look into it. See if they need any help this summer."

Taylor yawned and stretched her hands toward the headboard. She had enjoyed helping people learn how to read. It felt important, knowing that her grandmother struggled with it. She looked over at Reese, who had her eyes closed and a giant smile on her face.

"Reese! Are you sleeping?"

"No," she answered. "I'm picturing a tiny weed fairy delivering this high with little glitter sprinkles over our heads. She grants wishes too. But it never works out, because she's a bitter bitch. She twists your wish into something terrible while still giving you exactly what you asked for. I think I like her."

Taylor and Adrienne looked at each other and then burst into a fit of giggles.

"A fairy? What would you ask for?" Taylor asked, grinning lazily at her friend.

"For us all to still be friends like this in twenty years," Reese replied. Her usually large brown eyes looked small and sleepy. "You're the best person I know, Adrienne. Even if it is annoying at times. And Taylor, you're an unstoppable force of nature."

"I wish Levi felt that way."

"Hold up. Who?" Reese asked, lifting her head.

"Levi. New Guy."

"You're on a first-name basis with the maintenance man?"

"Wait, what maintenance man?" Adrienne asked.

"A new employee of my father's. He's gorgeous." Taylor sighed.

Reese sat up and scowled down at her friend. "Taylor, this is a new low, even for you."

"Whatever, Reese. Don't judge me. He's just so damn tempting. It's like I can't stay away."

"Why should she stay away?" Adrienne asked Reese. "If he's hot and she's available? Is your problem with his social status or lack of money?"

"Don't start with your Mother Teresa bullshit, Ade. Did you even try to stay away from him, Taylor?" Reese asked.

"He's been resistant to all my usual flirting. I'm going to have to step it up."

"I cannot believe we're even talking about this. He's disgusting."

Taylor sat up, facing Reese. She felt confused about the anger churning through her now. Of all the words she would use to describe Levi, "disgusting" was not one of them.

"Stop being such a snob," Taylor said. "I mean, he might be poor, but he's hot. And intriguing."

"Someone at your level shouldn't associate with trash. Stop slumming with the help just because you have abandonment issues."

Adrienne sat up and glared at Reese. "That was uncalled for."

Taylor flew off the bed and pointed to her door. "Get out!" she yelled.

"Excuse me?"

"You heard me. Get. Out!"

Reese climbed off the bed, grabbed her purse, and slipped on her shoes. She didn't give Taylor a second glance as she made her way to the door. Adrienne shrugged and followed her.

"Fine, Taylor, but you'll learn the hard way that just because you paint the sole of a shoe red, it doesn't make it a Louboutin."

"What does that even mean?" Taylor shouted.

Reese swung the door open and found Levi on the other side, fist poised to knock. She pushed past him and took off down the stairs. Adrienne gawked at Levi for a few seconds before scurrying around him and mouthing to Taylor, "Is that him? Wow!"

"Ade, are you coming?" Reese yelled from downstairs. Adrienne disappeared, and a few seconds later the front door slammed closed. Taylor motioned for Levi to come in, embarrassed that he might have overheard their conversation.

"Suzanne said one of your balcony doors is stuck."

His words were clipped, his shoulders stiff. Taylor could feel the hostility rolling off him. She nodded as he set his toolbox down next to the doors and checked the locks. He opened one side, but the other door didn't budge. Levi leaned into it with his shoulder, but it remained in place.

Taylor took a seat on the edge of her bed and watched him work. "It's been stuck for a while," she offered.

Levi ignored her and kept trying to free the door. He pushed and pulled, and checked the hinges and locks again. The more he struggled, the more Taylor felt his frustration grow. Whether he was upset with the door or with her, she didn't know. She also didn't know why she cared. Reese was right. He was the help, officially an employee of her father. But there was something there, something she wanted in the worst way.

Levi grumbled and slammed against the door again. The sound of breaking glass snapped her out of her buzz.

"Shit!" he yelled.

Taylor jumped from the bed and ran to find Levi's elbow through one of the small glass panes. There was a cut high on his biceps and blood soaked his shirt sleeve.

"I'm not really good with blood. Stay here," she said. She ran to the intercom and paged the entire house. "Suzanne, I need you in my room!"

There was no answer, so she ran to her bathroom and dug through the cabinet for the first aid kit hidden all the way in the back. By the time she made it back to Levi, he was leaning against the wall, pressing his hand over the wound while red seeped between his fingers.

"Levi, let me see it," she said, approaching him carefully.

"I'm okay. I just need a towel or something."

"You're not okay. Now let me see." He moved his hand and all she could see was a tear in the sleeve and more blood. She pushed the sleeve up, but it wouldn't go far enough. "Take off your shirt," she said, tugging the shirt out of his pants.

He fumbled with the buttons, before Taylor slapped his hands away and did it herself. She loved the way he watched her hands work down from his neck before peeling the shirt from his body. He wore a plain white T-shirt beneath and Taylor sighed at the sight. Who knew something so simple could be so sexy?

Her gaze traveled across his broad chest, where she could barely make out more ink beneath the thin shirt and down his stomach to his gunmetal belt buckle.

"Taylor," he said, snapping her out of her ogling.

Without a word, she cleaned the cut with antiseptic, applied a few butterfly bandages, and wrapped it in gauze. Her fingers smoothed the tape down and she let them trail down his biceps, skimming the inside of his elbow. The colorful art was smooth and warm beneath her fingertips. Continuing her journey, she traced the pads of his calloused fingertips with her own.

"Your hands are so rough," she said absently.

"A result of physical labor and guitar playing. Thanks," Levi said, checking out the bandage. "I thought you weren't good with blood."

"Huh, I thought so too. Maybe I just needed a distraction," she said, dragging one finger down his chest and thumping his belt buckle. Levi grabbed his shirt from the floor and threw it back on.

"You mind if I wash my hands in your bathroom?" he asked, waving the bloody hand at her.

"Go ahead." Taylor looked away and swallowed down her nausea.

When he reappeared, Levi started to pick up the glass from the floor. He threw it in the trash beside Taylor's desk. She sat on her bed, leaning back on her elbows.

"Sorry about your door. I'll fix it before I leave today."

"No worries. What you should be sorry about is killing my buzz."

He smirked at her and ducked his head. "Sorry about that, too."

"You could make it up to me."

"Taylor, I don't have any pot."

"There are *other* ways," she said, finally catching his attention.

Levi's hazel eyes seemed to shine as he stalked forward, coming to a stop between her knees. He leaned over, placing his hands on the bed, caging her in. His handsome face was a mask of seriousness, the muscles in his jaw clenched and released. Taylor shrank back into her pillows, unsure if she was turned on or afraid. He looked dangerous in the most beautiful way. Levi lowered his head, his lips just inches from her own.

"What would you have me do, Taylor?" The nearness of his body made her pulse spike. She fought to keep her hands still. "Should I take you right here on your thousand-thread-count sheets?"

Taylor nodded without thinking. Her fingers curled into the duvet, clawing at the material instead of his body. Suddenly, Levi stood and looked down at her in disgust. "Nah. You probably shouldn't hook up with poor trash like me."

He grabbed his toolbox from the floor and slammed the door on his way out. Taylor tried to catch her breath and calm the ache he'd left her with.

"Crystal, you there?" Levi said as he headed down the stairs.

"Yeah, I'm here. What's up?" Crystal asked.

"I've got to run to the hardware store for a piece of glass. We'll have to do recon later."

"Copy that. I'll let Kyle know. How's the arm?"

"It's fine. Just bled a lot."

"Good thing Nurse Taylor took care of you," she said.

"Shut it," Levi growled as he made his way out to his truck.

He walked around the hardware store for longer than necessary, just needing a break from Taylor Hudson and her scheming blue eyes. He stared at piles of lumber and stacked paint cans, but nothing seemed to make him forget the feel of her hands on him. Even one of his favorites, Shakespeare's Sonnet 57, could not clear his mind.

> Being your slave what should I do but tend
> Upon the hours and times of your desire?
> I have no precious time at all to spend,
> Nor services to do, till you require

When Levi arrived back at the house, he found a black Audi TT parked in the driveway. Its sleek lines and sexy curves made him remember why he was here—to take from the rich and give to the poor. He pictured himself in that car, flying down the road while the engine purred.

Making his way upstairs with the new glass in hand, Levi told himself to stop being so abrasive with Taylor. Sure, she was a spoiled girl who was too hot for her own good, but he needed to stay employed so he was going to have to play nice. Levi turned the corner and froze in front of Taylor's open door.

There she was, pinned down on her bed by a blond kid. The boy shifted his hips against her body as he kissed down her neck. Her hands gripped his shoulders as he started to unbutton her shirt. A lacy black bra was exposed, and Levi had to grab onto something to hold himself up. He'd seen her in far less—that tiny bikini left nothing to the imagination—but this seemed far more intimate. Taylor turned her head toward the door, finding Levi there. His grip on the doorframe tightened as she grinned before letting a small moan escape her lips. Her eyes were desperate, daring him to watch.

"Mmm, so good," she moaned.

"Baby, lift your hips so I can take your shorts off," the kid said.

His voice jolted Levi out of his staring. He turned and fled down the stairs and out onto the back patio. Throwing himself down into a chair, his mind reeled as he tried to erase those visions from his head. Taylor Hudson was proving to be quite the adversary. How could she try to seduce him one minute and have some other guy in her bed the next? Levi couldn't justify the feelings buzzing around his head. He was infuriated, jealous, and embarrassed. And unfortunately, hard as a rock.

6. mutual attraction and just friends

After he caught his breath, Levi took off across the lawn, past the tennis court and garden shed, into the woods. It was quiet out there and he could think without interruption. He sat on the top of the picnic table and lay back, staring up at the crisscrossing canopy of trees. Levi tried to calm himself, but he was too fired up, too on edge. No matter how long he lay there, nothing deflated but his erection.

Curtis emerged from the shed, a coiled hose over his shoulder, and gave Levi a wave.

"You okay, man? You look pissed."

Levi blew out a breath and nodded. "I'm good. Just needed a break."

"Well, my hiding place is your hiding place. Stay as long as you need."

Curtis gave Levi a knowing smirk and headed toward the house.

"I just caught up on the video feed," Kyle said, startling Levi.

"And?" Levi bit back, knowing his friend would have something to say about the peep show he'd just witnessed.

"And why did you run away? That's like turning off free porn. You never do that!"

"This girl is out of control," Levi said, leaning against a tree. "She's testing me, Kyle."

"Just avoid her for a while. It's okay for her to want you. That can probably work to our advantage. But you can't get distracted. We're here for the job, Levi. We'll go to Mavericks tonight, meet some girls—the kind with lowered inhibitions and nice racks—and forget all about Taylor Hudson."

"Right," Levi agreed. "The job. Let's just get the layout of the outside buildings now. I'll stay out of the house for a while."

"Let me set up all the outside cameras to redirect to a looped feed, and then we're go," Kyle confirmed.

The two worked diligently, mapping those buildings for most of the day. Levi took his time, moving purposely slowly. He knew he did not want to return to the house while the blond kid was still there. As much as he loathed everything Taylor Hudson represented, he couldn't deny the physical attraction. The fact that she was constantly throwing herself at him was going to test every ounce of his restraint.

When the pool house was finished, Levi stood staring out across the yard at the main house. It looked so ominous under a dark gray sky, a hollow shell of a house. In reality, the bricks and marble, stone and wood all added up to nothing significant. During Levi's childhood, it was the intangible things that made their house a home. The memories of growing up alone with his father, the dinners of cupcakes and french fries, the unbreakable bond between child and parent were what held them together. This house, with all its precious antiques and priceless art, held nothing.

"All right, Levi. Crystal and I are going to input the layout for today. Signing off," Kyle said.

"Later."

Levi checked to make sure the Audi was gone, grabbed the replacement glass and toolbox from the garage, and made his way back upstairs to Taylor's room. Thunder echoed through the house as the sky opened up, a rarity in Southern California. Suzanne passed him on the stairs and gave him a sympathetic smile. He barely returned her smile before wondering why all the women in this house were so strange. He stood outside Taylor's closed door for a few seconds and settled his frenzied mind. Focus on the job, he told himself before knocking.

"Come in, Suzy, but I don't want to hear about Beau."

He swung the door open, entered, and closed it behind him. Taylor was sitting at her desk typing on her laptop. She unwrapped a candy, popped it in her mouth, and continued typing. Her clothes were all back in place, but she looked ruffled.

"It's not Suzanne," Levi said. Taylor whipped around, surprised to find him there. She seemed to choke on her candy but recovered quickly. "I'm just here to finish the door."

Taylor pretended to return her attention to her computer screen. She felt a flaming heat in her cheeks when she thought of Levi seeing her with Beau. His fierce gaze had originally spurred her on, but when he'd disappeared, Taylor had felt guilty and ashamed. These were two emotions she was not familiar with. Beau's hands had felt all wrong, and before she knew what she was doing, she had asked him to leave.

Now, seeing Levi again, she was dying to be near him. Taylor struggled to think of ways to start a conversation, but she couldn't manage anything appropriate. She frowned and tried to remember when she had ever been unsure of herself around a guy.

Levi worked quietly. Taylor stole glances at him when she could, and he continued to ignore her. When she couldn't take it anymore, she closed her laptop and rolled her chair over to the balcony doors. He looked up from under the bill of his hat but made no effort to engage her.

"What are you doing?" she asked.

"Repairing the door."

"I know that." Taylor rolled her eyes. "I mean how are you doing it?"

He opened his mouth, but then closed it. She watched him take a deep breath and look up at her.

"I already replaced the pane of glass. Now I'm working on oiling the hinges and the upper and lower sliding locks." He sprayed something onto the locks and hinges. He tried the door again, but it didn't budge. "It may need to sit for a while. I'll try again in a few minutes."

A flash of lightning lit up the windows before thunder shook the house.

"I hate thunderstorms," Taylor said. "That's the best part about living here. This almost never happens."

Levi leaned against the wall and crossed his arms. "I was scared of them when I was a kid. Then my mom told me that thunderstorms were just people in heaven having a party." Levi grinned. "I know it's lame, but it worked."

She shook her head. "It's not lame. It's the perfect thing for a mother to tell her child." Taylor's chest squeezed tight at the thought of never hearing anything similar from her own mother. When the silence became too much, Levi broke first.

"So, where did your little friend go?" he asked.

"Who? Beau?" Taylor swallowed and tucked her hands beneath her thighs.

"The Ken doll with the nice car?"

"Yeah, that's him," she said. "He left right after he came." Taylor laughed at her own joke. Levi glared at her. "I'm kidding."

"Not one for sticking around, huh?"

"He's not invited to stick around, Levi."

"I thought he was your boyfriend or something," he said.

"I'm not a boyfriend kind of girl. We only started sleeping together again to piss off our parents. But, of course, none of them have even noticed. Our fathers are, like, mortal enemies."

"So you two are kind of like Romeo and Juliet?"

Taylor laughed, hiding her surprise at his Shakespearian reference. "I guess the warring families part is right, but take out all the love, devotion, and pointless suicide."

"Pointless?"

"Yeah. I mean, they didn't have to die. If just one of them had stood up to their families and declared their love, they could have avoided death. *Romeo and Juliet* is an overdramatic love story that ends in tragedy because of miscommunication and a lack of backbone."

Levi shook his head, an amused smile on his lips. "I disagree. It's my favorite piece by Shakespeare."

"Really?" Taylor asked. "I didn't know you could read."

"He showed us a realistic, chaotic portrayal of love," Levi said, ignoring the snobby jab. "Not a fancied-up, delicate version. They're thrown into this situation where they have to fight their families, their friends, and sometimes each other. Romeo was misunderstood. Rosaline left him wanting. And he's okay with his life until the moment he sees Juliet. I don't know if I buy the whole love at first sight thing, but it was something more than just lust."

"Oh, come on. He wants to bang her so he spits all this romantic bullshit to lure her in," Taylor insisted.

"Maybe. But the kicker is, she feels it too. Their attraction was mutual, and so intense that neither of them could fully comprehend or resist it."

"This so-called love"—Taylor used air quotes to make her point—"made them weak idiots who end up hurting each other, and eventually dead. I mean, the entire theme of the play is death."

"Romeo wasn't perfect." Levi threw his hands in the air before dropping them to his side. "He made mistakes. I get that. He was impulsive and volatile. He let his desire for this girl cloud his ability to make good decisions. You can't go around killing your new wife's cousin."

"And Juliet fell for all his lines when she could have had a nice cushy life with Paris," Taylor said.

Levi sighed and frowned at her. "A cushy life with someone her father appointed. She would rather die than do that. It speaks to the power of their love."

"Lust."

"Attraction," Levi countered. "As much as Romeo screwed up, he was also a victim of those crazy events he had absolutely no control over. Like he said, 'I am fortune's fool.'"

Taylor smiled up at him, amused at Levi's obvious passion. "Fortune? As in destiny and all that? I don't buy it for a minute. They were idiots who should have humped and said their good-byes."

He laughed, but it was cold and humorless. "I would expect nothing less from you, Taylor." With that, he turned to the door and pushed against it. Miraculously, it swung open.

Something about the tone of his voice set Taylor off. She jumped from her chair.

"What the hell does that mean?" she asked. Levi ignored her, moving the door back and forth. Taylor pulled it from his grip and threw it open, finally gaining his attention.

"It means that you're a spoiled, rich brat who takes what she wants and disregards anyone not in her tax bracket," he growled, stepping closer.

"I'm so tired of people making assumptions about who I am!" she yelled, poking Levi in the chest. His eyes followed her finger before returning to her fuming expression. "I'm sorry that you were born less fortunate. But I'm not apologizing for having money." She poked him again. "You think you have me pegged, but you don't know shit about me."

With the rain suddenly gone, her voice echoed through the room. The silence left them in an eerie standoff. "You decided you hated me right away. You think life's not fair because you got dealt a shit hand? Well, what's fair about the deadbeat parents I got? Huh? What's fair about your unfounded attitude?"

Taylor poked him in the chest again before dropping her hands to her sides, balling them into fists. She worked hard to pull in breaths as her head spun with words and thoughts she couldn't quite piece together. Levi dropped his eyes to the floor and shoved his hands into his pockets. His silence stabbed at her. Here she was, passionate and heated, while he stood motionless, unaffected.

"Say something!" Taylor demanded.

"You're right."

"I am?"

Levi nodded and shifted from foot to foot. His eyes scanned the room, avoiding her gaze.

"Money separates people. It's not your fault you were born into this life. My opinions of you are based on my general resentment of the wealthy, which stems from experience with other people, and not on you."

With no warning, Taylor launched herself at him. Her arms went around his neck as she pressed her lips to his. Levi's hands came up to hold her, but he stopped short. His fingers hovered around her waist as if there were an invisible force field restraining him. When she scraped her nails along the back of his neck, he was done for.

He parted his lips and sucked on her tongue. When his lips touched hers, he felt a jolt race through his body. It was that rush of kissing someone for the first time, someone that knows what you need more than you do.

His fingers curled around her hips and he pulled her closer. She tasted like watermelon candy and fit perfectly in his arms. Taylor hopped up, wrapping her legs around his waist. Levi's hands caught her and held her there before moving up her smooth thighs. He stumbled to the bed, needing more of her.

They fell onto the mattress with Taylor pinned beneath him. Levi pressed his hips against her, and she moaned at the feel of it.

"Levi, so good," she whispered.

Those words, spoken earlier in the day to another man, broke Levi out of his lust-induced haze. He pulled his mouth away from her neck and looked into her greedy blue eyes. Their mouths, inches apart, exchanged labored breaths. Levi's head and body battled between what he wanted and what was right.

"Don't," she said, her voice manic with need. "Levi, don't stop."

Levi shook his head, disappointed that he was willing to risk everything, ruin the plan, for a piece of ass.

"I've got to go," he said, pulling himself from her grip.

He packed up his toolbox and retreated as fast as his feet could carry him.

Later that evening, Levi sat in his favorite spot overlooking the ocean, and all he could do was think about Taylor Hudson. He strummed his guitar lazily and thought about the revolving heat and energy between them, the sort of lust and fury that pushed and pulled them apart. When the team learned of Taylor's existence, no one had given her a second thought. She was just a kid, they said. But Levi knew better now. With her wicked body and pretty face, she threatened everything they worked for.

Tempt not a desperate man.

Levi hummed along as he played "Sex and Candy," remembering the feel of her legs wrapped around him and the taste of her lips. He lifted his eyes to the sky and thanked God that Crystal or Kyle hadn't witnessed when he broke down and almost gave her what she wanted, though they would eventually watch the footage and find out for themselves just how weak he was. The Boss would not hesitate to cut him out of the deal if he jeopardized this job in any way. Levi finished the song and placed his guitar on the ground. He inhaled the cool, salty air and silently vowed to be strong, for himself and for his team.

The next morning, Reese called Taylor as if nothing had happened. That was the way the two friends operated. They fought, and the next day all was forgotten. She invited Taylor to the beach along with some friends. Needing an escape from the four walls of her room, Taylor agreed.

After she was dressed in her favorite bikini and new sundress, Taylor went in search of a beach bag in her mother's closet. One of the good things about Virginia always being gone was that Taylor had complete access to all her accessories. When she opened the bedroom door, Nadine was there, coming out of Henry's closet. Taylor raised an eyebrow at the woman and glanced back toward the closet.

"Is Henry in there?" she asked, expecting her father to stumble out half dressed.

"No," Nadine answered. "He's downstairs."

"What are you doing in here?"

"I'm just grabbing a few suits for your father since he'll be busy in meetings all week."

"How accommodating." Taylor sneered, while wondering where he was spending his nights.

Nadine pulled two suits from the closet and set them in a garment bag hung on the back of the door. "Just doing my job, Taylor. What are you doing in here?"

"That's none of your business. I live here," Taylor said.

Nadine stopped and put her hands on her hips. She tapped the toe of her knockoff shoe at Taylor.

"There's no need for you to be rude. I was only trying to make conversation. I think we got off on the wrong foot, Taylor. I'm not your enemy."

Taylor stepped forward, eye to eye with the petite woman. She'd never really looked at Nadine up close before, and even through her hate-tinted goggles, Taylor could see how attractive she was. She had a heart-shaped face, small button nose, and large almond eyes. Taylor thought she kind of looked like a cat, and by the tone of Nadine's voice, she imagined the woman had claws as well.

"Don't forget who you are. You're his assistant, not his wife. You don't get to ask me anything or make conversation. Do your job and get out of my house."

Nadine pulled her bottom lip between her teeth and held it there as she also held Taylor's gaze. She didn't seem rattled by the threat, only more determined to stand her ground. She returned to Henry's closet, retrieved two more suits, added them to the garment bag, and zipped it up.

Taylor found the bag she needed in her mother's closet, and by the time she exited, Nadine was gone. When she was finished packing, Taylor ventured downstairs to grab some breakfast before Reese picked her up. She found Levi, Suzanne, and Mandy sitting around the kitchen island drinking coffee. Taylor grabbed a banana and sat across from Levi.

"Is Henry still here?"

Suzanne shook her head. "Sorry, honey. He and Nadine left a few minutes ago."

Taylor hated the pitiful look on Suzanne's face, a look that said *I'm sorry your father is not much of one.*

"That's okay." Taylor shrugged halfheartedly. "Last time I saw him he patted me on the head like I'm the family dog. I'll take no interaction over that."

Suzanne threw her arms around Taylor from behind and wrapped her in a tight hug. She pressed her face into Taylor's hair and whispered the same words she'd been saying for eighteen years. "Thick and thin, tried and true. Against the world, it's just us two. Love you, Boo."

"Love you, Kitty."

Taylor swallowed the lump in her throat, remembering the words Suzanne had been telling her since she was a child. The nicknames were a reference to *Monsters, Inc.*, a movie Taylor had been obsessed with.

She was embarrassed to have this conversation in front of other employees, especially in front of Levi. Vulnerability was something Taylor was not used to showing. Suzanne released her and excused herself while Mandy scurried off mumbling about dusting.

"Don't everyone get to work on my account," she said. Levi didn't look up at her as he finished his coffee and stood. "Good morning, Levi." He dropped his mug in the sink and turned to go without acknowledging her. "Hello? Am I talking to myself here? Where are you going?"

"Outside," he answered in a short tone.

"Levi, you don't have to leave just because I'm here," Taylor said. He stopped, took a deep breath, and turned to face her. He wore a smile so fake it looked painted on.

"Don't flatter yourself, Taylor. I've got work to do."

With that, he turned and headed out the back door. Taylor sat motionless and stunned. She hated this avoidance, from her father and from Levi.

Reese's horn beeped twice and Taylor hurried out the front door. She tried to leave Levi and all unhappy thoughts behind.

"Hey, Reese," Taylor said, crossing her arms after buckling up.

"Well, good to see you, too, Debbie Downer."

Taylor pulled her sunglasses down over her eyes and put her best effort into a convincing smile. "Sorry, I'm tired today."

"No worries, kid. We're just lounging at the beach with the crew." Reese turned around in the driveway and pulled out into the neighborhood.

"Who's going to be there?" Taylor asked, trying to prevent more difficult subjects coming up.

"I don't know. I didn't get an official roster," Reese teased, poking her friend in the ribs. Taylor slapped her hand away.

For the entire ride to the beach, they talked about how great it would be to live on the opposite coast. Reese was attending Brown University, so she'd be about an hour away from Taylor and Adrienne. She was determined to land one of those old East Coast family frat boys, the kind with sweater vests and bottomless trust funds.

"I hear guys like that are boring and prudes," Taylor said, looking out the window at the passing scenery.

"He won't be when I'm done with him," Reese answered. "You know how these old-money boys are. They've got more dollars than sense. I'll just have to train him."

"Are we talking about a person or a puppy?"

"He'll be my good little puppy. Yes, he will," Reese said in baby talk while making smooching noises.

"And he'll probably have an overbearing mother who will be hostile toward you and make your life miserable. She'll say you're not good enough and call you a gold-digging whore."

"I don't care. I won't be able to hear a thing while sitting on top of my pile of money." Reese chuckled. "Stop killing my dream, Dream Killer. What kind of friend are you?"

Taylor shrugged and leaned back against the seat. "You'll make someone a terrific third wife one day."

"Don't I know it," Reese replied.

There was a shift in the air as they neared the beach. The cooler breeze and cawing seagulls greeted them, as if announcing their arrival to a better place.

Once parked, they grabbed their bags and made the trek across the sand to where the rest of the group had staked out some shade beneath beach umbrellas. It was the usual crowd, including Beau and a few of his teammates. Adrienne sat next to him. She laughed and touched his arm when she spoke—any excuse to get his attention. Taylor knew Adrienne had always had a crush on Beau. When she spotted them approaching, Adrienne stiffened and turned her attention toward the water. Taylor frowned at her friend's unnecessary guilt.

Beau jumped up and ran over. "Hey," he greeted, planting a kiss on Taylor's lips as he grabbed her bag.

She sucked in a breath and gawked at him. They'd never shown affection to each other in public. There were rumors of a relationship but never confirmation. It looked like Beau was upping his game. Taylor huffed and followed him back to the group, where everyone sat wide-eyed and waiting for an explanation. All conversations had been abandoned, all activities ceased.

"Are you guys together now?" Adrienne asked.

"No," Taylor answered. "We're just friends."

Reese threw her bag down in the middle of the blanket. "Thanks for offering to help a lady out," she said, breaking the tension.

"I don't see any lady," someone shouted before a chorus of "ohs" rang out.

The rest of the morning was spent catching rays or burying their toes in the sand while the guys kicked around a soccer ball. The sun was warm, the breeze was cool, and a soundtrack from someone's iPod kept them entertained. Taylor, Reese, and Adrienne discussed college boys and how different they would be. The three girls talked about their move cross-country in a couple of months while Adrienne filed her nails beneath the shade of her beach umbrella.

"It sucks that we have to live on campus. I applied for off-campus housing but was denied. I wanted to get an apartment," Reese admitted.

"It's a rite of passage, Reese," Adrienne said.

"Well, you guys have each other. I'll be living with a stranger," Reese pouted.

"It'll be okay," Taylor chimed in. "Unless your roommate is a serial killer or collector of human spleens."

"Spleens are pretty much worthless on the black market. It would probably be kidneys or livers. Much more profitable." Reese and Taylor gave Adrienne an incredulous look. Adrienne flicked sand off her nails, then turned to Taylor. "Oh! I checked on that literacy program for you, Taylor. It's on Tuesday afternoons."

Taylor stared out at the water, deciding that she shouldn't waste an entire summer being a self-centered brat. She certainly had the time and ability to help out.

"Will you go with me?" she asked.

Adrienne turned her face toward Taylor. She wore a smile reminiscent of their younger days. "Of course. We'll go next week. Any progress with your maintenance man?"

Taylor looked around, noting that Beau was too far away to overhear. Reese sat quietly, grinning at her friends.

"Maybe."

"Tell me," Adrienne insisted.

Taylor smirked at her friend and shook her head.

"Come on," Ade begged. When Taylor remained tight-lipped, Adrienne jumped up and tackled Taylor back onto the sand. She held her metal nail file in front of Taylor's face, laughing.

"Taylor Francis Hudson, if you don't tell me about that hottie's skills right now, I will stab this fingernail file into your medulla oblongata, therefore causing all your body's autonomic functions to cease and desist."

Taylor chuckled and pushed Adrienne off of her. "You are freakishly strong for such a tiny girl. And violent too."

"I'd call it persuasive," Ade answered.

"I'd call it psychotic," Reese chimed in, seeming disinterested.

"Tell us, Taylor," Adrienne demanded.

"Fine, fine. I kissed him yesterday."

Adrienne's eyes lit up and she scooted closer to her friend. "What was it like?"

Taylor couldn't help her growing smile. "It was pretty great. He's . . . intense."

"So was Jeffrey Dahmer," Reese pointed out.

Adrienne and Taylor rolled their eyes.

"So, just a kiss?" Adrienne asked.

The boys ran over, rejoining the group, and Taylor nodded at her friend, ending the conversation about Levi.

"I'm starving," Reese announced.

"Me, too," Taylor said. "No one thought to bring snacks?"

Beau hopped up and dusted the sand from his feet before sliding into his shoes. "Taylor and I will go get something."

"We will?" she asked. His expression was hopeful and she couldn't deny him. "Fine."

Taylor threw her clothes back on and followed him to the parking lot. She was nervous being alone with Beau and wasn't sure why. This was her childhood friend, the guy she'd lost her virginity to. She knew all his secrets. Nothing had changed between them, but something felt off. Maybe he was still upset that she'd turned him down the day before. After seeing Levi in her doorway, Taylor just couldn't stand the feel of Beau's hands on her anymore. She had stopped him and sent him on his way, along with the excuse of having her period.

"What's up with you lately, Tay?" Beau asked once they were on the road.

"What do you mean?"

"You've been weird . . . distant."

She leaned back into the leather seat and traced the door handle with her fingertips. "I don't know," she said. "You ever wonder if there's more to life than what we're doing?"

He chuckled nervously and kept his eyes on the road. "What *are* we doing?"

"I don't know. I mean, we're just kind of floating through life, taking what we want. We don't answer to anyone. We don't appreciate what we have. Or don't have," she added as an afterthought. "I graduated top of my class. I've been accepted to Harvard and I don't even know what I want to major in. I've got all these questions and no answers. I don't know what the hell I want to do with the rest of my life. Do you feel passionate about anything?" Taylor asked, watching his profile.

He shrugged and tapped his fingers on the steering wheel.

"I feel passionate about soccer. And you," he said.

Taylor frowned. His declaration felt stifling. What did he know about passion? In all their years of hooking up, she'd never felt the desperate need she felt with Levi. With Beau, it was easy and safe. The two had known each other since birth and had been friends just as long. So it seemed natural to end up together. They started sleeping together when they were sixteen. When they started dating other people, things kind of fell off.

A year ago, their fathers had a huge falling-out over a business deal gone bad. Taylor and Beau were told to stay away from each other. There were threats and promises made between the families, creating a definite rift in the social hierarchy of Newport Beach.

She rolled down her window and looked out at the passing cars. They were a blur of colors and sounds, a swirling mess of nothing solid or static. She hung her arm out the window and basked in the sun. Taylor flattened her hand and used the wind to lift and lower it like a dolphin diving in and out of the surf, letting go of all the tension that plagued her.

7. hustler and quivering jelly

Levi spent his entire morning avoiding Taylor's room, still undecided on how to deal with her. He completed a more thorough search
of the attic space after Crystal rerouted the cameras, ruling it out as
a place for the safe. They repeated the same process with the gym
and theater in the basement, eliminating them from the list as well.

He threw himself down in one of the plush home theater chairs.
A relaxing sigh slipped from his lips as he let himself get too comfortable. Levi pushed a button and the chair reclined, kicking his
feet out in front of him. His worn-out, dirty boots had no place on
leather this soft. Still, he didn't move.

"What are you doing?" Crystal asked through his earpiece.

"Seeing how the other half lives."

"Other half? Try the one percent."

"Here we go," Levi huffed, rolling his eyes and hopping out of the chair.

"What? The rich get richer and the poor stay poor. It's an endless cycle meant to keep people like us in our place."

"That's why we're here, right? To make our own rules."

"Amen, brother."

"And what if we don't find the safe? Or what if there is no safe, Crystal? It's like we haven't even considered those options."

"You can't think like that. Positive energy out into the universe, Levi. There is a safe. We will find it. Get rich or die tryin'."

"You're quoting 50 Cent now," Levi pointed out.

"Seriously, man. I know you think this job is worth the risk. Otherwise, you wouldn't have pulled us in. This money will change our lives, Levi. It'll give us a voice where we had none before. Thank you for your generous donation, Henry Hudson III."

Levi laughed at his friend before signing off. He took a break for lunch only to be met with another plate of food and a smiling, flirty Mandy. While her affection was annoying, the food was just too good to turn down. Levi hadn't had home-cooked meals in years.

He spent the rest of the afternoon completing his work list and avoiding the leaky showerhead in Taylor's bathroom. When he ran out of excuses, he stood at the bottom of the stairs, one hand on the banister, trying to gather his wits before facing her.

"She's not here, you know," Suzanne sang as she walked past him through the foyer. He exhaled and heard her chuckle as she exited the room.

Levi made his way to Taylor's bathroom and got to work on the leak. While he was in there, Mandy came in.

"Hi, Levi." She gave him a shy wave.

He nodded and watched her dart around Taylor's room, making the bed and picking up dirty clothes. She entered the bathroom and threw an armload of clothes into a small door on the wall.

"What's that?"

She leaned against the wall and eyed Levi through the glass shower door now closed between them. "That's the laundry chute. Goes down to the washroom."

He nodded and turned back to the showerhead. As Mandy left, Levi told himself to just finish the job and go home. Another day over and still no safe, but they were making great progress. He tightened the fixture, stepped out of the way, and tested the shower. No leak.

As he turned to leave, the glass door flew open and a very naked sunbaked Taylor Hudson appeared in front of him.

"Levi!" she yelled, grabbing a towel to cover herself. "Shit! You scared me to death!" Taylor leaned against the stone wall of the shower and tried to catch her breath. Meanwhile the vision of naked flesh and soft curves flashed in Levi's brain, taunting his resolve.

"You look alive to me," he said, forcing his hands into his pockets.

Taylor saw his wavering and took advantage. She stepped to Levi and pressed her body against his with only the towel between them. She weaved her fingers together behind his neck and pulled him down to her waiting lips.

Levi stopped short and inhaled deeply. The memory of their kiss made him want to lean in and take want they both wanted, but there was always this nagging reminder that he was here for the job.

"What's stopping you?" Taylor asked. Her voice was breathy and just a whisper between them.

"I'm your employee, Miss Hudson, not your newest conquest."

She scowled at him, a deep V appearing between her brows as she tamped down the rage boiling just below the surface. He unhooked her arms from around his neck and pushed past her. He grabbed his toolbox and made his way through the bedroom.

"Try not to steal anything on your way out," she yelled.

Levi smiled at her jab, finally satisfied he'd gotten under her skin.

The next morning, Levi sat having coffee with Mandy and Suzanne. It had become a habit for them to share this ritual. Mandy was her usual flirty self, but Suzanne sat quietly, just enjoying the company. Levi sipped his brew and watched Suzanne. He wondered how she'd maintained her sanity in this house for eighteen years. She seemed like a genuine and caring person, and he thought she deserved so much more than being Taylor Hudson's shadow.

Her sweet smile and motherly instincts reminded him of the few memories of his own mom. Levi pictured Suzanne living a different life, where she was a mother and wife and not someone to be used by these shallow people. He wondered if she wanted those things for herself, or if she was fulfilled in serving this family.

His work list was short today, and that afforded him the opportunity to search more of the house. Levi stayed quiet and kept out of sight as he made his way from room to room on the first floor.

In the pretentious dining room, his calloused fingers slid behind centuries-old plates and silver platters that probably served food worth more than his truck. The china held a complex pattern of gold and pearl designs. Frankly, it reminded him of the print on his Dixie paper plates at home. In the main room, he lifted end tables and checked under floor lamps while steering clear of the back glass wall. Crystal was rerouting only inside cameras at the moment. The one on the back patio would be able to see him if he went anywhere near that glass.

Kyle helped guide him, making sure to check every place where a safe could be hidden. As he slid his hands over imported furniture and crawled on their expensive rugs, Levi thought about how much this money would change their lives.

There would be no more worrying about where their next meal would come from or how rent would get paid. No more slaving away to make someone else a profit. They would control their own destiny and settle into the kind of life they were meant to have.

Of course, there would be sacrifices. Each of them would have to disappear once the job was complete. Levi had already chosen his place, a small town outside of Florence, Italy. His father had always talked about this town when he was a child, telling stories about their family's roots. He said their heritage and bloodline resided there and he'd always wanted to visit. Levi's dreams of making that happen died with his father. He never got the chance to go, but Levi was determined to follow through.

"Okay, this floor is complete except for the study and Suzanne's bedroom. I'm getting kind of nervous that we haven't found anything yet," Kyle said.

"It's only been a week. Before we start to panic, let's work on the second floor. I'll check in with you after I grab some lunch," Levi said, heading to the kitchen.

"You mean from your girlfriend?" Kyle sang.

"Really? What grade are you in?"

Kyle laughed and made kissing noises in Levi's ear. "Later, bitch," Kyle said before signing off.

Levi was surprised to find the kitchen empty. He made a sandwich for himself and was disappointed when it didn't taste as good as the ones Mandy made. After eating, he cleaned the pool, restocked the chemicals, and cleared out the filter. He swiped the sweat from his forehead with the red rag and made his way inside.

He decided to pass through the study again and stopped to look at all the shelves of books. Surely it would be an easy place to hide a sliding panel or secret door. He let his eyes scan over each shelf carefully as he looked for a seam or anything out of the ordinary.

"If you're looking for something to read, you'll have to find it elsewhere. There are no Dr. Seuss books up there."

Taylor's voice surprised him, and he turned to find her lounging in one of the oversized chairs, her legs thrown over one side. Levi glared at her. He was a lot of things, but he wasn't stupid.

"Actually, I prefer the pages of *Hustler* to all the pretentious bullshit in this room."

She smiled and returned her attention to the book perched in her lap. "I would expect nothing less from you, Romeo."

It didn't go unnoticed that she was using his own words against him. She was testing him, trying to break him down and conquer him.

"I'm actually surprised that you guys own books. Don't you just pay someone to read them for you?"

"Henry wouldn't waste his time with such things, and I'm sure Virginia reads nothing more complicated than *InStyle* magazine. These books were my grandfather's. We inherited them when he died. Henry added this room just to house them. The craziest part is, my grandmother could barely read. I think she was dyslexic or something. She had all these books at her disposal and didn't use them."

Levi was surprised that she'd shared such personal family information with him. The look on her face showed that she was surprised at herself as well. He filed the information away for later use.

"There are some great books of poetry in here," he said.

"I wouldn't know. I don't read that stuff."

He took a seat in the chair across from her. Taylor ignored his presence, returning her focus to the pages of her book.

"*This is the female form,*" Levi recited, "*a divine nimbus exhales from it from head to foot.*" Taylor's head snapped up, her eyes meeting his. "*It attracts with fierce undeniable attraction.*" She sat up, placing her bare feet on the floor. Levi slid forward to the edge of his seat, his knees now between hers. "*I am drawn by its breath as if I were no more than a helpless vapor.*"

Taylor's book dropped to the floor, but her eyes stayed on Levi's face. He placed his rough hands on her knees and slowly slid them up her bare thighs to the edge of her shorts and back down. Her fingers dug into the arms of the chair, her breaths came faster.

"*All falls aside but myself and it, books, art, religion, time, the visible and solid earth, and what was expected of heaven or fear'd of hell, are now consumed,*" Levi continued. Taylor leaned forward as if tethered to his words.

"*Mad filaments, ungovernable shoots play out of it, the response likewise ungovernable.*"

Levi's hands traveled up her legs again, his thumbs rubbing slow circles on her inner thighs, just short of where she wanted him most. "*Hair, bosom, hips, bend of legs, negligent falling hands all diffused, mine too diffused, ebb stung by the flow and flow stung by the ebb, love-flesh swelling and deliciously aching.*"

Levi paused when she closed her eyes and exhaled a stuttered breath. He moved his hands down to her knees again and pushed them wider. Leaning forward, he eliminated the last bit of space between them so that his words were only a whispered secret between the two of them.

"*Limitless limpid jets of love hot and enormous, quivering jelly of love.*"

Taylor's eyes remained closed as her fingers dug deeper into the leather of the chair. A tiny whimper escaped her lips when Levi stood abruptly, ending their intimate moment.

"Don't you just love Whitman?" he asked.

Her eyes popped open, a look of confusion and lust pooling in them. As Levi exited the room, he heard three little words that gave him a victory in this battle of wits.

"I do now."

Taylor lay in bed reading a collection of poetry by Walt Whitman. After her encounter with Levi, she'd searched every shelf in the room to find it. She flipped through the pages, searching for the poem he'd recited, hoping to relieve the flaming current racing through her. The title alone, "I Sing the Body Electric," had Taylor panting in excitement. But no matter how many times she read it, the words on paper never relieved the ache inside.

Frustrated, she threw the book aside and closed her eyes. She pictured Levi and the way his lips formed the devious words. She saw his smirk and burning hazel eyes cutting through her. Once again, she could almost feel his hard hands against the skin of her thighs. The feeling turned her insides to liquid.

"Quivering jelly of love," she said aloud.

It was then that Taylor realized it was not the poem itself or the words that made her burn. It was Levi, and him alone. As she turned off the light and drifted off to sleep, she wondered if she'd ever get to consume him the way she so desperately needed to.

"Taylor. Wake up, baby girl," Suzanne said.

"Too early. It's Saturday, Suzy." Taylor rolled over and buried herself beneath the covers.

"Come on, Taylor. Your father's here and he wants to see you for breakfast."

"Tell him to fuck off," she groaned.

"Taylor Hudson, if you are not out of that bed and dressed in ten minutes I will take a razor blade and Sharpie to every pair of shoes in your closet."

Taylor sat up, stretched her hands over her head, and yawned. "You wouldn't dare."

"Wouldn't I?" Suzanne asked, placing her hands on her hips.

"All right, all right. I'm up, bossy lady."

Taylor scurried out of bed, brushed her teeth, threw on some sweats, and made her way to the formal dining room. Outside the door, she took a deep, calming breath and tried to ready herself for this torture.

As usual, Henry was sitting at the head of the mahogany dining table, rattling off orders to Nadine. Taylor scowled at the woman, wondering if she'd arrived this morning or last night. Henry was dressed in one of his custom-made signature Armani suits, a powder blue tie that matched his eyes knotted tightly around his neck. He looked freshly showered and clean shaven, his permanent scowl firmly in place.

Taylor took a seat at the table across from Nadine, around the corner from her father. As always, the formal china, silverware, and crystal water glasses were set out at her place, breakfast already on the plate. Nadine gave her a smile while taking notes. Taylor's eyes darted back and forth between them. Henry had nerve bringing her into their house. It was one thing to diddle the assistant at work, but to bring her into the bed you're supposed to share with your wife? That's just ballsy.

"Good morning, Taylor," Nadine chirped from across the table.

"Why are you here?"

"Taylor," Henry warned.

"Henry," she shot back.

"Just getting started on some work here so that your father could see you before he left for the week. Remember, he's headed to San Francisco for that project?" Nadine said.

Taylor ignored her and looked to her father, expecting some sort of greeting, but he offered nothing. Instead, he quietly ate his breakfast and never looked up from his newspaper. The most interaction she ever got was a curt nod or a quick glance, but, today—nothing. It had been ages since she'd seen him. Taylor stared at him in disbelief. She wasn't sure why this man still held so much power over her or why she even wanted to be acknowledged, but she did.

Finally, Henry's eyes met hers. "Eat your breakfast, Taylor. It is getting cold."

She gripped her fork tightly and forced it toward her plate instead of stabbing it through his heartless chest.

"Don't assistants get a day off, Nadine?" Taylor asked through gritted teeth.

"I certainly make good use of my downtime, Taylor. Thank you for your concern." Though she smiled, Nadine's words were cold and implied things that Taylor would rather not know. "Okay, Henry, I'll head to the office now and start on the proposition documents," she said. Henry nodded and she stood to leave.

"Henry? She calls you Henry? Why don't you just invite her to move in?" Taylor scoffed.

"It was great to see you again, Taylor," Nadine said before leaving the room.

"Wish I could say the same," Taylor answered. She eyed her father and waited for a reaction—a cold glare, a stinging slap, sharp words. "Nothing to say? Guess you're not blessed with conversation from Henry Hudson unless you're making him a profit or sucking his dick."

"Watch your mouth, Taylor."

Tears stung her eyes and she dropped her head, not wanting to let him see her cry.

"Have you seen Beau Upton?" Henry asked.

Her head snapped up. "What? No."

"We had a break-in at my office. I've kept it quiet, because I don't need the media breathing down my neck. I don't know what they were looking for, but I'd bet that bastard father of his was behind it. Do you know if George is in the country?" He watched her closely. She wasn't sure what he was looking for, but she kept her expression neutral and shook her head. "I'd better get going," Henry announced as he stood and threw his napkin on the table.

When there was nothing left of him but a swinging door, Taylor looked around at the empty room and two plates of half-eaten food.

"Thanks for breakfast, Dad," she said before pushing her plate away and laying her head on the table. She stayed there for a while as tears blurred her vision and dotted the linen place mat.

Vanessa, the weekend employee, entered the room to clear the dishes and found her there.

"Are you okay, Miss Hudson?" she asked.

Taylor straightened up and turned to go. "Yeah, I'm fine." The lie slipped from her lips easily, because it had been told so many times before.

8. on the prowl and passion theory

Taylor sat on her balcony reading her way through *Leaves of Grass*. Whitman now held a certain appeal, and she wouldn't deny herself the pleasurable memories. She closed the book and stared out over the lawn, cursing how everything seemed to remind her of Levi. The pool, the garage, even the sprinklers made her mind snap back to visions of his strong arms and memories of his lips on hers. They'd only shared one kiss, but it had been enough to make her crave more.

Her phone blasted from inside and she raced to answer it.

"Reese!" she said excitedly.

"Hey, babe. What's on the agenda today?"

"Oh, I'm thinking binge drinking and half a dozen cupcakes."

"Yikes. Did you have another monthly visitation breakfast from Henry?"

"Yeah, only this time he brought along his employee side dish," Taylor said.

"That man is such a loser. I know it's kind of random, but my brother's friend is throwing a party and I promised I'd go. You in?"

"Hell, yes. See if Ade wants to go."

"Already did. She's got some lame family stuff tonight. I'll pick you up around eight," Reese said before ending the call.

The afternoon dragged by slowly as Taylor took her time getting ready. She went through the motions of preparing for a night out but just didn't feel her usual excitement. If this was a result of Levi being on her brain, she would be so disappointed in herself. So she refused to explore the reasons behind this new attitude. Still, Taylor stood in her closet for almost thirty minutes, trying on outfit after outfit. With a heap of designer duds at her feet, she finally settled on her favorite jeans and a simple off-the-shoulder top.

When Reese arrived, Taylor scurried down the driveway in her heels and hopped into the car.

"Lookin' good, Tay."

"As do you, my sista. I mean, you turned it up tonight, huh?" Taylor took in Reese's short shirt and knee-high boots. She leaned over and fingered the dangling diamond earrings sparkling from beneath Reese's curls. "What's the occasion?"

"I'm on the prowl."

"Did the last one die on you or something?" Taylor asked.

"Shut up," Reese said with a laugh. "No, he started talking about leaving his wife. I had to pull out. I'm not trying to ride that Hot Mess Express."

"Ahh. Got it."

"You look très casual for this outing."

"Fuck you. I look hot and you know it," Taylor answered.

"You always look hot, Taylor. But I'm sensing no effort."

Taylor sighed and leaned her head against the window. "It's true. I'm not on the prowl. I just want to have a good time with my BFF."

The party turned out to be total bust. Reese abandoned her as soon as they got there, somehow finding the only adult in the room to chat up. Taylor moved around the party, beer in hand, dancing like she was the only one there. After three drinks, she used her buzz as an escape. She ignored every guy who approached and slapped away roaming hands, intent to focus solely on herself. In this mind space, she was free and completely content.

After a few hours, Reese spilled beer down the front of her dress, forcing them to leave—but not before slipping her number into the back pocket of the middle-aged guy with the golden tan and a line where his wedding band should be.

In the car, she tried to listen objectively as Reese rambled on about her potential new conquest.

"He's got a sailboat and two vacation houses. He said he and his wife separated a few weeks ago . . ."

Taylor nodded and stayed quiet. She tried not to point out her friend's naïveté. When they were looking to land a girl, they all had a sailboat and two vacation homes. They all claimed to be separated from their wives. Taylor had no idea what Reese saw in these older men, or what Reese could get from them that she couldn't get with a boy her own age. Being a part of the privileged club as they were, they all had their own issues. Taylor would never judge her friend.

When they finally arrived at the Hudson house, the two girls stripped out of their clothes and passed out in Taylor's bed.

"Well, this is the hottest thing I've ever seen," Beau said.

Taylor rolled over and found morning light pouring in through her window. Beau stood next to her bed, his grin impossibly wide. She turned her head to find Reese sprawled out next to her in only her bra and panties. Taylor's hands slid down her own body, finding the same state of dress. She groaned and rolled away from Beau, trying to ignore the pounding in her head.

"Oh, God, don't move. It's so hot. I want to remember it just like this," he said, holding his phone up and snapping several photos.

Taylor threw a pillow at him and nudged Reese awake. "We have company," she whispered.

"Ugh! Stop it. Let me sleep," Reese grunted.

"Reese, is that any way to treat me after the magic we shared last night?" Taylor asked.

Beau coughed and dropped his phone.

"What?" Reese asked. Taylor rolled on top of her and laid her head on Reese's chest.

"You mean you don't remember?" Taylor asked, seeming offended. Reese stared at her friend and then at Beau, whose wide-eyed expression was expectant.

"Shut up. We didn't do anything," she said, pushing Taylor off of her. Taylor laughed and climbed out of bed, heading to the bathroom.

"Not last night, we didn't," she said, turning to wink at Beau.

Knowing that Beau would still be in her room, Taylor dressed before exiting the bathroom. Now that she wasn't sleeping with him, teasing and flirting would be cruel. She also didn't want to explain her sudden change of heart. If challenged, she wasn't sure she *could* explain it.

"Took you long enough. Damn," Reese griped. "How many orgasms can you have in one shower?"

"I wouldn't know. You're the one with the twelve-speed-turbo-charged-burn-your-clit-off shower massager."

"Touché," Reese said. "Well, I'm out. You two behave." She gave a wave, slipped into her shoes, and was through the door before they could respond.

"What are you doing here?" Taylor asked, sitting on her bed next to Beau. He seemed too comfortable in her space, and she wasn't ready to admit why she suddenly didn't like him there.

"What? We can't hang out?" he asked, sliding his phone into his back pocket. He tapped the end of her nose and gave her a smile. It was a simple gesture, something he'd done since they were kids.

"Yeah, we can hang out. What did you have in mind?"

"I don't know. I just had to get out of my house. My dad's been busting my balls lately."

Taylor leaned on his shoulder, knowing exactly how he felt. She hated that they could relate.

"Okay. I say we watch a couple of movies. Lots of blood, bombs, and bad guys."

"I get to hold the remote?" Beau asked.

"In my house? Ugh. Fine. But I get the center chair."

"Deal."

When the credits rolled on the second Tarantino film, Beau let out a sigh and turned the lights up using the remote.

"Why can't life be simple like that? Don't like someone? Shoot him in the face. Your family members are assholes? Blow them up," Beau said.

Taylor let out a laugh while she chewed on the end of a cherry licorice stick. "Wow. Your dad's that bad? At least mine is gone most of the time."

"He's been up my ass lately. He wants a report of where I've been and where I'm going. And what George Upton wants, George Upton gets. Like, suddenly he decided to be a parent or something. Keeps asking me tons of questions about you, and Henry too. He's so paranoid."

"George and Henry need to get in a boxing ring and hash this shit out and leave us out of it," Taylor said.

"Yeah."

"Hey!" Taylor jumped out of her chair. "Let's go smoke a bowl and try not to drown in my pool."

Beau blew out a breath and smiled up at her amused face. "Sounds awesome."

An hour later, they both lay drifting on rafts in her enormous pool, peaceful and content in their high state. Every once in a while, they would bump into each other before floating off again. Taylor adored having this time with her old friend. She loved that they could have these quiet moments with no awkwardness.

After a while baking in the sun, Taylor's stomach rumbled.

"You hungry?" she shouted from her end of the pool.

"Hell, yeah."

Not wanting to bother the weekend housekeeper with cooking, the two were left to fend for themselves. They raided the fridge and the pantry, before settling on a buffet of junk food. Sitting across from each other at her formal dining room table, they ended the meal with a shared pint of mint chocolate chip gelato.

"I'm stuffed," Beau said, leaning back in his chair.

"More for me."

"I'm going to head home. Or maybe somewhere else."

"Okay," Taylor said, giving him a smile. It was halfhearted, because she didn't really want to be alone in this big empty house again so soon. "I had fun."

"Me, too. Thanks for today, Tay." He tapped the end of her nose and disappeared through the door before she could respond.

The next morning, Suzanne woke her up with a shake of the shoulder.

"Taylor, your mother's on the phone."

"So?"

"She wants to talk to you."

Taylor blew a breath into her pillow, wanting to scream. Instead, she just held her hand out for the phone.

"Hello," she said.

"Taylor! Darling!"

"Yes, Virginia, it's me."

"You know I disapprove of you calling me that. I'm your mother, Taylor. Mom will do just fine."

"Okay, *Mom*," Taylor said, stressing the word. "Where are you?"

"Madrid, sweetheart. How's your summer going? I hope you and Reese are having fun. How's Beau? Has he been around? I heard his father's company is going to fold soon if they don't find an investor. You know how the rumor mill works. Could be all talk. I ran into the Conrads in Monte Carlo. They had a lot to say about George and his company's demise." There was a beat of silence as Taylor tried to formulate an answer to at least one question. "Oh! Fernando, stop that!"

A man's voice came over the line and then her mother's giggling and moaning.

"Mom! I just threw up in my mouth."

"What, dear? Well, I'll see you in a few weeks. Adios!"

Taylor handed the phone back to Suzanne, avoiding her pitying look. Taylor loved her mother, but spending any extended amount of time with the woman would be an excruciating penance she did not deserve. They were opposites in every way possible. Her mother's jet-black hair and huge rack made Taylor, with her honey blond waves and C cups, look adopted. Virginia was all about spray-on bronzer, tattoo eyeliner, and gel nails while Taylor enjoyed real tan lines, going natural, and biting her cuticles. They had nothing in common except for a shared strand of DNA, and most days, Taylor questioned even that.

"I'm going back to sleep," Taylor announced.

"It's Monday. Your yoga instructor will be here at ten. Go get calm estate."

"What? You mean namaste?"

"Yes. That's what I said. Now get up."

"I'll get up in an hour."

Suzanne nodded and left the room.

After a few minutes of lying in bed and staring up at her ceiling, Taylor got up and showered. She threw on some yoga pants and a tank, wanting to be comfortable for the torture that was to come. As she made her way to the seldom used gym in the basement, she ran into Levi at the top of the stairs.

"Hi," she said as they descended together. Levi offered only a nod, though she caught his gaze roaming over her body. When they reached the first floor, Levi turned to walk away. Taylor grabbed him by the wrist, the feel of his skin beneath hers forcing memories to play out in her mind. "Levi, that kiss," she said. "I can't stop thinking about it—about you."

Those weren't the words she had wanted to say, but suddenly she couldn't remember the right ones. This confession left her open and vulnerable. It showed her weakness instead of her prowess. His eyes met hers, alight with some emotion she couldn't place—or didn't want to. Here, beneath the grand chandelier, they displayed a kaleidoscope of colors.

"That kiss was a mistake. It won't happen again."

He yanked his arm from her grip and disappeared down a hallway. Taylor frowned at the floor and continued down to the basement.

As hard as she tried to meditate while stretching her body in pose after pose, all she could think about was Levi. Nothing had ever been this hard for her. She never had to be the pursuer. Taylor wasn't sure she liked having to do all the work. Then Levi's handsome face and poetic words came to mind during Warrior pose, and as she transformed into Mountain pose, she had a feeling he would be worth every bit of effort.

For lunch, Taylor met Reese at their favorite sushi place. After being seated on the patio, they sat quietly and watched people pass by.

"Oh, look at him," Reese said, nodding to an older gentleman in the corner of the restaurant. "He's hot."

Taylor laughed, "No, he's not. He looks like Beau's dad." She focused harder and realized it was George Upton. "Wait, that *is* Beau's dad."

He was seated alone, sipping scotch. Taylor knew this not from the color of the drink but because she had once been a part of his family. His tan skin, too-white smile, and black hair with gray at the temples made George Upton look like money. He had soft but masculine features that reminded her of Beau. Taylor smiled, remembering all the times spent at his house as a child. George had been around a lot. Consequently, Taylor had more memories of this man than of her own father.

George caught her gaze and grinned, raising his glass in her direction. She gave a slight wave and returned her attention to her menu. There was something off about his smile; it was not the warm good-to-see-you smile she usually received. This one was dark, as if he held secrets behind his perfect teeth.

"Damn, if that's what Beau is going to look like when he grows up, you better snatch him up now." Reese plastered on her best smile and gave George a tiny wave.

"Stop that! Beau and I are better off just being friends."

"What's up for tomorrow? Want to go with me to the Plaza? I need to get a new phone."

"Can't. I'm going to do that volunteer thing with Ade."

"You were serious about that?" Reese said, her eyes flicking over to George Upton and back to Taylor.

"Yes. Why not?"

"Girl, I could think of a million reasons not to go to Santa Ana."

"Snob," Taylor said, hitting Reese's shoulder.

"I'm not a snob. I'm just better than everyone else."

Taylor rolled her eyes and took a sip of her drink. She loved Reese, but sometimes the girl just needed to be slapped around a bit.

"Whatever. Okay, check out this girl's hair," Reese said discreetly. "Nineteen ninety-five called, they want their scrunchie back."

Taylor laughed and looked around for their next victim. "Forget the scrunchie, look at that waiter at the bar," she said.

The man was tall and lean with dark hair and light eyes. His muscled arms flexed and strained as he opened a bottle of wine. Reese watched Taylor watching him and shook her head.

"What?" Taylor asked.

"You're pathetic."

"Oh, come on. He's hot. You can't deny that."

"I'm not sure what your attraction is to service industry workers. He looks just like your little maintenance man crush."

Taylor looked again and noticed the resemblances to Levi, the strong jaw and tattoos peeking out from his uniform sleeve.

"He does not," Taylor insisted, crossing her arms and scowling at her friend.

"So I guess you haven't slept with him yet?"

"No. Resistance is strong with this one."

"Maybe he's gay," Reese said, pouring soy sauce over a piece of sushi and popping it into her mouth.

"Definitely not. But he's got a big I'm-poor-and-life's-not-fair chip on his shoulder." Taylor shrugged and used her chopsticks to grab some noodles.

"Look, I've seduced my fair share of men and, believe it or not, I've had to work for it a time or two." Reese sat back and lifted her sunglasses to the top of her head as the waiter refilled their drinks. "There are two ways to approach a situation like this. Not that I approve," she clarified.

"Not that I need your approval," Taylor countered.

"One, you could invest time and actually get to know him. Find out what he likes, what makes him tick. But in this case, I think that's probably not necessary."

"So what's the second way?"

"Piss him off."

"What? That's it?" Taylor asked, gesturing wildly with her chopsticks. "I piss him off all the time."

"No, I mean really make him angry. You've got to get him so worked up that he loses control. Anger is a powerful, passionate emotion, Taylor, and as long as you don't let him run off, you'll get what you want."

Reese chewed on another piece of sushi and smiled. Taylor thought about her theory. She knew that Levi was a passionate person. She knew that she could use that against him. Taylor could read the signs clearly. Levi wanted her as much as she wanted him. She just didn't understand what was holding him back, why he wouldn't surrender to those desires. Maybe it was their four-year age difference, or maybe the fact that he was an employee of her father's. One way or another, she would find a way to break him down.

"Ladies," George said, approaching their table.

"Hello, George," Taylor answered. "Aren't you breaking the rules right now?"

"Some things are worth breaking the rules for," he said, his eyes never leaving Reese.

"Oh, George, this is Reese Sutherland. Reese, George Upton."

"A pleasure," he said, shaking her hand, his fingers stroking the skin on the inside of her wrist. "Quite a pleasure."

Reese gave him her best seductive smile and released his grip.

"You girls have a fantastic lunch. It's on me. Taylor, it was good to see you."

He smiled at Reese, not a friendly kind of grin between strangers but a seductive smirk. George gave Taylor a squeeze on her shoulder before making his way to the door.

All morning Levi and Crystal searched the two guest bedrooms and one accessible office on the second floor. Still unable to get into the locked office, Levi knew their search could not be complete without it. Each time they cleared a room without finding the safe, his frustration grew. It ate away at him and brought feelings of inadequacy and failure.

"Just take a break, man," Crystal said. "Find somewhere to chill."

He made his way to the pool house and looked back at the Hudson residence. He knew it was just a building, but he felt as though it was a live being taunting him, proving him incompetent. It slept at night and formulated new plans on how keep Levi out, how to keep its secrets hidden.

Rain began to dot the concrete outside, creating a pattern until it was completely soaked. Levi tapped out the melody to Amos Lee's "Night Train" on the window. He blew out a breath, creating an instant patch of gray condensation on the glass and watched it disappear just as quickly. Behind him, the door opened and closed. He didn't need to turn around to know who it was.

"I've been looking for you," Taylor said. There was no sound besides the rain outside.

"Well, you found me," Levi answered, keeping his back to her and emotion out of his voice.

"What are you doing out here?"

"Thinking."

"About?" Taylor asked.

"Nothing important," he said, shrugging and looking over his shoulder. He turned back toward the window. Levi stood a better chance against her if he wasn't faced with the wet, sheer fabric of her T-shirt clinging to her body or the way slick tendrils of hair stuck to her face and neck. "Did you need something, Taylor? Or are you just here to give me hell?"

"Why do you do that? Why do you always assume the worst from me, Levi?"

"Because you haven't proved me wrong yet." His words were strong and delivered the blow he hoped they would. Silence engulfed them until Taylor stepped toward him.

"So let me prove you wrong now," she said, her soft voice directly behind him. Taylor's body molded to his from behind. She slid her hands over his shoulders and dragged them down his biceps. "Let me in, Romeo."

Her touch felt comforting, and for a few seconds he let himself enjoy it. But then her hands continued their journey around his body, over his stomach and down to his crotch. He stepped away and spun to face her.

"Stop," he groaned. He hated how much he wanted her and that it was evident in the strain of his voice.

As if a switch were flipped, something changed in Taylor. She went from smoldering temptress to raving bitch in two seconds flat.

"Are you gay? Is that the problem?"

He shook his head, smirking at her attempt to break him. Taylor knew better; she was just trying to push his buttons. He wouldn't allow it. "That's it, isn't it? I knew you were too pretty to like girls."

"Taylor, stop being a brat."

"What happened to you, Levi? Did you have an abusive childhood? Did you have a drunk for a mother?"

"You shut the fuck up!" he yelled. His voice seemed to echo in the small room, and Taylor cringed. Levi stepped to her, his hot breath fanning down onto her face. His hands formed fists and he shoved them in his pockets to maintain control. "Don't say another word about her."

He could see a fire inside her now and knew this would not end well. Taylor squared her shoulders and stood up taller.

"That's it. You have mommy issues, right? Did she smack you around a bit? Did she whore around on your dad?"

"No, Taylor!" His loud voice boomed and she shrank away from him. "None of that shit happened, because my mom was dead!"

Never in his life had Levi wanted to hit a woman so badly, so he did the only thing he could—he threw open the door and ran away from that house, away from his failure, his dead mother, and the infuriating Taylor Hudson.

"Levi!" she yelled, her voice getting lost in the pelting rain. "Levi! Stop running!"

Taylor ran after his retreating form as fast as her legs would move. She stumbled a few times but refused to take her eyes off his back, terrified that she would lose him. She wrapped her arms around her waist, completely soaked and chilled from the rain. Her now transparent shirt stuck to her skin, and the wet denim of her jeans weighed her down. She kicked out of her shoes and kept moving.

"Levi, please!" she yelled again, her desperate voice wavering.

Levi's pace slowed and he finally stopped, but he didn't turn around. The green material of his uniform was like a second skin, the rain making it appear black. His fists clenched and uncurled, the ligaments in his arms raised like cords. For an instant, she questioned herself. Had she pushed him too far?

Taylor caught up to him near the edge of the property. She never came out here and was surprised to find a picnic table and an old metal shed. Levi stood before her, his shoulders rising and falling with each breath. She moved close enough to touch him but didn't dare.

"Levi," she whispered. "I'm sorry." He shook his head, still refusing to face her. "Stop running from me. Stop denying what you want, what we both want," she said between panting breaths.

Taylor trembled when he finally turned toward her, a fierce look in his eyes. His jaw ticced, the muscles of his neck strained beneath the taut skin. He looked like a predator, and if she hadn't wanted him so badly, she would have had been terrified.

He stalked toward her as if she were his last meal before execution. Taylor stumbled backward until she was pressed against the shed. Under the cover of trees, they were not completely exposed to the downpour.

The closer Levi got, the quicker her pulse thundered in her ears. Taylor's breaths came faster and she felt dizzy from the need and the want churning inside.

Levi stepped forward and closed the space between them, pressing his body to hers. The warmth of his skin penetrated their cold, wet clothes and soothed Taylor's shaking body. His green-gray eyes held hers. They displayed worry and doubt and fuming anger.

The need to touch him took over. She reached up and removed his hat, throwing it into the trees. His messy brown hair fell into his eyes, beautiful and imperfect. Taylor ran her fingers through it, scraping her nails against his scalp. She wrapped her fingers around a handful and refused to let go. Time seemed to stand still as they held on to each other and exchanged bated breaths and heated glances. Fat drops of rain fell around them in a melodic *plunk, plunk* countdown.

Taylor lost her breath when Levi leaned in and attacked her lips. The force bumped her head into the wall, but she didn't care. His kiss, the taste of his tongue and the nip of his teeth, made her indifferent to anything that wasn't Levi. She moaned into his mouth. He swallowed it and pressed her harder, held her tighter. His fingers clawed into her ribs before sliding down and cupping her ass through her soaked jeans.

Levi's lips left hers. Taylor gasped for air, turning her face to the sky and welcoming the rain that fell between the branches. He traveled down her neck, licking and sucking, his warm tongue igniting her. She scraped her nails along his scalp and grabbed a handful of hair, pulling him back to her lips.

Taylor's fingers fumbled with the buttons of his work shirt, but her lips never left his. When she got them undone, Levi peeled the soaked shirt from his body before reaching behind his head and yanking off his white T-shirt as well. Taylor took in the sight before her. Beautiful ink covered his upper right arm and shoulder. The smooth skin of his defined chest was a stark contrast against the images of fire and water inked into his flesh. Taylor traced the line between them.

Levi fisted the thin material of her V-neck T-shirt and pulled. The fabric ripped easily in his hands, and the sound shocked them out of their frenzied lust. Levi took a step back and watched Taylor. They were mirror images of water-slicked skin and heaving chests, swollen lips and desire. The art of his arm and shoulder looked like glossy wet paintings on a marble canvas.

Levi reached out for her again and pulled her in for another kiss. His hands and lips were punishing, and Taylor loved the feel of it. She slid her hands down his chest and stomach, drifting over hard muscle to find his belt buckle. Her hands worked quickly to get his offensive pants out of her way. Soon she was granted the beautiful sight of his tented gray boxer briefs.

Levi kicked out of his pants and stood like a shrine among the trees. Their eyes met again as Taylor tried to say everything she wanted to say—yet she couldn't. *She wanted him. She wanted this.* His expression was still one of lust and fiery hate. Levi let out a hiss as her cold hand skated down his body and grabbed hold of him. He was soft skin and hard warmth in her hand, everything she imagined.

Reluctantly, she let go and moved her hands to her own jeans. Taylor unfastened the button and slid the zipper down, working hard to push the wet material from her legs. Naked and cold, she went to him. Taylor pressed her lips to his chin, his jaw, and then just below his ear.

"Levi, please," she said.

His arms slid around and lifted her off the ground. Levi walked her over to the picnic table and placed her on top. He didn't hesitate or ask permission before entering her. Taylor cried out against his shoulder, biting down on the salty skin there.

At that moment, Taylor felt like a circuit that had been completed. As if this was what she'd been missing her whole life. The smell of rain and nature mixed with Levi left her dizzy. She lay on the table as Levi held her thighs around his waist. His rough fingers dug into the flesh of her thighs, pulling Taylor against him with every thrust. The combination of their bodies crashing together, the biting pain of the wooden table on her back, and the complete fulfillment of Levi inside her sent a blissful kind of pleasure through her. It was an erotic pulse that originated at her center and radiated outward, stinging her fingers and toes. Levi slid one hand between them and pressed his thumb to her sensitive bundle of nerves. Taylor gasped, her back arching up.

"Give it up, Taylor," Levi growled into her ear, his first words since all this began. "It belongs to me and I want it so fucking bad."

Those words sent Taylor flying over the edge. She cried out and clung to him as he continued to take her body relentlessly.

"Is this what you wanted, Taylor? Is it?" he asked, his voice a low and feral snarling sound.

"Yes, yes," she answered on each breath. "Yes."

Levi's rhythm increased now, divine and punishing at the same time. She clawed at his skin, needing him harder and faster—just needing him.

"Fuck," he breathed. "See what you do to me?"

He slammed into her roughly and lay over her, pinning Taylor between his hard body and the harder table as his climax took over. He stared down at Taylor, a beautiful, angry kind of frown gracing his lips. One hand slid beneath her hair and gripped the base of her neck while the other fist beat against the table. Levi bit down on his lip as a strangled moan escaped and water dripped from his hair onto her face. She was overwhelmed, the entire experience burned into her memory—every sight, touch, taste, scent, and sound.

Their chests pressed together, each fighting for breath against the other. All this time Taylor wanted him, wanted to have him. She thought once she did, it would be out of her system and she could move on. But this felt too right, too wild and comforting at the same time. She knew she would need more.

Levi pulled out of her and Taylor sat up, her feet finding their place on the wet ground. He didn't look at her as he pulled his pants back up over his thighs and buckled his belt. There was a looming finality to this dance of redressing, something that Taylor already dreaded.

She struggled into her wet jeans as Levi searched for the rest of their clothes. He pulled on his T-shirt and handed her his green uniform shirt.

"I tore your shirt. You'll need something to wear," he said, his eyes not meeting hers.

She nodded and slid it over her freezing skin. Even through the perfume of rain and sex, she could smell him on the shirt.

Levi retrieved his hat, slicked back his wet hair, and placed it on his head. A sinking feeling kicked her in the gut, a desperation that she didn't want to own up to.

"Levi . . ." Taylor started, but she stopped when she didn't know how to finish.

She watched him turn and walk through the drizzling rain toward the house. She regretted how they got there, but she wasn't sorry about what happened. When he was gone, Taylor recognized the feeling haunting her, the sick nervousness that ignited. She wanted him to hold her and whisper sweet words against her mouth. She wanted to make him smile and watch him pluck at the strings of a guitar. She wanted something she'd never wanted before. She wanted him to stay.

9. radiohead and hurricanes

Levi turned out of the driveway and hit the accelerator, trying to put as much distance as possible between him and Taylor Hudson. At the stop sign at the end of the street, he slammed his hand on the dusty dashboard until it cracked beneath his fist.

"Fuck!"

He was disgusted with himself, disappointed in his weakness. In this game of cat and mouse, no one was declared the winner. When he waved the white flag and finally took her, Levi felt more alive than he had in years. All of their flirting, foreplay, and fighting came together and erupted in the most satisfying and sadistic experience he'd ever had. Levi didn't want to want Taylor, but the more he touched her, the more evident it became that he would always lose this battle.

A horn honked from behind him and Levi gave an apologetic wave before proceeding through the intersection. Kyle called on his way home, concerned when they'd lost visual and audio over an hour ago. So Levi confessed his crime and waited for the worst.

"This changes nothing, man. You've still got a job to do and it's still yours. You've got to get back in there. The house, I mean. Not Taylor," Kyle said. Levi gave a hollow laugh. "Too soon?"

"Too soon."

"Well, no one could have held out forever. She was throwing herself at you. I am kind of disappointed, though."

"Why?" Levi asked, pulling onto the highway.

"I owe Crystal fifty dollars now."

"You guys were betting on whether I would sleep with her? Assholes." Levi hung up and concentrated on getting home.

Inside his apartment, he let the door seal him off from the rest of the world. His first inclination was to go out and pick a fight with someone. He needed to get rid of this hostile energy. But he couldn't take that risk. Instead, Levi took a scalding hot shower before sliding into bed with his guitar and a bottle of whiskey. He ignored his phone and let the strumming hum of steel strings drown out the feelings of panic hurtling around his head. The whiskey kicked in and Levi welcomed the numbness with a satisfied grin.

The next morning, he woke with a killer hangover and an empty bottle as a bedmate. Levi placed a call to Mandy, letting her know that he would be out sick for the day. She gushed over him, offering to deliver soup or anything he needed. He politely refused.

Levi spent his entire day trying to deny his desire for Taylor.

He told himself over and over that she was just a kid, a manipulative, beautiful kid. But he knew better. Her fierce words and the way she clawed at his skin represented all the want and pain of a woman. That afternoon, when the buzzing frustration beneath his skin became too much, he headed to the nearest YMCA. Levi tucked himself into the back corner of the gym and beat a punching bag into submission. He swung and connected with the leather over and over, letting this inanimate object bear his irritation. When his shirt was sweat soaked and his arms shook from his effort, he finally gave up.

Back at his apartment, Levi showered and ate a sandwich while flipping through television channels. Nothing appealed to him. He felt suffocated and too alone here. He grabbed his father's guitar and headed out to Mavericks.

He added his name to the lineup for open mic night and took a seat at the bar.

"Hey, man. Where you been?" Gregory asked.

"That new job keeps me busy," Levi replied.

"You all right? You look like shit."

"Fine." Levi shook his head and looked up at the stage.

"Let me guess. Female troubles?"

"Am I that obvious?"

"I been around the block with enough shorties to recognize girl troubles. How 'bout a drink? On the house," Gregory offered.

"Nah, I'm still recovering from last night."

Gregory tucked his dish towel into his back pocket and leaned over the bar top.

"I don't know if you're trying to get rid of one or trying to keep one. Either way, use it, man."

"Use what?" Levi asked.

"That feeling. Forget the excuses and bullshit. Use it onstage."

Levi nodded. When it was time, he took his place on the

single barstool set beneath a white-hot spotlight. The mic stood before him, ready to serve. Levi flipped the switch to power it on and cleared his throat. His pick slid across the strings, and the crowd's roaring conversations dropped down to a whisper.

His random plucking turned into the sounds of Radiohead's "Talk Show Host." The eerie notes lulled Levi as he closed his eyes and pictured Taylor. His voice was strained but hard as he played the melody between lines. He heard no clinking of glass, no murmured conversations, only his song.

You want me, fucking come on and break the door down

Levi dropped his head and opened his eyes. They stayed trained on his fingers working the new strings of the old guitar. He wondered how many times this guitar expressed things his father couldn't. He wondered if he sang now for Taylor . . . or for himself.

One more chord and the last notes faded out of the speakers. There was a sobering moment of stillness and silence. Levi lifted his eyes to a muted crowd. Gregory gave a whistle from behind the bar and everyone broke into applause. They clapped and cheered until he was uncomfortable up there, until he had no choice but to start a new song.

After a few more, Levi gave a quick nod and exited the stage. As soon as he was out of the spotlight, he felt lighter, freer. He slid his guitar onto the bar and signaled to Gregory.

"I'll take that drink now."

The bartender smiled and grabbed a beer for him, sliding it down the bar into his waiting hand.

"Good job up there, man. You got real talent. Not that auto tune bullshit," Gregory said. Levi grinned and took a long pull from the ice-cold bottle. The liquid cooled his insides. "Every girl in this place wants to fuck you or marry you. Want me to be your wingman? I spotted a pair of hotties drooling near the stage."

"Ha. What I don't need is any more women in my life, but thanks."

Gregory let out a giant cackling laugh and headed down the bar to serve someone else. Levi finished his beer and left a tip for the free drink.

Twenty minutes later, he lay in bed and mentally prepared himself for work tomorrow. When his phone rang a little before midnight, he knew exactly who it was.

"Boss," he greeted.

"Levi, I hear you didn't go to work today."

"I wasn't feeling well." His voice went up at the end like he was asking a question. He cleared his throat and tried again. "Stayed in bed all day."

"I don't suppose this has anything to do with the fact that you fucked the Hudson girl, does it?"

He slammed his fist down onto his mattress and mouthed the word "shit."

"No," was all he said.

"Good. Frankly, I don't care who you stick your dick in, Levi. But if you jeopardize this operation, I will not hesitate to end you. You fuck with my money, I'll fuck with your life. Do you understand?"

"Loud and clear, Boss."

The call ended and Levi stared at the glow of his phone screen. As much as he tried to deny Taylor Hudson, she'd found a weakness in his armor and went in for the kill. He'd taken her in anger and frustration, but there were no words to describe the feel of them finally coming together. It was like being connected to something bigger than himself, something out of his control, something completely terrifying but also exhilarating.

———

Adrienne picked up Taylor around one o'clock. The drive to Santa Ana was quiet. Taylor fidgeted in her seat and adjusted the air vents a few times before Adrienne spoke up.

"You don't have to be nervous," she said.

Taylor dropped her hands to her lap and pasted on an easy smile. "I'm not nervous."

"These kids are not much younger than us, you know? We should be able to relate to them better than an adult."

"Yeah, you're right," Taylor answered. "I'm just distracted. I thought this summer would be really chill, and it's turning out to be . . . well, a little crazy."

"Does this have anything to do with your handyman crush?"

Taylor leaned her head back and kept her eyes on the road ahead of them. "Maybe."

"Well," Adrienne said, pulling up to the youth center, "I'm here if you want to talk. I know we haven't been super close in the past few years, but I'm still your friend, Taylor."

"I know, Ade. Thanks."

The girls hopped out of the car and made their way inside. Adrienne led Taylor around the basketball courts to the back side of the gym. They entered a set of double doors that led to an open room with tables and chairs.

"We have to go to the director's office first," Adrienne said, pointing toward a long hall.

Taylor nodded and followed. There were lots of framed awards and certificates on the wall, and Taylor found herself reading over each one.

"Whoa," she said, when someone bumped into shoulder. Taylor turned to face the offender and saw a tall redheaded girl standing there, gawking at her. She rubbed her shoulder and frowned.

"Sorry," the redhead offered. Her eyes widened and she let out a choking kind of cough. "I didn't see you there."

"Oh, hey, Crystal," Adrienne piped up. "This is my friend Taylor."

Crystal gave a tight, forced smile showing too many teeth. "Taylor, nice to meet you. For the first time. Ever." She gave a small wave and pointed over her shoulder. "I've, uh, I've got to go. See you around."

"Bye," Adrienne sang.

"Do I have something on my face?" Taylor asked, continuing down the hall.

"No, why?"

"She was just staring at me. It was weird."

"Well, Taylor. You are incredibly beautiful. Maybe she's a lesbian."

"Ha ha. So funny. How do you know her?"

"Just through volunteering. I participated in a program last summer and she was a volunteer with me."

Taylor nodded and followed Adrienne into the office. They were introduced to the director of the reading program and sat through a short training video.

"Since you girls have some experience with this, I think you'll do just fine. These kids have somehow slipped through the cracks. Most of them are between twelve and sixteen but aren't reading beyond a third-grade level. They all have assignments from us, so you won't be going in completely blind. You'll work to help them complete at least one section of the assigned work each time you're here. We appreciate your volunteering to help give them a shot."

Both girls nodded and were led into the reading room. Adrienne was assigned to a boy named David, while Taylor was introduced to a teenage girl named Dee.

"Hi, Dee. I'm Taylor."

"Hey." Dee seemed shy, keeping her eyes on the table while doodling around the edge of her assignment.

"Tell me about yourself," Taylor said, trying to get a conversation started.

"Not much to tell. Got two older brothers locked up and a baby sister. My mom works two jobs, so I take care of the little one a lot. Just moved from Florida."

"Do you like it here?"

"It's different. The weather's nice, I guess. No hurricanes."

"Nah, just earthquakes." Dee's eyes widened and Taylor couldn't help but smile. "Well, I've lived here my whole life. I think you'll love it."

Dee stuck a finger through a hole in the sleeve of her T-shirt and nodded.

"Let's get started on your assignment."

"I really don't think it's gonna help. I just don't get it," Dee murmured.

"Well, that's why I'm here, right? To help you get it?"

Dee shrugged and slid the paper toward Taylor. After reading the instructions, Taylor worked hard to engage Dee and get her to complete the assignment. The girl's heart just wasn't in it. The entire two hours were a struggle, but Taylor remained cool and persistent. By the end of their time together, she wasn't sure if she'd made any headway at all.

"That was fun," Adrienne said excitedly as they headed home.

"I'm not sure I'd use the word 'fun.' My kid doesn't want to learn the material. It was like she would rather be anywhere but with me learning that stuff."

"She'll come around, I'm sure. Why did you enjoy it so much last time?"

"I don't know. I guess I didn't take it so seriously. The kid I worked with was the same age as me and we mostly talked about music."

"There you go," Adrienne said. "Find something you have in common or something she's passionate about."

"Right," Taylor said, thinking it over and having no idea where to find common ground with Dee.

"Just don't give up on her, Tay. She's where she's at now because people gave up on her."

Taylor nodded. Those words sank in and stayed with her. She would show up again next week and the week after that, until Dee understood that she could depend on Taylor. She would be an advocate for that girl. She would help her to grow and learn so that she had a fighting chance in this world. She would convey how important an education was, and she would be an example for Dee.

When Taylor crawled in bed that night, she lay in the dark and, for the first time in hours, thought about Levi. For some reason, after the day's events, she felt closer to him. She felt like she understood him a little more. With him missing work today, she didn't know if she'd ever see him again. Taylor vowed to make sure he knew how sorry she was for the terrible things she'd said to him, to make sure he knew that she wasn't the person he assumed her to be. She was something new every day, changing and evolving, seeing the world through different eyes. Taylor fell asleep with her head full of thoughts and her heart full of good intentions.

10. carnal desires and plan b

Taylor woke early, full of nervous energy. She threw on a sports bra and running shorts, and headed straight to the gym in her basement. Willing the physical exertion to numb her thoughts of Levi and feelings of guilt, Taylor pushed herself until her legs felt like jelly and her lungs burned. When she was exhausted, she turned off the treadmill and headed upstairs. With her earbuds still in place, she pulled a bottle of water from the refrigerator and gulped it down in three long swallows. Her hips swayed back and forth, still moving to the music in her ears. Beads of sweat ran down her back and soaked into the band of her shorts.

"Ugh, I need a shower," she said to herself.

She threw her bottle into the recycling bin and crossed the kitchen. When she passed the pantry, two strong arms wrapped around her, one at the waist and the other over her mouth. She screamed but soon recognized the calloused fingers on her lips and the hard body pressed against her back.

"Shhh," Levi whispered. "It's just me."

She let out a breath and relaxed against his chest. Levi removed his hand from her mouth and slid it down her neck and shoulder. Taylor spun in his arms, looking into eyes she never thought she'd see again.

"Levi," she said. "Thank God." Her hands grabbed on to his shoulders, her fingers digging into the muscles there. "I'm sorry. I'm really sorry about the things I said to you. I didn't mean them. When you didn't show up yesterday, I thought you weren't coming back."

"I'm here. I'm not going anywhere," he whispered.

Taylor gave a tiny smile and stretched up on her tiptoes to reach his lips. Their kiss started off slow and hesitant, a question of forgiveness. It quickly escalated to something heavier and pleading.

"Meet me in my shower in five minutes."

She pressed a kiss to his hard jaw and made an escape before he could deny her. Taylor practically sprinted up the stairs. She took off her sweaty gym clothes in the bathroom and tossed them into the laundry chute.

Stepping under the warm spray of water, Taylor let it wash away everything from the past two days. The desperate longing, the anxiety—it all circled the drain and slipped away.

She quickly soaped up her body, scrubbing the sweat from her skin. Taylor lathered her hair, and as she leaned back to rinse, she wondered where Levi was. She kept her eyes closed, letting the water take the soap and bubbles down her body.

When she was done, Taylor toweled off, disappointed that Levi hadn't joined her. She slipped into her favorite shorts and a navy T-shirt and then eyed herself in the full-length mirror. She wasn't sure what she was looking for. Over the years, she had studied her face and her body enough to know what she looked like. She wondered what Levi saw when he looked at her.

Leaving her closet, Taylor walked into her room to find Levi there. He stood leaning against her closed bedroom door. She smiled before she even thought to. His large arms were crossed over his chest, and his hat hung on her doorknob.

"You didn't join me," Taylor said. "Are you still mad?"

He shook his head, though his expression was serious.

"Come here," she said, needing him closer.

Levi stepped toward Taylor, meeting her near the foot of her bed. She pushed the hair away from his face and scratched her nails along his scalp. Finally, he slid his arms around her waist and pulled her against his body. His lips found hers, teasing and tasting, demanding. Taylor held on to his shoulders while his mouth dominated hers.

They were a frenzied mess of roaming hands. He greedily swallowed every mewling sound that came from her, while Taylor couldn't get enough. She wrapped her hands around his collar and tried to tug him toward her bed. Levi did not move.

"What's wrong?" she said, looking up into his cautious eyes.

Levi sighed and rubbed the back of his neck as her hands fell away. "What are we doing?" he asked.

She wrapped one arm around her middle and the other hand rested on her hip.

"We're doing what we want to, Romeo."

A tiny smile pulled up on one side of his mouth at the nickname. "You're my employer's kid," he said, taking a seat on her bed. His hands scrubbed his face and he blew out a breath.

"I'm not a kid," Taylor said, sitting next to him.

"Don't I fucking know it."

Taylor slid into his lap, her knees on either side of his hips. She rested her forearms on his shoulders and laced her fingers behind his neck.

"Don't make this complicated," she whispered before kissing his jaw. "We're just giving in to our most basic" *kiss* "carnal" *kiss* "desires."

Levi's fingers gripped her waist and he kissed her fully. His aggressive actions made her even more desperate, and she couldn't resist grinding down onto his lap. Taylor leaned against him, pushing him flat on his back.

"Taylor, I've got your—" Suzanne's voice stopped short.

Levi shot up, sending Taylor flying to the floor.

"Ouch! Shit!" Taylor yelled. "What the hell?"

Levi stood up and tried to smooth his rumpled clothes. He stuck a hand out and helped Taylor to her feet. Suzanne stood with her hands on her hips, a dark frown on her usually chipper face. She looked from Levi to Taylor and back to Levi. There was no surprise in her expression.

"I have a letter from Harvard," Suzanne finally said, holding up an envelope.

She walked to Taylor's desk and set the letter there. Taylor shrugged and stepped onto her balcony in an effort to avoid a lecture.

"Levi," Suzanne said. Her eyes glanced to the balcony and back to his face. "I need your help with something downstairs."

Levi nodded and shoved his hands in his pockets. "I'll be there in a minute," he said, looking back at Taylor.

Suzanne left and closed the door behind her with a soft click. His hat swung back and forth from the doorknob.

"Taylor," Levi said, his voice scratchy and thick, "I'm going to go."

She turned to find him leaning against the door, regarding her with his careful gaze. She wanted to wrap her arms around him and curl up in his lap. She wanted to breathe him in and make promises that this wasn't a mistake, that they were good for each other. But those things were fantasy, she knew that this would never end well. She knew that she'd never have all of him and he wouldn't want all of her. All the chasing, all the seduction had been a game to Taylor. *This* did not feel like a game anymore. And that scared the hell out of her.

"Yeah," she answered. Levi looked away, making it easier to say what came next. "You should get back to work. You've got a job to do, right? I'm sure you don't get paid to stand around all day and flirt with the boss's daughter."

His eyes snapped back to hers, cutting through her game. She planned to wave her hand to dismiss him, but something inside her wouldn't do it. *Not this one*, her brain said, *not him.* The tendons in his neck strained as he fought to stay calm. Taylor could see the rage bubbling just below his surface. Without a word, Levi threw on his hat and slammed the door behind him.

Levi knew that Taylor was pushing his buttons, trying to regain control. Still, it didn't quell the fury that made his pulse beat like a drum inside his head. He ran down the stairs and across the foyer, feeling relieved when he reached the front door. Pulling it open, a familiar voice stopped him.

"She'll destroy you, Levi. I love that girl. She won't mean to do it, but it'll happen, because she's a Hudson."

He turned to find Suzanne standing in the foyer. Her arms were crossed, but her face was soft and pleading.

"I know what I'm doing, Suzanne."

"How long do you think Henry will let you two be together?"

"I don't want to be with her. It's not like that," Levi said. He couldn't even tell if he was telling the truth or not.

"Well, I clearly see what neither of you can. In any other circumstance, this could be the greatest thing to happen to either of you, but this is going to end badly. You should stop it now."

He shook his head. "There's nothing to stop."

"If you say so," she said, disappointment evident.

"I do."

That evening, the Boss called a roundtable meeting to discuss the team's progress. Levi, Kyle, and Crystal waited for the Boss to arrive.

"I met Taylor Hudson," Crystal blurted out. Both guys turned toward her. "She was at the Center. I acted like a complete freak."

"What was she doing at the Center?" Levi asked.

Crystal shrugged. "I don't know. She's even prettier in person than through Levi's hat cam. I can see why lover boy would want to hit it." She gave Levi a wink.

"You should be keeping better tabs on your piece of ass," Kyle teased.

"Shut up," Crystal and Levi replied in unison.

The Boss pushed through the door and took a seat, getting them right down to business.

"We've done a background check on every employee that works at the Hudson property and don't foresee any problems with them," Kyle stated. "There are only a few people who come and go, mostly friends of the daughter, Taylor. We've checked each of them, as well."

"Good," the Boss answered, giving the group a sly grin before piercing Crystal with an icy glare.

"Using the camera and Levi's footwork, we've done a grid-pattern layout of the entire property. After finishing that, we started detail work of each room. We've checked and cross-checked the entire first floor, basement, attic, garage, shed, and pool house for the safe and found nothing," Crystal said.

The Boss turned to Levi. "What's the holdup on the second floor?"

"As you know, the only resident in the house right now is Taylor, and she spends most of her time in her room on the second floor. Henry comes and goes, but I've never seen him there," Levi said. "I've done a thorough search of the master and guest bedrooms along with one of the offices up there. I didn't find anything."

The Boss frowned and took a swig of beer, addressing all of them. "Our progress is slower than I'd planned, but I have faith we'll find it. Meanwhile, I will keep working on my end. I know there have been some distractions." The Boss looked directly at Levi. "But if you stay focused, we should be inside that safe in the next few weeks. If not, we move on to Plan B."

"Wait. What's Plan B?" Kyle asked.

"Let's just say it's a more violent way to get what we want." The team was quiet and glanced nervously at each other. "We're done here. I'll be in touch."

The Boss stood and exited the room, leaving them in a whirl-wind of confusion and determination. Levi knew the more violent solution was not what any of them wanted. But he also knew if it came to that, the Boss would not hesitate. They were in too deep and would be held accountable if they abandoned the job.

"What does that mean, a more violent way?" Levi growled.

"It means we have to find that safe. Or else," Crystal said.

"Or else what? We didn't agree to anything like that!"

Kyle stood and faced Levi. "We'll do whatever the Boss says. That's what we signed up for. Stop thinking with your dick and get your head back in the game."

Levi shot up, towering over Kyle, but his friend did not back down. They stood face-to-face, daring each other to make a move or say the wrong thing. Hard breaths and cold stares connected them. Even in his frustration and fury, Levi had enough sense to not take it out on Kyle. He turned, grabbed the wooden table's edge, and flipped it over. It crashed against the floor, along with glasses of water and a beer bottle. Levi took a deep breath and looked at each of his friends before releasing it.

"This is bullshit and you both know it," he said before storming from the room.

The rest of the week was uneventful. Levi went to work each day, trying his damnedest to steer clear of Taylor. He didn't see her or any of her friends, so he assumed that she was spending her time elsewhere. He was hopeful that she was avoiding him too. If they were too weak to deny each other, it was best to just stay away. Levi knew it wasn't a foolproof plan, but it was the best he had.

He completed a search of every room on the second floor except Henry Hudson's personal office. With the locked door and keypad entry, he would have to find another way in.

Friday night, with past disagreements behind them, he met the team at Mavericks for more beer and strategizing. Levi gave a wave to Gregory, grabbed a beer, and took a seat in the corner booth along with Crystal and Kyle.

"You feeling better?" Crystal asked.

"Yeah. Sorry I hulked out on you guys," Levi offered.

"No worries, man," she said. "We're all stressed out. We just handle it differently. You fight. I drink. Kyle plays with his Ninja Turtle action figures."

Levi laughed while Kyle flipped off both of them.

"So?" Kyle asked. "How was it?"

"How was what?" Levi asked.

"You know. Banging the Hudson girl. I bet it was hot. Was it hot? She seems like she'd be crazy in the sack."

Levi drank half his beer and looked at his expectant friend. "I'm not discussing this with you."

"Aww, come on, Levi. I'm too busy working on this job to get laid. Let my dick live vicariously through yours."

"Drop it. And I'd appreciate if you'd abandon all thoughts of my dick."

Crystal laughed and slapped Kyle on the shoulder.

"Stop acting like the job is keeping you from getting laid," she said. "It's more about your general lack of social skills and disregard for hygiene."

"Hey!" Kyle shouted. "I bathe!"

"Once a week doesn't count," Levi piped up.

The two of them laughed while Kyle pouted like a toddler.

"I'm getting another drink," Crystal said, sliding out of the booth and heading to the bar.

Gregory gave a wide smile and flexed his arms for Crystal. Levi saw an opportunity and made his way over to the bar. When Gregory returned with the drink, Levi put his arm around Crystal's shoulders and smiled.

"Gregory, I don't think you've officially met my very good friend Crystal."

He stepped to the counter and held his fist out. Crystal hit it with her own, returning the gesture.

"Nice to meet you, cutie," she said. Gregory only nodded. It was rare to find him speechless.

"He's a Sagittarius, likes graffiti art, that old denim jacket, and has a not-so-secret crush on Mariah Carey," Levi said.

"Aww, man. How you gonna play me like that? What can I say? I like the older ladies. Always have."

"You're terrible," Crystal said to Levi. "Besides, there's nothing wrong with having a crush. Personally, I'm a fan of Lenny Kravitz."

"While I like your appreciation of a brotha, he's tired. I got more game than Lenny."

"Let's hear it, then," she demanded, twirling a piece of her red hair around one finger.

Gregory stared at the woman, unusually quiet. Levi laughed and hopped off the barstool. "Well, my work here is done."

Monday morning brought a mix of emotions from Levi. He had an ounce of hope, because there weren't many more places the safe could be hidden—they'd find it soon for sure. On the flip side of that, dread weighed heavy on his chest. No one had even questioned what if there was no safe? Plus, he was a mess when it came to Taylor. He wanted to see her, to touch her, but when she opened her mouth he wanted to strangle her. He felt himself getting too close to the girl but couldn't deny wanting to be there.

When he pulled into the drive at work, he immediately spotted the Audi TT. Levi's fingers gripped the steering wheel until his knuckles turned white from the force. He cringed as images of that boy up in Taylor's room, his hands on her body, flashed through his mind. The thought drove him insane with jealousy, which he worked to redirect as anger at himself. He had no right to Taylor. He had no reason to possess her, yet the thought of that kid touching her made the blood in his veins boil.

Levi tore into the house, slamming the door behind him. He stood in the foyer for a minute, trying to compose himself and squash down his irrational feelings. He heard laughter and voices from the kitchen.

"Beau, we miss you around here, but you know how Henry feels," Suzanne said.

"Our parents are acting like children. I have a plan to end all that, though."

"What on earth could make those two see eye to eye again?"

"Well, if their only children are in love, what can they do about it? I'm going to make Taylor finally see that she feels the same way about me as I do about her."

Silence fell over the kitchen, and Levi hoped it was as awkward and uncomfortable as he imagined it to be. Levi entered to a familiar scene. Suzanne and Mandy were in their regular spots, but Beau sat on Levi's usual barstool.

"Morning, Levi," Mandy said, waving him in. "Let me get you some coffee."

"Thanks," he replied, eyeing Beau before taking a seat on the opposite side of the counter. The only sound was clinking spoons against ceramic mugs.

"Oh! Where are my manners? Maybe I left them wherever I left my glasses," Suzanne said, patting the top of her head and each pocket before returning her attention to the two men. "Beau, this is our new head of maintenance, Levi. Levi, this is Beau Upton, a longtime friend of Taylor's." She seemed to rethink her statement. "A friend of the family, really."

Levi nodded at him before sipping his coffee. Beau barely gave him a glance. Levi had the sudden urge to get upstairs before Beau could. He slid off the stool, abandoning his coffee.

"I'm off to work, ladies."

He grabbed his work list from the laundry room and hurried toward the stairs. At the top of the landing, he noticed Taylor's bedroom door open. She flitted around her room dancing to some chick rock music.

Levi was hypnotized as he watched her endless legs, fully exposed by the shirt she wore, move and sway to the beat. When she spun and shook her hips, Levi sucked in a breath. A deep, burning desire filled him as he realized Taylor was wearing his work shirt.

The dark green material complemented her skin and the white stitching of his name on her chest made him instantly hard. The few buttons that were fastened left a deep V between her breasts and a slight peek of white lace panties when she moved. It was the sexiest thing he'd ever seen.

"Enjoying the view, buddy?"

Levi spun to find Beau at the top of the stairs, glaring at him. He shoved his fists into his pockets and stepped toward Beau.

"I'm not your fucking buddy."

Beau pushed past him. "Loser."

Every muscle in his body was pulled tight, like a rubber band stretched to its limit. Levi was ready to snap. He controlled his temper long enough to let Beau get by, only because he knew what the boy was about to find. It wouldn't take long for him to piece together the puzzle. Levi knew he should be concerned about anyone finding out about their secret, undefined relationship, but the part of him that wanted to lay claim to this girl didn't care. He pressed himself against the wall outside Taylor's bedroom and waited.

"Hey, Tay," Beau said.

Taylor jumped and turned to find Beau sitting at her desk. She threw her hand over her heart.

"Shit, Beau. You scared me. Stop sneaking up on people, creeper."

"Me? You need to talk to your maintenance guy. He's the creeper. I found him watching you when I came upstairs. Don't worry, I took care of it."

Taylor rolled her eyes and walked over to the desk, lowering the volume of her music.

"What did you do?" she asked as she crossed her arms and tapped her bare foot.

"I just told him . . . Wait. What the fuck are you wearing?" he squeaked out.

"Huh?"

"Taylor, is that his shirt?"

She looked down at the shirt and smoothed her hand down the front. "Yeah, it's his," she answered honestly.

"What? Why?" he yelled, jumping up and knocking the desk chair over on its side.

"Beau, stop being so dramatic," she said, tossing her hair over her shoulder.

He grabbed her shoulders roughly and turned her to face him. His gaze dropped down to Levi's embroidered name and back to her face.

"Are you fucking him?"

"Beau," Taylor warned.

"That's disgusting. He's your employee. He looks like a goddamn criminal!"

"Shut up!" she yelled back. "You know nothing about him."

Of course, she realized that she didn't know much about Levi either, but she wanted to. Taylor shrugged out of his grip and turned away, changing the music to something slower. She closed her eyes and inhaled deeply.

Beau approached her slowly, his footsteps steady. "Taylor, you don't have to go slumming with someone like him. I'm here," he said in a softer, kinder voice.

Taylor faced him again, this time unable to tamp down the anger. "Beau Upton, the only slumming I've been doing was with you, you jerk. Get out of my house!"

"You're kicking me out? Seriously?"

"Go!" she yelled.

He held up his hands in surrender, but she saw the shock in his eyes, the pain barely hidden by outrage.

"Fine. But don't call me when you're done with your charity case. I wouldn't touch your filthy ass now."

Beau stalked out of her room and down the stairs. Taylor grabbed the closest thing she could reach—the Whitman book—and threw it at the open doorway.

"Ugh! Stupid boys!" She picked up a shoe and hurled it in the same direction. "Assholes!"

"Ouch!"

She looked over her shoulder to find Levi, holding the book and shoe.

"You dropped these," he said as he gave her a slightly crooked smirk.

Taylor walked over and snatched them from his hands. "Thanks," she grunted.

Levi followed Taylor back into her bedroom and shut the door behind him, the whole while keeping his eyes glued to her bare legs.

"That's a nice shirt you have there."

"Yeah, I like it," she said, looking up at him through her lashes, her cheeks reddened from the argument.

"It looks really fucking good on you." Levi took a step closer. "But it's mine. You're a thief, rich girl."

Taylor dragged her fingers through her hair, across her chest, and down to the buttons, where she began to unfasten them.

"I'm sure you need it back, then, don't you?"

Levi nodded, exhaling at the sight of her exposed skin and tiny white panties.

"Well? What are you waiting for? Come get it."

He stepped behind her and pulled the uniform shirt from her shoulders, tossing it to the floor. "This is mine." Levi swept her hair to one side and placed a light kiss on her neck. "This is mine." His mouth was hot against her skin.

Taylor gasped at his domineering voice and possessive declarations. His warm breath fanned over her skin like a man marking his territory. Something about him made Taylor want to throw her charmed life away and live in the shadows. So she gave herself over to his command. She knew she belonged to him, if only for these few stolen moments.

Levi's hard hand slid around her waist, and Taylor sighed. When his fingertips slid beneath the lace of her panties, she raised her arms and ran her hands through his hair. He curled his fingers to cup her sex, and Taylor whimpered.

"What's this?" Levi asked, his breath hot in her ear.

Taylor bit her lip, and when he shifted his hips into her backside, she let out a stuttered breath. "Yours."

He hummed, satisfied with her answer, and gently bit down on her neck. Levi tossed Taylor onto her bed and let his lips and tongue taste every inch of her body. He sucked on the pulse beneath her ear before sliding down to worship her breasts. Levi scraped his chin along her stomach and his teeth along her inner thighs. He left kisses behind each knee and on each dimple at the base of her spine. He teased her to the point of complete abandon. Each breath expelled a plea or his name, and it only spurred him on.

"I love making you beg," he rasped.

When Taylor finally gave in and outright begged him, Levi took her fast and hard on her fluffy white bed. The need to crawl over her, inside her, ate at him as he gave her everything he had. Their melody was a greedy, rushed pounding of flesh and satisfied moans. The dirty words that usually came to him in a time like this seemed to be trapped in his throat. He claimed her body while Taylor chanted his name and scratched lines into his skin. He took the punishment for claiming what could never truly be his.

When they were both spent, they gasped for breath and clung to each other. Her head lay on his chest as she traced her fingers over his tattoos. Levi grew uncomfortable in the intimate position, so he shifted and rolled away from her. He could think more clearly when she wasn't touching him.

"How do we do that?" she asked, folding her hands together and tucking them beneath her cheek.

"Do what?"

"Have something so . . . physically intense when we can barely have a conversation. That was amazing," she said.

"I can't explain it." Levi kept his eyes on the ceiling. "I'm just that good."

Taylor propped her head up on her hand and stared at him. "You don't always have to be an asshole, you know."

"And you don't always have to be a bitch," he countered.

She didn't say anything for a while, just watched him squirm beneath her gaze.

"Why do you have such an aversion to me, Levi?"

He exhaled and rolled on his side to face her. As much as he didn't want to have this conversation while naked, Levi couldn't deny her any longer. Taylor had always been up front and honest with him about her intentions. His job here was a farce and his objective a secret, and he was beginning to feel guilty for all the lies.

"After that you think I have an aversion to you?"

"I know that there's no problem with physical attraction," Taylor said, tracing a pattern inked onto his biceps.

"It's not you specifically. I hate what you and your family represent. I hate that your life has been so easy, everything handed to you, while my dad struggled so hard to support us. I've always been treated like shit by people like you." Levi stopped and contemplated whether he should continue. He wasn't sure how much he was willing to share. With Taylor's expectant eyes on his, the words spilled out like a confession. "My mom died from cancer when I was seven. I barely remember her."

Taylor frowned at him, her eyes shining. Levi rolled out of bed and started pulling his clothes back on, unable to deal with her pitying gaze.

"What about your dad?" she asked.

"He raised me alone. My dad always blamed himself for my mom's death, because we were too poor to afford the best hospitals and advanced treatment. He used to apologize to me when I was a kid. Told me it was his fault I didn't have a mom. Then he was killed in a car accident last year." After his father's death, Levi felt truly alone in the world. That's what sent him looking for more.

"I'm sorry. But my life wasn't so easy, you know," Taylor said, watching him redress. "I know what you're saying. Because of our money, I didn't want for anything. I had more opportunities than someone . . . like you. But it all came with a price, Levi."

He pulled on his T-shirt and then his uniform shirt, standing at the edge of the bed tucking them in. Taylor sat up and scooted over to him so that he was between her knees. Levi's eyes skimmed over the thin sheet covering her naked body and he found it much more difficult to keep putting clothes on. Silently, she reached up and slid his belt into place, buckling it for him. Her fingers smoothed over the leather before dropping down to hook on to his pockets.

"At least when you had your parents, they were good to you. Since I was born, I've been nothing but a burden to mine. They don't love me. They pay my bills and buy me things. That's not love."

Levi stepped away and grabbed his hat from the floor. He felt guilty for making such rash assumptions about Taylor and her life.

Her parents were worthless shits that didn't appreciate the life they had or the family they could have.

"I guess we didn't see each other very clearly," he said.

She shook her head and offered a weak smile. Levi walked around the bed, but before he reached the door, Taylor called out his name. He turned to find her sprawled across the bed on her stomach, her crossed ankles in the air.

"Does this mean we're calling a truce?" she asked.

Levi laughed. "Hell, no. Where's the fun in that?"

11. sexual pun and 1989

Levi grabbed a beer from Gregory and joined Kyle around a pool table. He was glad to be back in the company of men. Working in a house full of women left him feeling emasculated. He feared he'd soon be reading *Glamour* and talking about his feelings.

Kyle grabbed a stick from the wall and chalked the end. He nodded at Levi. "You break."

Levi lined up the cue ball and hit it. He knocked two striped balls in, made the next shot, but then missed the three ball.

"Now that you're getting laid, you're a much more likable guy, Levi," Kyle said before sinking his shot.

"Can we not discuss my sex life?" Levi begged. "And for the record, I've never had trouble getting laid. I just have standards."

Crystal joined them, taking a seat near the table. "I got twenty on Kyle."

"Damn. Thanks for the vote of confidence," Levi said.

Gregory appeared and delivered a drink to Crystal. She thanked him with a kiss and a slap on the ass when he turned to go.

Kyle threw his hands up in the air. "Am I the only one not getting laid?"

"Yes," Levi and Crystal answered in unison before pounding fists.

Kyle huffed and returned his attention to the game.

"Thanks for introducing us," Crystal said to Levi. "He's adorable."

"No worries," Levi said.

"How do you know him?" Crystal asked, looking down at her drink.

"He used to hang out with these kids down at the park by my apartment. I'd play basketball with them every now and then."

Crystal smiled. "I'm trying to picture this."

"Don't laugh. I've got skills."

"I'm sure you do."

"Anyway, I noticed that he never went home. Never had anywhere to go. I'm pretty sure he was homeless. I hooked him up with Mattie down at the Center. They set him up with a job as busboy here."

"And now he's serving drinks," Crystal said, her eyes on Gregory behind the bar.

"Yes, well, he's a charming motherfucker. And the ladies seem to like him."

Crystal grinned and watched Kyle continue to clear balls from the table.

"So we're now assuming that the safe is in Henry's personal office on the second floor, right?" Kyle said. "How do we get in there?"

"It's a typical ten-key entry pad, but I'm not sure of wiring or safeguards. If the safe is in there, I assume that it is not only tied to the main house alarm but also to some sort of secondary system," Crystal said.

Kyle missed the eight ball, giving the table back to Levi.

"Right," Kyle agreed. "And it probably has the default lockdown after three incorrect entries. We can't afford to set that off, because then he'd know something's up."

Levi worked his way around the table, sinking every ball. He looked up at Kyle and called his last shot.

"Eight ball, side pocket," he said, tapping the pocket with the end of his stick.

Levi made the shot and held his hand out toward Crystal, a victorious grin on his face. She sighed and slapped twenty bucks into his hand.

"If we shut off the power to the house, we'd have a six-second window before the backup power kicks in and resets the alarm," Crystal said.

"I can't get in there in six seconds," Levi muttered, tucking his winnings into his pocket.

"That's what she said," Kyle joked.

The other two looked at him and shook their heads.

"That doesn't make any sense," Crystal pointed out.

"That's why you're the only one not getting laid," Levi said, punching his friend in the arm. "You don't even understand sexual puns."

Kyle grabbed his crotch and gestured at them. "I've got your sexual pun right here."

Levi and Crystal groaned and headed toward the bar for new

drinks. They finished the night with an agreement to brainstorm a way into Henry Hudson's office and headed their separate ways.

With a nice buzz, Levi lay in bed and revisited his conversation with Taylor about her parents. When he was fourteen years old, Levi had gone to work with his uncle Zach at the Hudson property. They were supposed to be heading to the beach, but Zach was called in for an emergency. He shadowed his uncle all day, asking questions and learning about all the tools they used. Levi remembered being so impressed by the enormous house, and his uncle had reminded him time and time again to keep his hands to himself.

"Uncle Zach, I gotta pee," Levi said.

Zach sighed and gestured to the hallway. "There's a bathroom down there. Second room on the left. Go there and come right back. Don't touch anything."

Levi nodded and took off in that direction. When he passed a large, open room, he stopped. There was a girl, younger than him, lying on her stomach on the floor. She had a book propped open and was reading as her lips quietly mouthed the words. She had blond hair that hung down around her shoulders and a blue dress on. Her ankles were crossed in the air, swinging back and forth.

An older man and woman stormed into the room wearing matching frowns. Levi slid to the side of the door.

"I'm leaving for Barbados in the morning, Henry. You'll have to go." The woman sneered.

"I can't. I have meetings all week." The man's voice was jarring but calm. He seemed uninterested in their conversation. "I don't have time for menial shit like this."

"Well, I'm not canceling my trip just to watch Taylor graduate from fifth grade. I mean, I just thought one of us should be there."

Levi peeked around the corner and spotted the little girl. She had abandoned her book and was now watching the couple argue from her hidden spot behind the sofa.

"It's only fifth grade, Virginia. Not much of an accomplishment. Besides, that's why we hired Suzanne. She'll be there," Henry said.

"You're right," Virginia responded. "Taylor won't even notice. That Caribbean rum isn't going to drink itself. And God forbid your secretary gets a night off from faking her orgasms."

Henry moved forward now, he towered over the woman. "Watch yourself, Virginia. With that prenup, I'll have you out on your ass before you know what hits you. Then you and the brat will have nothing."

Levi gasped at the hateful words. The girl turned toward him, catching him listening, tears painting her cheeks. He panicked and ran to the end of the hall in search of the bathroom.

When Adrienne picked her up after lunch, Taylor was determined to get through to Dee. After an hour of the same poor attitude and minimal effort, she was ready to pull her hair out.

"Dee, you're not even trying."

"You don't know me. Don't act like you know me. I am trying." Both girls wore matching expressions.

"Okay, let's take a break," Taylor suggested.

"Fine by me."

"What's your favorite subject in school?"

"I hate school."

"Okay, but surely there's something there that you don't hate."

"Phys ed, I guess."

"So, you like sports?"

"Not all of them. I like basketball."

"What's your favorite team?"

"Miami Heat, all the way," Dee said, a new excited tone in her voice.

Taylor smiled and held up her finger to the girl. "I'll be right back."

She spoke to the director and asked to borrow a computer. Taylor searched online for a few basketball articles involving the Miami Heat and printed them out. She stapled the papers together and went back to her place across from Dee.

"Okay, so let's read about basketball."

Taylor slid the papers toward Dee and waited for a reaction. The girl glanced at the photo above the article and looked back to Taylor.

"You want me to read about the Heat? I can get behind that, blondie."

The second half of the session went much better than the first. Whether she was inspired by Taylor's effort or simply interested in the subject matter, Dee made a brilliant effort to read through each article. Taylor helped with the more difficult and foreign words, trying not to patronize her with elementary phonics.

In the car on the way home, Taylor had been in much higher spirits, and she found herself feeling proud of the job she'd done today.

As soon as Taylor made it in to her room, Suzanne came barging in.

"Taylor? Your father called about an hour ago."

"And?"

"He said he's been calling your cell all afternoon, but you're not answering."

"Yeah, I couldn't find my phone before I left." Taylor shrugged.

"Well, Henry said if you don't call him back by five o'clock today, he's cutting off your AmEx card."

"What?" Taylor squealed. "What the hell did he want?"

"I don't know, but he sounded serious," Suzanne answered.

"How serious?"

"Like when your mother buys another house in Mexico or when the stock market plummets serious."

"Shit!"

Both of them began a frantic search of Taylor's room. They opened every drawer, searched every bag, moving around the room like a tornado. Taylor was out of breath, bent over her desk, when Levi showed up.

"What are you doing?" he asked. Levi pulled off his hat and hung it on her doorknob. This had become habit for him. Though the camera and mic were offline now, Kyle or Crystal could tap in whenever they wanted to. Leaving the hat there gave him a sense of privacy.

Taylor's heart leapt into her throat and a smile graced her lips at the sight of him.

"It's not polite to linger in doorways, Romeo. Come in," she said, before turning her attention back to her desk. "I'm looking for my phone. I've got like ten minutes to find it and call Henry before he cuts off my AmEx."

Suzanne ignored the two and kept searching through Taylor's closet.

"Now, that would be a tragedy."

"Shut it, Levi. I don't have time for your attitude today," she grumbled.

"I was stopping by to tell you I'm leaving. I can just go now," he said pointing toward the door.

"No!" Taylor yelled. She took a deep breath and held up one finger. "Stay."

Levi nodded and took a seat on her bed. "Why don't you just use the house phone?"

"Because we're idiots," Suzanne shouted, stepping out of the closet and smacking her forehead with the palm of her hand.

"Yes! I found it!" Taylor said, holding the phone up and waving it at him.

Before leaving, Suzanne held up two fingers and pointed them at her eyes and then at Levi and Taylor.

"What was that all about?" Taylor asked.

"She doesn't approve."

"Ah, it's a new variation of the Look."

Taylor jumped onto her bed and threw her feet into Levi's lap. She raised a finger to her lips to make sure he stayed quiet and dialed her father on speakerphone.

"Hudson," he answered, his voice echoing through the quiet room.

"You said I needed to call before five."

"Taylor, it is four fifty-two."

"That's still before five. What could be so important as to receive a personal phone call from Henry Hudson and not his assistant? Did you get tired of Nadine and trade her in for a younger model who doesn't know how to work a phone?"

"Cut the attitude, Taylor. I received a rather disturbing phone call from Beau Upton this morning."

Taylor stilled, her eyes flashed to Levi.

"What did he want?" she asked, her voice wavering.

"He informed me that you're sleeping with the new maintenance man." Taylor slapped her hand over her mouth as Levi sucked in a breath. "Nevermind how he may know this information, but Taylor Hudson, so help me God, if you are involved with that man, I will . . ."

"You'll what, Henry? What?" she asked, barely containing her fury. "Of course I'm not sleeping with that loser, give me some credit."

Taylor's gaze shot to Levi and she mouthed a 'sorry' to him and frowned.

"For once, think before you act. Consider how this would look, Taylor. If you embarrass this family, in any way, I will not hesitate to take action."

"And do what?" she said, running her hand through her hair. "Cut me off? Send me away? You can't possibly ignore me any more than you do now!" Levi placed his hand on her leg and ran it up to her knee and back down, trying to soothe her.

"Watch yourself, young lady," Henry's deep voice shouted, catching them both off guard.

"Are you threatening me? I'll tell you what, Henry, why don't you worry about who you and your wife are fucking and not me!" Taylor yelled, throwing her phone across the room. It broke into several pieces, ending the call.

Taylor covered her face with her hands and inhaled deeply. Her whole body trembled beneath Levi's touch. He felt wrong and out of place being a witness to something so personal.

"Are you okay?" he asked after a few minutes.

"That man makes me crazy."

Levi sat, unmoving, unsure what to do or say. He felt as though he should comfort her, but maybe that was crossing a line. As a tear slipped from her eye, ran over her cheek, and dropped onto her shirt, he decided he couldn't be what she needed.

"Should I go? I should go. I'm going to head home."

"The hell you are."

Taylor yanked Levi toward her. Their lips came together in a heated kiss that begged to make her forget. He kissed her back, no longer able to deny her addictive taste. He inhaled the tiny, desperate whimpers that escaped her lips. When Levi moved to crawl on top of her, she pulled back, her chest heaving, her red eyes dry and determined.

"Not here," she said.

A new, devious smile tugged at Taylor's lips. She grabbed his hand and pulled Levi after her. His eyes darted up and down the hall, looking for other employees.

"Taylor, where are you—"

His words were cut short as she stopped directly in front of Henry's locked office door. Levi's heart raced as he watched her punch in 1-9-8-9 on the keypad. A grin split his face and he looked away to hide it.

They entered the office quickly, Taylor pulling him in behind her and closing the door. It was a large room with several bookshelves, filing cabinets, and an enormous wooden desk in the center of the room. Taylor led him over to the desk and pushed Levi down into the leather chair.

"This is Henry's personal office," she said, smiling. "What do you say we defile it just a bit?"

The smile on his face represented more than a craving for the beautiful girl before him. His eyes scanned each wall, frantically searching for the safe. There were shelves, cabinets, and a closet—not to mention the desk he sat at. So many places to search. A clattering noise brought his attention back to Taylor. She had swept most of the things off Henry's desk and planted herself on the top after sliding out of her clothes.

Taylor leaned over and placed hurried kisses along his jaw up toward his ear. When her panting breaths ghosted over his neck, a chill ran down his spine. A low, satisfied moan left his lips when her fingers raked through his hair. He reached up and pulled her lips down to his, wholly losing himself in the pleasing taste of Taylor Hudson.

Levi slid his lips between her breasts, causing Taylor to throw her head back, arching her body toward him. His hands circled her hips and brought her to the edge of the desk. He placed a kiss on the inside of each ankle before propping her feet on the arms of his chair. Pressing her knees apart, Levi gave her a wicked grin from between her thighs.

"Lie back, Taylor."

His demand was simple and she followed it without question. Immediately, Levi lowered his mouth to her center. He closed his eyes and reveled in the scent of her arousal, the way she slid against his tongue, the absolute sinful taste. Hooking his arms around her thighs, he held her there while he continued to please and torture her with his mouth.

Taylor begged for more as she rocked her hips against him, curses shouted toward the ceiling. He doubled his efforts, taking her higher and making her legs twitch until she was a writhing mess. She was breathless when her orgasm took over, her entire body rigid and shaking from the release.

Levi sat back in the leather chair and swiped his mouth with the back of his hand. He was hard and aching for her and wouldn't wait another minute.

"I like seeing you come apart," he said, watching her chest rise and fall, mesmerized by the sight of her skin. "It makes me want to see it again."

He stood and unbuttoned his work shirt, throwing it to the floor. Taylor watched from her place on the desk, like a sacrificial virgin on an altar. She was beautiful and perfect, and all his.

"Come here, Romeo."

Taylor crooked her finger at him, summoning Levi closer. He removed the rest of his clothes, then leaned over her and kissed her waiting lips. He knew she could taste herself on his tongue, and the thought drove him wild.

"Hold on, Rich Girl," Levi warned.

Levi grabbed her hands and placed them over her head, curling Taylor's fingers around the edge of the desk. She braced herself but looked surprised when Levi entered her slowly. He covered her body with his own and created a steady, torturous rhythm. He fought hard to keep his eyes open, to watch her face and her little smiles interrupted by mind-numbing bliss. Levi covered her lips with his, swallowing all her breaths and words that pleaded for more. He could read her body like one of his poems, recognizing the way she teetered on the edge of what he wanted most.

"Levi, please. Oh, God."

"You want more?"

Levi gave her more, quickening his pace. He gave her everything he had. The sound of their bodies colliding was an erotic melody and accompanied only by the *tick, tick, tick* of the Tiffany lamp that rocked near the edge of the desk. Lowering his lips, Levi placed sucking kisses between her breasts before tugging one nipple between his teeth.

"Levi!" Taylor screamed.

His name from her lips sent them both spiraling over the edge, each grasping and pulling and pushing at the other until the wave of ecstasy had passed. Levi collapsed, careful not to crush her beneath him. Their sweat-slicked skin moved together as they fought to catch their breath. Taylor released her grip on the desk and ran her nails through Levi's hair. A low rumble sounded through his chest, vibrating both of their bodies.

"Did you just purr?" Taylor asked, raking her nails down to his back and over his shoulders.

Levi gave her a smirk and stood, separating them. He pulled his clothes on while Taylor sat up on her elbows, watching him redress.

"Are you going to stay here?" he asked, while buckling his belt.

"No," she answered. "I just can't move quite yet."

Levi's smile grew bigger as he leaned over her body and kissed her. It was hard and biting, passionate and possessive. He pulled back, hovering just above her lips and whispered the first words that came to mind.

"Love-flesh swelling and deliciously aching, quivering jelly of love."

With that, he grabbed his hat from the floor and slipped out the door.

"We're in! We're fucking in!" Levi yelled into his phone.

"What?" Crystal asked.

"The office, Crystal! Henry Hudson's office!"

"Holy shit! You're my hero. How'd you do it?"

"Uh, let's just say that Taylor and I violated his desk in every way possible."

Crystal laughed. "Damn. That's ballsy. I bow down at your greatness. We'll have to hack the security feed and delete the footage now."

"That's right," Levi said. "The damn cameras. I'll be home in thirty. You guys meet me at Mavericks later."

"Will do," Crystal said.

A couple of hours later, Levi arrived at Mavericks and slid up to the bar. Gregory added his name to the lineup and brought him a cold beer.

"Thanks," he said, smiling. "Get yourself one, on me."

"Whoa, big baller. What are we celebrating?" Gregory asked, pouring a shot of tequila.

"Small victories," Levi answered, lifting his bottle.

Gregory clinked the shot glass against it. "Small victories."

"Celebrating without me?" Crystal asked, taking a seat next to Levi.

"Don't worry, shortie. We'll have a private celebration later," Gregory said, winking at Crystal.

Kyle saddled up on the other side of Levi and ordered a beer. Gregory took care of them and left to serve other customers.

"So? We're in the office because you got into Taylor?" Kyle asked.

Crystal reached over and slapped him on the back of the head.

"I'm not even mad at that," Levi said.

"Hey, Levi. I know I clown you a lot, but good job. No matter how you got into that office, all that matters is that you did."

Crystal and Levi stared at him, open-mouthed and dumbfounded.

"Thanks," Levi said, though it sounded like a question.

"An office pass and a piece of ass. Nice."

The two groaned at his rhyme.

"Now there's the Kyle we know and love," Crystal said.

"Did you erase the footage?" Levi asked, hopeful.

"Yeah. And I didn't even watch it. What a shame." She gave him a wink. "The security company's system was a little more advanced than I'm used to, so at a quick glance they'll never notice it. But if there is a reason to go looking, they'll see there are almost thirty minutes missing."

"Here's hoping they don't have a reason to go looking," Levi said, raising his beer and clinking it against hers.

Levi signaled Gregory for another beer and tapped his fingers on the bar, echoing the beat of the overhead music. Gregory delivered his beer and scooted over to Crystal. Levi watched their carefree interaction, the way they looked at each other, and immediately thought of Taylor. The idea of not seeing her, not being able to taste or touch her, made him groan. Though he couldn't be happier about getting into that office, he knew this meant they'd be completing the job and leaving soon.

He sipped the amber liquid and mentally justified sacrificing Taylor for a few million dollars. While it felt like a small sacrifice, something inside him did not agree. A tight feeling in his chest radiated out through his limbs and centered back on his heart.

"Penny for your thoughts," Crystal said, slapping the bar and jarring Levi out of his reverie. He gave her a fragile smile and met her eyes.

"You've been asking me that since we were fifteen," Levi said.

"It was the only way to distract you when you were in fight mode."

"Fight mode?" Levi asked. "You make it sound like I'm a robot."

"I used to wonder. You liked to play guitar and fight. There wasn't much else for a while, Levi."

Levi nodded. "I guess you're right. I was an angry kid. Still lose my temper pretty easy."

Crystal chuckled and bumped his shoulder. "You don't say," she teased. "I don't think it's your temper, man. We've all got ways to relieve stress, fighting happens to be yours."

He drained his second beer and set the empty bottle down. "I do love it. I'm good at it too."

"I know. Remember Ryan Douglas? He broke my heart, you broke his nose." She gave him a smile. "Not sure I ever thanked you for that."

"No need. That douchebag had it coming. Is that how we became friends?" Levi stared at her freckled face, waiting.

"It was that day in detention. We were pretty segregated. There were the cool kids, then there was us. It was natural for you, Kyle, and me to fall in together."

"The rest is history," Levi mumbled.

The pair sat in silence a few minutes, before Gregory got Levi's attention and pointed toward the stage. He turned to Crystal and bumped her shoulder like she'd done to him earlier.

"The Beatles or Tracy Chapman?" he asked.

"I gotta go with the Beatles. Always."

"Blackbird it is," Levi said, and carried his guitar to the stage.

Levi arrived at the house, waved hello to Suzanne and Mandy, and checked the laundry room for his work list. As soon as he stepped in the room, he spotted Taylor. She jumped into his arms and attacked his lips.

"Mmm, you taste like coffee and mint," she whispered as he lifted her up and set her on the counter. "God, you smell so good. How do you always smell so good?"

Taylor pulled off Levi's hat and tugged at his hair. He moaned into her mouth before pulling away for a much needed breath.

"Morning," he said.

"Good morning, Romeo," she said, locking her legs around his waist.

"Have I thought long to see this morning's face, and doth it give me such a sight as this?" he quoted.

Taylor sighed and pulled him toward her again.

Levi smiled against her lips, but inside he battled the regret of leaving this house and never seeing her again. He leaned away and she frowned.

"Why such an eager greeting today?" he asked, his hands resting on the counter.

"I'm leaving for the day, but I wanted to see you first. How about a quickie right here?" She giggled.

"Where are you going?"

"I promised Reese I'd go to visit her brother with her. I won't be back until late and you'll already be gone."

Levi felt the weight of her words and the honest need behind them. It set off alarms in his head. He reached behind his back and unhooked her legs, taking a step away so he could think clearly.

"What's wrong?" she asked.

"Taylor, we don't have to see each other every day." His mouth formed more lies before he could even stop. "I've got so much work today, I doubt I would have noticed you were gone," he said, gesturing to his work list on the corkboard.

The light in her eyes changed, and he braced himself for the worst. Taylor's hands pressed hard into her thighs. Levi knew it was cruel, but he felt himself on a slippery slope and needed to regain control.

Instead of yelling and screaming or resorting to physical violence, the strangest thing happened. Taylor ducked her head, hid her face from him, and slid off the counter. She left the room without a word or backward glance.

Levi ripped his list off the wall and cursed. He wanted to tell her he felt it too, the comfort and ease of being with her. He wanted to tell Taylor that she drove him wild and ruled his thoughts. But he could barely admit those things to himself. There was no way he could say them out loud.

Besides, it would be pointless, like leading her on and making promises for a future that could never exist. Levi would be gone soon, and she'd be better off without a mess like him. She'd move to Massachusetts, graduate from Harvard, and reminisce about how she once went slumming with a guy from the wrong side of town.

Taylor lay back against the leather seat, letting the wind whip around her. Reese had yet to inquire about her foul mood today, and she was grateful for it. What would she say? The maintenance guy hurt her feelings?

He wasn't just the maintenance guy anymore. He was Romeo, the surprising man who quoted poetry and had stories tattooed into his flesh. When he said he wouldn't notice if she was gone, it shot straight through her. Taylor hadn't realized she had feelings for him until those words hit her.

There was no future with Levi. There was only the here and now. There was only the unyielding, intense need to be in his arms and the unexpected desire to know more about him. She woke up this morning wanting to see his face and kiss those lips. Since she'd met him, Taylor thought it was the thrill of the chase that held her to Levi. She realized now that there was something deeper and more powerful pulling them toward each other.

Even though those feelings frightened her, she was willing to embrace them and throw caution to the wind. It seemed that Levi was not on the same page. Her only option this morning was to take those cutting words and slink away, because she deserved it. Taylor had hit him with hurtful words too many times to blame Levi for the attack. She recognized it for what it was—a defense mechanism.

"Why are you being so emo? I haven't seen you in, like, a week and you show up all sad faced."

"It's nothing. PMS I guess." Taylor shrugged. "Speaking of being MIA, where have you been?"

Reese smiled and pushed her curly hair behind her ear, displaying large diamond earrings.

"Whoa, those are nice. I assume you've found a new sugar daddy?"

"You assume right."

"Is this one married?" Taylor asked.

"Does it matter?"

"Not to you."

"Spare me your judgmental attitude, Taylor. At least I don't want to fuck the help."

Taylor crossed her arms and frowned at her friend.

"I'm sorry. That was harsh. It's just . . . this one is different. He's so passionate and strong. He listens when I talk, totally interested in what I have to say. And he does this thing with his tongue that—"

"Stop! Eww. TMI!" Taylor shouted.

Reese laughed, dispelling the tension between them, and

Taylor smiled back. While she would never understand it, she could see how satisfied her friend was.

Hanging out with Reese and her brother proved to be just the distraction Taylor needed. It was light and fun with no pressures or expectations. They went to a picnic at one of the frat houses, where Taylor and Reese joined a volleyball game and promptly got their asses handed to them. Still, being surrounded by strangers and having the pleasure of anonymity kept her smiling. While Taylor was happy to flirt with some of the boys, she didn't touch a single one of them. She didn't even want to.

They were almost home when Reese finally brought up Taylor's earlier pouting.

"Do you want to talk about it?" she asked.

"Talk about what?"

"Whatever had you so pissy this morning."

"No," Taylor answered, shaking her head.

But she *did* want to talk about it. She wanted to confess. The words formed themselves on her tongue and she tried to spit them out. But the fear of her best friend's rejection made her chicken out.

"You're not still pouting because maintenance man won't sleep with you, are you?"

"No, that's definitely not it," Taylor said, hiding her guilty face.

"Good. He's not worth it."

Taylor glared at her friend but kept her mouth shut. Reese didn't know that Levi was totally worth it. She didn't know that he was strong and smart and kind. Taylor had only seen small glimpses of those things, but she knew they added up to make him a great man. Reese didn't know how passionate he was or how much he missed his parents. She didn't know that he was funny and could easily put Taylor in her place.

As Taylor crawled into bed that night, she thought of nothing but Levi. She thought about his hands and what it felt like to be kissed by him. She thought about learning more about his childhood and his surprising love of poetry and music. She thought about his beautiful ink and the stories hidden behind those images. But most of all, she wondered if Levi thought about her at all.

12. false bottoms and friday

Levi threw himself into his work. After a couple of hours, he did a quick sweep of the house and pinpointed each employee's location. With Taylor gone and everyone else occupied, he let Crystal and Kyle know they were on for office infiltration.

Approaching the office door, he checked the hallway one last time. Levi reached into his pocket, pulled out a pair of latex gloves, and slipped them on. Yesterday, as hard as it had been, Levi's fingers had touched nothing in the office besides Taylor. His fingerprints were legitimately everywhere else in the house, but he had no excuse to be in this room. He wanted to leave no evidence.

"You guys with me?" Levi asked.

"We're both here," Kyle answered.

He punched in the code 1-9-8-9 to the keypad and exhaled when the light switched from red to green. He checked the hall one last time and slipped into the office.

"Damn, what happened in here?" Kyle asked, seeing the mess of papers and the knocked-over lamp on the floor.

"That's from Taylor and me," Levi said, chuckling.

"Oh, did you guys play sexy librarian? That's hot!"

"Can we focus on why we're here?" Crystal piped up.

Levi scanned the room and gave them the measurements before turning to his right and facing the first wall.

"Okay, Levi, start the detail work. We'll be your second and third set of eyes," Crystal said.

"Copy that."

He slid his hands over every inch of that wall, pulled artwork down, and checked behind and under each piece of furniture. It was a slow, tedious process, but he knew that they needed to be especially meticulous with this room.

When the first wall was clear, he moved to the next. Kyle and Crystal had no comments or conversation while Levi searched, but he knew they were still there, probably holding their breath. This wall held two bookshelves and a large flat-screen monitor mounted between them. It took awhile for Levi to check and recheck each space. Again, he slid the books aside, and when he found nothing, replaced them exactly as they were.

The monitor was tricky to pull down. It was heavy and awkward, but it did not hide a safe. Once that was mounted back in place, he turned to the third wall. It was the easiest, with only two large windows and a framed print. Levi's rough hands ran over the expensive drapes and he checked behind the canvas. Still, no safe.

The final wall held more shelves and a small closet. He continued his exploration, checking the closet closely. There was nothing inside but a few suit jackets.

"What the fuck?" Levi growled as he shut the closet door. "You guys didn't see anything?"

"No," Kyle said. "Nothing."

Levi dropped to his knees and pulled back the antique rug covering the floor. He found nothing beneath it, not even dust. He moved around the mess and eyed the large desk with fondness. He could almost see Taylor now, lying across the top with her blond hair hanging over the edge while her fingers clawed at the smooth surface.

"Hello? Levi? You haven't moved for a while. You okay?" Crystal asked.

"Sorry."

He stepped to the desk and pulled open each drawer, searching for hidden panels or a release button. The first drawer was useless, filled with fancy pens and monogrammed paper. The middle drawer was a flat tray that held a laptop. Levi powered it up, but it was password protected. He shut it down and placed it back in the drawer.

The third drawer contained a few receipts for hotels, restaurants, and airline tickets. As Levi pulled the items from the desk, he noticed that the drawer seemed shallower than the others. He pushed on the bottom. When it didn't budge, he knocked on it.

"What's up, Levi?" Kyle asked.

"I think this drawer has a false bottom," he said as he tried to pry the edges up.

"Push down on the corner," Kyle suggested.

Levi followed his instructions and the bottom popped up, revealing a small compartment below.

"Sweet!" Crystal yelled.

"Let's not get too excited, Crystal. There isn't anything in here but a file folder," Levi said.

He flipped the folder open to find an old label across the top that read HUDSON, JULIA. He flipped through the stack of papers, finding what looked like medical records, receipts, letters, and an old black-and-white photo of a young girl.

"Again with this Julia," Levi said. "You guys ever find information on her?"

"Nothing," Kyle answered. "Maybe you should take it."

"And what if Henry goes looking for it before we find that safe?" Crystal asked. "I say leave it. We can always come back for it."

Levi agreed with her and replaced the folder. He put the false bottom back into the drawer and returned the papers before slamming the drawer shut. He pulled off his hat and tugged at his hair.

"Nothing!" he growled. "We found nothing."

After a quick lunch, Levi found it hard to concentrate on the rest of his work. He left in the early afternoon and waited for that inevitable call to come in. Two hours later, it did.

"Levi, the Boss wants to meet tonight. Usual place. Eight o'clock."

"What's the verdict, Kyle?"

"I'm not sure. I'm just as much in the dark as you are."

Being the last to arrive, Levi took a seat at the table and greeted each of them. There was a tense, choking air surrounding them. He knew it would get worse before it got any better.

"What's the update?" the Boss asked, not one for pleasantries.

"We completed a detailed search of the Hudson residence this afternoon, including Henry's personal office. We found nothing," Kyle answered as he shifted in his seat.

The Boss glared at Levi, as if he was personally responsible for the safe not being there. He held his own, not wavering against the gaze, but he felt transparent.

"If you're positive the safe cannot be located, then we move to Plan B. I'll still need you on the inside, Levi. You may be able to orchestrate a suitable setup for a simple kidnapping and ransom scenario. But I've got my own guys for this."

Levi frowned, slamming his hand down onto the table. "We weren't prepared to be involved in something like this."

His friends eyed him as though he'd lost his mind. Levi knew he was taking a risk challenging the Boss, but he also knew he had to.

"It's too late for that, Levi. I suggest you check yourself before I cut you out completely."

"Give us until Friday," he countered. "If we don't find the safe by then, we'll move on to Plan B."

"It's just a few more days," Kyle hedged. "We'll figure out a plan to get inside with Levi and triple-check the entire house. It could work."

It was dangerous to tread on the Boss's toes like this, but Levi had to risk it. The thought of Taylor being in any kind of danger sent his mind reeling. The Boss eyed each of them at the table before nodding.

"Friday."

The Boss stood and left them without another word. When the door slammed shut, they all exhaled and relaxed into their wooden chairs.

"You are either the dumbest son of a bitch that ever lived, or you've got balls of steel," Kyle said as he slapped Levi on the shoulder.

"The Boss won't do anything to us. We know too much," Levi said, though he wasn't sure he believed his own words.

"Do you really believe that?" Crystal asked. "If we screw up, we're cut out of the deal. I don't know about you, but after six months of working on this, I'd like a damn payout."

"I know. We've got to find that safe," Levi said.

"What if there is no safe? What if we're just wasting time here?" Kyle asked.

"The Boss said this information was reliable," Crystal said. "I'll go over the layout one more time, but I don't think we've missed anything."

Levi nodded and scratched the back of his neck.

"Well, I've got to go. It's my turn to referee at the Center. Let's meet tomorrow to work on a plan," Kyle said, hopping up from his chair.

"How's that going?" Levi asked.

"It's good. These kids remind me a lot of us, man. They just need direction, you know? Someone to tell them, 'Just say no to drugs,' 'Wrap it before you tap it,' 'No drinking and stealing your mom's car to go to Disneyland in the middle of the night because you think Donald Duck needs to be called out on his no-pants situation.'"

"Wow. That last one is specific," Levi said.

"Well, it's best these kids learn from my mistakes."

"You sound like a damn after-school special," Crystal said, chuckling.

"Yeah," Levi answered, "but I wish we had had that."

"Maybe we wouldn't be thieving criminals now?" Crystal chimed in.

"Hey, we're not thieving criminals. We're aspiring thieving criminals," Kyle said. "Livin' the dream, baby. Later, guys."

"See ya tomorrow," Crystal replied.

Kyle gave them each a fist bump before pushing his way out the door.

Crystal looked at Levi. "What on earth led you to believe negotiating with the Boss was a good idea?" she asked.

"I have no idea. I panicked. My mouth seems to be functioning without any assistance from my brain lately."

"Does it have anything to do with a certain blonde at the Hudson house?"

Levi blew out a breath and ran his fingers through his hair. "You know it does."

"You're falling for her," Crystal said.

"Whoa!" Levi jumped up and leaned over the table. "I'm not falling for anybody. She keeps things interesting. And she's the best piece of ass I've had in a while. That's it."

He felt guilt seep into his mouth with those words. Levi knew that he was trying to convince himself more than anyone. Crystal called him out on it.

"The sooner you admit it, the better off you'll be. It's a dangerous game you're playing now, Levi."

These violent delights have violent ends.

Levi shook his head and dropped his chin to his chest. "I've got two fucking days to find that safe, Crystal. If I fail, she'll be in danger and I can't protect her. Why is the Boss so determined to get over on this family? Seems like there may be more to this job than just the money."

Crystal shrugged and the two said their good-byes. Levi pointed his truck toward Mavericks, where he knew he could find solace and a strong drink.

Thursday morning, Levi woke to the feeling of a two-ton weight on his chest. With their new deadline, the pressure was inescapable. He supposed they always knew this was an option, though they never fathomed it would actually happen. The team had been overly confident coming into the house. They'd underestimated Henry Hudson, and now, if they failed, Taylor would pay the price.

"Good morning, ladies," Levi greeted Mandy and Suzanne at the kitchen counter.

"Levi," they answered in unison.

He gave them his best smile and took a seat while Mandy poured him a cup of brew.

"Oh, I saw a celebrity yesterday at the Plaza," Suzanne said, bouncing in her seat.

"Who?" Mandy asked.

"Ice T Cube."

Mandy and Levi stared at Suzanne, wearing matching blank expressions.

"You mean Ice-T?" Mandy asked.

"Or Ice Cube?" Levi added. "Because that's two different people."

"Oh, you know, the one who's on that crime television show with the initials."

"That clears it up," Mandy said, her face squished up. "*SVU? CSI?*"

"Oh, I don't know," Suzanne said flippantly. "I don't watch that stuff."

"What does he look like?" Mandy asked.

"Tall, bald head. Nice lips. Handsome guy."

Levi rolled his eyes. "LL Cool J?"

"Yes!" Suzanne exclaimed. "That's what I said, right?"

Mandy laughed and poured herself another cup of coffee. "Hey, Levi. Saturday is Suzanne's birthday. We're going to do a small dinner party here at the house. Would you come?"

Her eyes held so much hope, Levi felt helpless. "You're having the party here?" he asked, gesturing to the house.

"Yeah. We figure the residents never use it, so we can."

"It's not a big deal if you're busy," Suzanne said.

"I'd love to come."

"Great!" Mandy exclaimed, a bit too enthusiastic. "It's at seven o'clock. No gifts. And bring your guitar." She winked and left the kitchen before he could reply.

Levi turned to find Suzanne red-faced, her hand over her mouth as her shoulders shook. "I'm glad you find this amusing. And how does she know I play the guitar?"

"She may or may not have Googled you and found your name on an open mic night list at some bar. She also may or may not have watched a video of you singing on YouTube. Several times. Back-to-back. At full volume."

Suzanne shrugged and mimed locking her lips and throwing away the key. Levi shook his head before sliding off his stool and grabbing his work list from the laundry room.

The list consisted of his normal weekly maintenance chores and a loose tile on Taylor's balcony. He groaned and read over the list again before leaving the room.

Levi prioritized his work in order to get things done as quickly as possible. He decided he'd put off the safe search until after lunch. He was hoping to avoid Taylor completely.

As he made his way to the garage, Levi shook his head. If he was being honest with himself, he wanted nothing more than to see Taylor. The hurtful words he'd thrown at her circled his head. He had wounded her, and he knew Taylor would make him pay for it.

When Beau Upton's name appeared on Taylor's new phone, she couldn't believe his audacity. Fueled by insecurity and anger and more unidentified feelings, she felt compelled to take it out on him. So she answered.

"You've got some fucking nerve, Beau."

"You sound upset," he said. His voice was light but cautious.

"You ratted me out to Henry, you asshole! You haven't even seen angry yet!"

"That's why I'm calling, Taylor. I want to apologize."

"You don't get to apologize, Beau. What you did was unforgivable," she said, her voice turning from rage to disappointment. "You know how I feel about Henry. How could you?"

"Come on, Tay. We've been friends since birth. Just let me explain. Please, Taylor."

Taylor was quiet. She swung back and forth in her desk chair. She contemplated cutting Beau out of her life for good without giving him a chance to explain. She felt that he deserved that and worse. But she couldn't do it. Until recently, he had been on the very short list of people Taylor trusted and cared about. She hated what he did, but she also hated to lose her friend.

"Go ahead. Tell me how you could possibly justify outing me."

"Not over the phone. Meet me at the country club for lunch?" Beau asked.

"Fine. One o'clock. Don't be late," she said.

Beau was right. They had known each other since birth. They had been the best of friends and more until this falling-out between the families when they were forbidden from seeing each other, a rule they'd enjoyed breaking.

Taylor stayed in her room all morning, mostly trying to avoid Levi. She didn't know what she would say to him if she saw him, so this was the best option. She would steer clear of the man who invaded her every waking thought. She would try to forget the man who made her body sing and looked at her like she was the most complicated and tempting thing. She would try.

It had all started as a game. Now she wondered if she'd gotten in over her head with Levi. When she wasn't with him, she dreamt of his smooth voice and craved his touch. It was inexplicable. And for once in her life, she didn't care to understand.

———

After a morning full of work, Levi sat in the kitchen scarfing down chicken and dumplings while Mandy rambled on about the dinner party. Levi nodded and hummed in the right places, all the while thinking about how much he would miss this cooking.

"So, I think we'll have wine and beer and a few hors d'oeuvres. What do you think?"

Levi slid his empty plate toward her and pasted on his best smile. "Sounds great," he said, hopping up from his seat. "Thanks for lunch."

He took off upstairs as Mandy's voice followed him through the house. When Levi reached the landing, he turned toward the master bedroom and ran right into Taylor. She clutched the fabric of his shirt to keep from falling over. Levi's hands grabbed her waist to steady her. The feel of her body beneath his fingers set forth a torturous mirage of images in his mind.

He wanted to pull her lip from between her teeth and suck on it. He wanted to kiss away her frown and apologize for his cruel words the day before. He knew it was best not to. Instead, Levi took a step away and dropped his hands, instantly able to think more clearly.

Taylor released his shirt and looked up into his eyes. Her face was unreadable, caught in limbo between anger and caution. He hated being responsible for either.

"I'd better get to work," he said after the silence stretched on too long.

Taylor nodded. "I was just on my way out." She pointed to the stairs. "I'm meeting Beau for lunch."

Levi turned his face away, not wanting to show her what he knew she wanted to see. He stuffed his hands into his pockets and curled his fingers in until his short nails made lines in his palms.

He closed his eyes and took a deep breath. All he could see now were images of Taylor and Beau, his hands on her body, the way his gaze adored her.

"Don't go."

He frowned and stared down at the floor, surprised that the words had left his lips. Taylor looked up, trying to catch his gaze. When Levi finally met her eyes, she stared without apology. She was looking for something in him, looking so hard it made his skin prickle. She must not have found it, because she shook her head and took to the stairs.

"Later," she called over her shoulder as she disappeared from view.

Levi retreated to the master bedroom and leaned against the door. He banged the back of his head against it and cursed his stupidity. Sliding down, he let his back press against the door and his forearms rest on his bent knees. He tried to reason with himself. This was a good thing. It was best to stop whatever they had now, before neither of them could deny it. Soon, he'd be gone and she'd leave for college. All would be right in the world. But it didn't feel right. It felt like searing pain in his chest and an emptiness that ached.

13. foreshadowing and home services

On the drive to the country club, Taylor worked out everything she wanted to say to Beau. Her frustration and disappointment made it hard for her to concentrate on her practiced words. Of course they had fought before. It had always been over stupid things, mostly Beau's jealousy. But he had never gone to Henry before. Beau, of all people, understood the contempt Taylor had for her father. She needed to hear how he could justify this breach of trust.

Twenty minutes later, Taylor took a seat across from Beau. There weren't many people in the restaurant at this hour, so they would have their privacy. Taylor tucked her napkin into her lap and watched him fidget with the silverware. The waiter appeared, took their order, and disappeared again. Beau had yet to make eye contact.

"Well?" she said after their drinks were delivered. "Let's hear it." She leaned back and crossed her arms while tapping her toe against the table leg. The soft knocking sound counted off the seconds of silence.

"When I came over that day, I'd just gotten in a fight with my dad," Beau started. "I was already pissed off. I met that maintenance douche bag downstairs and then I caught him watching you in your room. I didn't like the way he looked at you, Taylor," he finished, finally meeting her gaze.

"It's none of your concern how anyone looks at me."

Beau nodded his head. "I know I have no claim to you. You've made that perfectly clear. But when I saw you wearing his shirt? I lost my damn mind."

Even now, Taylor could feel the hostility rolling off him while he thought back to that day. His expression remained calm, but the muscle in his jaw twitched.

"You're damn right, you did."

"It's just that . . . I know we've never been exclusive. I know about the other guys you've gone out with. But the thought of him—this loser, who probably has a gun rack and parole officer—touching you drove me crazy. I know you've always said you'll never settle down with one guy. I think that's because you don't believe you deserve that. I wish you'd see that you can be happy—"

"Beau," she tried to interrupt.

"Seeing his shirt on you, like his brand on you, broke me, Taylor. I've never seen you let a guy claim you in any way. Somehow he got to you. This older guy . . . probably *manipulating* you. I didn't like it and I was worried. That's why I called Henry."

"So, if I had never worn his shirt, we wouldn't be having this conversation?"

Beau shifted in his seat and scrubbed at his face. Their food was placed in front of them, and when the waiter was gone again, he continued.

"No. It's not about the clothes. It's the sentiment behind it." He stopped and took a long sip of his water. The condensation rolled down his glass and dripped onto his plate. "I figured Henry would ground you or fire him. And you'd want me back. That's why I called Henry."

"You should have just talked to me—like you're doing now. You know how I feel about that man. He may be my father, but . . ."

"He *is* your father. You love him. That's why he can hurt you so much. But I am sorry, Taylor. I was jealous and I acted like a jackass."

"Jealous of what?" she said as she stabbed some lettuce in her salad and took a bite.

"Taylor, you have to know what you mean to me. I want to be with you."

She swallowed her food and felt panic push up from her stomach, threatening to choke her. She should have known it was coming. Taylor should have known that he'd never let her go off to Harvard without a big declaration. This had been brewing since they were twelve years old. Suddenly, she felt terrible for letting it get this far. Taylor regretted all the times she'd led him on, even if not intentionally.

"That's not an option, Beau. I can't give you that," she said.

"But you're willing to give it to him? The hired help? Some delinquent you barely know?"

Taylor shook her head and gulped down her sparkling water.

"Taylor, I'm in love with you. I love you."

Beau reached for her hand that rested on the table, but she

pulled it back and tucked both hands into her lap. Tears wet her lashes as she worked up the nerve to say what she had to.

"I love you too. As a friend. That's all," she said. "I'm sorry if sleeping with you misled you. That was never my intention. I thought my feelings were clear."

"I can be what you need, Tay. I can take care of you and give you anything you want. I will always love you."

"I know, Beau," Taylor answered, her voice surprisingly shaky. "And you will always be special to me. But I can't force myself to fall in love with you. I'm so sorry. It would be a lie."

He dropped his head, and Taylor watched as his chest rose and fell quickly. He slammed his fist down on the linen-covered table, making the plates and glasses rattle.

"So this is it? It's over?" he whispered angrily.

"Yes. Us sleeping together is over. It's not fair to either of us. But you'll always be my friend, Beau."

He pointed a finger at her as his eyes grew cold. "I won't wait for you. I won't be around when he takes what he wants and breaks your heart." She didn't say a word, just stared into his face, twisted with jealousy and resentment. "Good-bye, Taylor."

Beau threw his napkin onto the table, dropped a few twenties, and disappeared. Tears dotted her own napkin and she wiped her cheeks quickly. Beau, one of her only true friends, was gone and now she was alone. She sat there for an hour, food untouched, and wondered if this was some kind of sick foreshadowing of the rest of her life.

"Okay, down to business," Levi said, sipping his beer and joining his team in the corner booth of Mavericks. "I checked the master suite and basement today. Any other ideas?" Crystal and Kyle shrugged. "Come on! We've got one day to find that fucking safe!"

"Levi, calm down," Kyle said. "It's not do or die by tomorrow. I mean, if we don't find it, what's the worst that happens? Some thugs hold Taylor for ransom? That's not so bad."

"Not so bad? These are people we don't know, more people to split our money with. Who knows what kind of assholes the Boss has for this job?"

"Levi's right," Crystal chimed in. "We don't want the Boss to resort to Plan B. We need to prove that we were the right choice for the job."

"I understand all that. But I think Levi's a little short-sighted because of his hot piece of ass," Kyle said, tapping his beer bottle on the tabletop.

Levi stood. "Fuck you, Kyle!"

Kyle shrank in his seat but grinned up at his fuming friend. "When are you going to own up to letting Taylor Hudson distract you from the real job?"

Levi grabbed Kyle's shirt collar and twisted it, lifting him out of his seat. "Taylor Hudson was not, is not, and never will be a distraction. I'm in that house five days a week working my ass off for this job. Don't talk to me like I'm fucking up."

Kyle wrapped his hands around Levi's and pried the strong fingers from his shirt. Kyle dropped back down into his seat. "I don't want to have to worry about your priorities. That's all I'm saying."

Blood rushed through Levi's veins, the sound of it like thunder in his ears. There was a fire in his gut now, a fire stoked by someone who knew what he was doing. "Get off my balls and worry about your own priorities, limp dick."

"Dude! That was one time!" Kyle yelled.

"Can you both calm down?" Crystal asked. "Kyle, stop antagonizing Levi. Levi, you're at a nine. I need you down to around a three." Crystal tugged on Levi's arm until he sat back down. "Whatever is in your head needs to stop. You've got to focus on the job."

Levi glared at Kyle and picked at the label on his beer bottle. "I know," he said. "I know," he repeated more for himself.

"Damn, I thought I was finally going to get to kick your ass," Kyle said, emptying his bottle and cracking the knuckles on his right hand.

"As if, bitch. I beat you down in tenth grade and I'll do it again."

"Please. The sun was in my eyes and I had a cold that day. Otherwise, I would have killed you."

The three of them laughed, and just as it is with true friends, the tension was gone.

Friday morning hit Levi like a sledgehammer. Consciousness brought feelings of inadequacy and failure. A mental clock counted down the hours until Plan B would be initiated. He spent the entire day rechecking the house while Crystal rerouted all video feeds. By that afternoon, hopelessness felt like a heavy weight on his shoulders.

As he climbed the stairs to the second floor, he confirmed with his team the bad news. "No safe. I found nothing."

"Copy that." Kyle sighed. "Plan B it is."

Levi stood at the foot of Taylor's bed. Minutes ticked by as he stared blankly at the messy sheets and all the soft white pillows. He pictured her there pinned beneath him, chanting his name in breathy whispers.

The door flew open and Taylor came barreling in, her phone pressed to her ear. She stopped and gave Levi a confused look.

"What are you doing here?" she asked, ignoring Reese's continued talking in her ear.

"Repairing a tile on your balcony," he answered. Levi stepped onto the balcony and knelt next to the tile.

"So who's going to be there?" she asked.

"I don't know. It's a party in the valley. The usual crew will be there."

"Fine. I'll go."

"I'll drive," Reese offered.

"All right. I've got to go. See you at nine."

Taylor stepped onto the balcony and took a seat in one of the lounge chairs. She watched Levi pull the tile from the floor and brush out the dirt around it.

She could tell her nearness made him nervous—his body was tense and on edge. She almost enjoyed the effect she had on him. It meant that he felt something too, that she wasn't alone in whatever was happening between them.

"So who are you today, Levi? It's exhausting keeping up with your moods," Taylor said. Levi remained quiet and continued to clean the area. "Well, that sucks. Guess you're just Maintenance Levi today. Do you have any other personalities? Cross-dresser Levi? Magic Mike Levi?"

He shook his head and pressed his lips together, fighting a smile. He applied some goo to the floor and placed the tile back down. She hated being this close to him when his mind was so far away. She hated that he worked hard to deny what was so easy to embrace. Taylor looked out over the lawn and sighed up at the gold and pink sky.

"I get that you don't want me anymore, Levi. But you don't have to ignore me. You are still capable of conversation, right?"

Levi turned and looked at her now. Taylor crossed her legs, and her skirt rode up dangerously high. A gust of wind blew across them and the gauzy material fluttered around her thighs. Levi's gaze was transfixed there.

"Yes, Taylor. I'm capable of conversation," he said.

"Good to know. The world is not ready to lose your poetic words or your views on Shakespeare."

"It would be a shame." Levi pushed down on the stone tile.

Taylor watched his arms flex and move as he worked. The art on his skin seemed to glow in this afternoon light.

"I broke it off with Beau," she confessed. "The friendship. Everything."

Levi didn't look up, though she saw his shoulders relax. It shouldn't matter that he was relieved. But it warmed her just the same.

"Is that what you wanted?" he asked.

"Yes." Taylor leaned forward now, resting her elbows on her knees. "Whether you realize it or not, you helped me figure that out."

Levi raised his hands in front of his chest, one of them holding a red rag.

"Whoa. Taylor, I didn't—"

"Calm down, Romeo. I just meant that you made me see how nice it could feel to be with one person." She paused and looked at him. "The right person."

Levi nodded and continued to keep his eyes focused on the tile below him.

"Not every relationship is like your parents'."

"Suzanne told me for years that I'm worth more than sex with these random boys. I never really understood. I felt like I was just using them to get what I wanted, like I was in control. But they were using me, too. I never had control over anything."

She sat back now and looked at him, the colorful sky painting Levi's handsome face in warm colors.

"You can change that," he said.

"I'll be leaving soon, starting over on the other side of the country. I can be whoever I want to be, right?"

"Right," Levi agreed.

"Therapist Levi deems it so."

Taylor laughed at her own joke and Levi smiled. It wasn't the tight, reserved smile he usually gave her. He wore it freely and it made her heart stutter.

Suzanne appeared, poking her head outside.

"Levi, your *girlfriend* is requesting your assistance in the kitchen," she said with a smirk. "Something about the ice maker. I swear I think she's sabotaging appliances just to get you down there. Come quick before she sacrifices the coffeemaker."

"Girlfriend?" Taylor asked, sitting up straight in her chair.

"Tell her I'll be down in a few," Levi answered.

When Suzanne was gone, Taylor looked at Levi again, waiting for an explanation. When he didn't offer one, she pushed again.

"Girlfriend?"

"Mandy," he said, wiping the tile down with a wet sponge. "She has a crush on me or something. Suzanne finds it fucking hilarious."

Taylor leaned back in her chair. "She would."

"Why do you say that?"

"Suzanne knows everything that goes on in this house. She mothers us and finds it all very entertaining."

"Does she have kids of her own?"

Taylor looked out over the lawn again and shook her head. "No. It's always just been me and her."

"She had no idea what she was in for, huh?"

"Not a clue." Taylor smirked. Levi started to pack up his tools, and she scrambled to keep him there longer. "Do you remember your mom?"

He twisted his lips and squinted up at the sky. "Yeah, somewhat. I remember her eyes. They're the same as mine. I remember her singing in the kitchen while my dad played guitar. I remember her being sick and I remember her funeral."

"I bet she was pretty," Taylor said, picturing a softer version of Levi. He nodded. "What about your dad? He never remarried?"

"No. My mom was his only love. After she died, he took care

of me and worked to keep a roof over our heads. When he was around, he smothered me with attention. Taught me lessons on becoming a man and how to play guitar. It was always important to him that I become something better than what he was."

"Sounds like you had a decent childhood," Taylor said.

"I did. But all good things must end, right?" He finished packing up his tools and stood to go.

"Why, Levi? Why do all good things have to end?"

He turned to face her. His usually cool eyes reflected the sky in hues of orange and amber light. His lips were set in an indifferent straight line, not giving anything away. She leaned toward him, drawn in by his closeness.

Levi tucked a stray piece of hair behind her ear. Taylor closed her eyes at his touch and kept them closed as his deep, velvety voice washed over her.

"Nature's first green is gold, her hardest hue to hold. Her early leaf's a flower; but only so an hour. Then leaf subsides to leaf. So Eden sank to grief, so dawn goes down to day. Nothing gold can stay."

When she finally opened her eyes, he was already gone.

14. file folder and eye candies

Taylor was flitting around her room, readying herself for the party tonight, when she heard the footsteps on the stairs. She went to the landing and leaned over the top banister, frowning when Nadine's face came into view.

"Hello, Taylor," she offered in her usual cheery tone.

"You don't live here, you know. You can't come and go as you please."

"I'm well aware that I don't live here. I come and go as your father pleases. And right now, he's asked me to retrieve something from his desk."

"Guess he's too busy to come get it himself?"

Nadine lifted one shoulder in a shrug. "We've got a huge acquisition coming up. He's at the office day and night."

"I'm sure he is."

Taylor stared as Nadine gave her a smile and turned down the hall. She watched the woman punch in the code to Henry's office and step inside. Knowing what Nadine would find, Taylor was all too happy to explain. She tiptoed toward the office and hid herself just outside the door.

"What on earth . . ." Nadine whispered.

Taylor grinned, remembering the mess that she and Levi had made in there—papers scattered, pens strewn about, and the antique Tiffany lamp on the floor. She peeked through the crack in the door and saw Nadine pull out each desk drawer. There was a noise from downstairs, and before Nadine could look up, Taylor hid herself against the wall.

She cursed herself, feeling ridiculous spying on Henry's assistant in her own house. So she pushed the door open. Nadine's cheap shoes stepped around the mess and over the lamp, making her way to the door. She held Henry's laptop and a file folder clutched to her chest—the name HUDSON, JULIA written on the tab. The name seemed familiar to Taylor, but she couldn't place it.

"Have a good night, Taylor. I'll tell Henry you said hello."

"Is that part of your job? Reporting on me?"

Nadine sighed and pulled the door closed and tested the knob to be sure it was locked. "No. Just thought I'd pass it along."

"Well, I didn't say hello. But you can tell that asshole—"

"Taylor."

They both turned to find Suzanne approaching.

"Good evening, Suzanne. How are you?"

Suzy gave Nadine a genuine smile as she wrapped her arm around Taylor's waist.

"I'm great, dear. Haven't seen you in a while."

Nadine looked at her feet and back to Suzanne. "Yes, well, Henry keeps us working nonstop." A moment of silence stretched between them. "Well, I'm off. Good night, ladies."

"Good night, Nadine," Suzanne offered before nudging Taylor in the ribs.

"Good night," Taylor forced out.

The sound of the woman's high heels faded down the stairs and out the front door.

"What the hell, Suzy?"

"You were being rude."

"She deserves it!"

"That woman has never been anything but polite to you. I think she has put up with enough of your verbal bashing over the years. I taught you manners, now use them."

Taylor sighed and made her way back toward her room.

"You also taught me how to use aerosol hairspray as a flame-thrower, but I'll never use that."

"You'll be thanking me when the zombies come," Suzanne replied coolly.

Taylor slammed the door between them and leaned against it. She shook her head and smiled.

"She's nuts. Absolutely nuts."

The thumping bass of the music felt like a hammer driving nails into Taylor's skull. The people dancing in the crowded room bumped into her with no regard for personal space. She was three drinks in, and still nothing could soothe her scattered brain.

Taylor made her way to the edge of the crowd and looked for Reese. After checking the room and downstairs bathroom, she came up with nothing.

Not wanting to navigate through the horde of people, Taylor slipped out the front door and took a seat on a wooden swing on the porch. On the outside, this place was just a nice suburban home, complete with a fenced-in yard and blue shutters. Inside, the smell of sweaty bodies and alcohol, the drumming of the music, and the roar of conversation made it feel like Taylor's own personal hell.

She kicked off of the ground and let the swing carry her back and forth. The cool night air against her skin felt like a reprieve from everything inside her head. Taylor leaned back and thought about Levi and the Robert Frost poem he quoted. She was familiar with its meaning, but she wasn't convinced of its accuracy. She refused to believe that nothing good could stay. If that was the case, then what the hell was life all about? What was the purpose of finding happiness only to know it'll be ripped from you? After surviving childhood and adolescence, Taylor was holding out for something better. And she was willing to fight for it.

Tipping back her cup, she finished her drink and gave in to the numbing bliss that pulled down over her. She let go of all those heavy thoughts, releasing them into the black sky like balloons. Her thoughts drifted to Levi. She knew where he was tonight and she wanted to see him. Before she could talk herself out of it, Taylor called a cab.

An hour later, she stood in the dimly lit bathroom eyeing the place with disgust. If this is how the other half lived, she was glad to have no part in it. She leaned over the counter and applied her favorite lip gloss before adjusting her cleavage. Of course the bouncer hadn't questioned her fake ID when she'd handed it over with a $50 bill. Money talked in a place like this.

She strode over to the bar and ordered a vodka tonic like she'd been doing it for years. Making her way through the space, Taylor found a dark spot near the stage. She listened to a woman fumble her way through an acoustic version of Katy Perry's "Dark Horse" and applauded exaggeratedly when it was over.

From this corner of the wide-open room, Taylor took in the crowd. She loved people watching, and this was, by far, more interesting than the snooty dinner parties and country club brunches she was used to. There was a gaggle of groupies gathered near the stage. These girls varied in age but not wardrobe. They wore their highest heels, low-cut shirts, and bras that pushed their tits up to impossible heights.

In back of the bar, staking claim to a large corner booth, were the hipsters. They looked too cool in their throwback fashion and detached attitudes. She imagined that they sat around drinking cheap beer and quoting Tolstoy and Bob Marley. Taylor liked this group and envied their autonomy. She couldn't imagine being so comfortable with who you are and not caring what other people think.

The majority of the population were generics. Average looks and the ability to disappear in a crowd were the trademarks of these people. They hung with their generic friends and drank generic drinks, happy in their generic existence.

Scattered throughout the bar were the eye candies. They didn't travel in packs. This group was secure on their own. They were beautiful and sexy beings who radiated confidence and demanded attention. Some of them didn't even realize what they were.

A couple of guys were giving Taylor looks from across the room, but they weren't who she was looking for. She came here for Levi, that bad boy eye candy.

When her glass was empty, Taylor took a seat at the very end of the bar and ordered another drink.

"Do you believe in love at first sight, or should I walk by again?"

She turned to find one of the generics breathing down her neck.

He had shaggy blond hair and smelled of cheap liquor. Taylor was nauseated by his mere presence.

"Excuse me?" she said, shifting in her seat to put more space between her and the encroacher.

"You're so damn sexy. Those lips would look good around my . . . name."

"Not interested."

"Come on, beautiful. I know you're just playin' hard to get," he slurred.

"Be gone, loser."

He leaned in closer now and Taylor could not escape quickly enough. She wanted to scream when he pressed his sloppy lips to hers, but that would only give him access to more of her. Her hands pushed against his solid chest, but the jerk would not move. And suddenly, he was gone.

The drunk was held against the bar, a hand around his throat. Levi was beautiful in his anger. The tendons in his inked arm flexed as his fingers wrapped tighter around the asshole's throat. Taylor wiped her mouth with the back of her hand and watched silently as a threat was delivered.

"When a woman tells you to get lost, that is not an invitation to kiss her."

"I wasn't—"

Levi shoved harder, cutting off the guy's air supply.

"Save it. Now get the fuck out of here."

He swung the asshole away from the bar and shoved him before running his hands through his hair. Taylor's breath was stolen by her savior. She'd only seen Levi in her home, in his uniform. Here, he was a completely different being. A threadbare black T-shirt and jeans made him a simple kind of sexy. His gorgeous brown hair was just long enough to fall in his eyes. His face was all hard lines and tension. Dark stubble covered his cheeks and jaw, and Taylor immediately remembered what it felt like between her thighs.

"Thanks for that," she said. "I thought he was going to club me over the head and drag me into a dark corner before anyone noticed."

"I noticed." His eyes connected with hers, a bright mix of hazel among his dark features. "What are you doing here, Taylor?"

"I heard you on your phone today, saying you were coming here. I wanted to see you in your element."

"My element?" Levi frowned at her and tapped his fingers on the bar. "You treat me like I'm a fucking experiment."

Taylor dropped her eyes to the floor and let out a sigh. She didn't mean to treat him that way, but she felt the truth in his words.

"How'd you get in here, anyway?" he asked.

"I have my ways."

She trailed her hand down his chest. Levi jumped back and looked around the bar, his eyes sweeping the space frantically.

The house music was cut off and the bartender stepped onto the stage. He held his hand over his eyes, shielding them from the blinding spotlight.

"What's up, party people? I'm Gregory. We're going to finish up our open mic night with a friend of mine. So keep quiet. Listen up. And don't forget to tip your bartender," he said, pointing to himself. "Levi? Where you at, man?"

Levi left Taylor at the bar, grabbed his guitar, and stepped onto the stage. He shook hands with Gregory, and Taylor was mesmerized again by the colorful inked images on his arm. Beneath the spotlight, the art seemed to glow and move, as if animated.

Alone on the stage, he took a seat on the stool. She was enamored with the way his lithe fingers danced back and forth along the strings of his guitar as he strummed. She thought of those fingers playing her body and had to bite back a knowing groan.

"Hi, I'm Levi," he said into the microphone as he adjusted the height. "Can you lower this light?" He waited a beat while the spotlight softened. "This is 'I'll be Your Lover, Too' by Van Morrison."

When Levi started singing, Taylor felt lost in his voice. He sang line after line of sexy prose and promised adoration, and she felt like it was all for her. With no conscious decision, she left the bar and made her way to the front of the stage. Taylor didn't care that she was huddled up with the groupies; she needed to be near him.

When the last chord was played and his voice faded away, Levi finally looked up into the crowd. Their eyes did not meet in some kind of soul-baring connection. In fact, he didn't look her way once. It didn't matter. Taylor felt possessed.

She watched closely when Levi began the next song. There was so much pleasure in the way his lips pursed together in concentration when he wasn't singing and how his eyes fluttered closed on certain lyrics. She felt herself swaying to the melody, getting lost in his sound. This was something so new, so surreal, it felt like she was floating above it all.

A couple of the groupies started whispering about Levi. They planned their seduction and encouraged each other with fist bumps and devilish smiles. Taylor wanted to make sure they never got a piece of him.

After a couple more songs, Levi announced that this would be his last. Taylor left the groupies and took a seat at the bar, ordering another drink. The bartender delivered it with a smile and flirtatious wink.

"Thanks," she said. "This place sure got quiet."

"It always does when Levi's up there. He's the real deal, ya know?"

"Seems like it. I'm Olivia," she said, holding out her hand. The name on her fake ID felt wrong in her mouth.

"Gregory," he answered, shaking her hand. "Nice to meet you. Don't see many ladies of your kind around here."

"And what kind is that?" Taylor fingered the edge of her glass.

"The kind whose shoes cost more than my whole paycheck."

She glanced down at her feet and tucked them beneath the bar-stool, surprised that he had noticed.

"It's okay, shortie. Your secret is safe with me."

Taylor offered a weak smile and turned toward the stage. Levi's voice floated over the crowd and returned her to her happy place.

"He is so talented," she said mostly to herself.

"Yep. And he's pretty popular too," Gregory replied, wiggling his eyebrows.

A roar of cheering, whistling, and applause got their attention. Taylor turned just in time to see Levi hop down off the stage. She followed his movements through the shadows as he dropped his guitar into a case and latched it closed. The house music was turned back up and the lights over the stage faded to black. The groupies dispersed, along with the generics, while the hipsters remained un-impressed.

Taylor smoothed down her hair and stared straight ahead as Levi approached the bar. She forced herself to not look when he stood beside her and ordered a beer. The whole time, Taylor kept her eyes on the shelf of liquor bottles along the wall across from her. Gregory delivered the bottle and Levi paid for his drink.

"You did it big, man. Like always."

"Thanks. Nice crowd tonight," Levi said, taking a sip of his beer.

Taylor felt the pull of gravity as her body leaned slightly closer.

"Speaking of the nice crowd," Gregory hinted, "here's one now." He turned toward Taylor and waved his hand. "Levi, this is my new friend, Olivia. She drinks vodka tonics and thinks that you are so talented. My work here is done."

Gregory stepped to the end of the bar to fill more drink orders. Taylor's cheeks flamed and her heart beat wildly against her chest when Levi turned his eyes on her. Even though she knew him in-timately, this felt so different from their stolen moments in the house. This felt real.

"Olivia?"

Finally, she turned to meet his gaze. The corner of his mouth lifted up on one side, and she realized that she'd been caught wordlessly staring.

"It's the name on my fake ID," she said. Taking a sip of her drink, Taylor recrossed her legs toward Levi, letting the hem of her dress slide higher on her thighs. She did not miss his gaze landing there before moving back up to her face.

"So how would you pick up a girl here?" Taylor asked.

"I don't usually have to try."

"Humor me. Pretend we don't know each other," she said.

"Do we know each other?" Levi raised one eyebrow and took a sip of his beer.

Taylor leaned forward. She ran her hand up the side of his neck and pulled his ear down to her lips.

"I know how you feel inside me and the sound you make when I kiss beneath your chin. I know what every inch of your body feels like and the way your fingers dig into my hips. Now, play my game, Levi."

He straightened up and finished his beer, meeting her challenging eyes.

"I haven't seen you here before," he said.

"Is that the best line you've got? You're not doing much better than the pencil dick who tried earlier."

He laughed and Taylor almost forgot to breathe. Until that moment, she'd almost forgotten what a hold he had on her. She'd almost forgotten the dark moments of hurtful words and the shining moments of passion and desire. Taylor wanted to make him laugh again, because it was the quintessential fuzzy feeling she'd been searching for since their last shared moments together.

"It's not a line. It is an observation."

Taylor trailed her fingers along the neckline of her dress before sliding her hair behind her shoulder. His eyes followed her every move. "Please. It was a sad variation of 'Do you come here often?' Come on, you can do better."

Levi stared at her, his quiet intensity driving her crazy.

"You want a line? How about, '*Spirit of Beauty, whose sweet impulses, flung like the rose of dawn across the sea, alone can flush the exalted consciousness with shafts of sensible divinity*'?"

Taylor blinked a few times. "While impressive, quoting poetry is still not inventive."

He stepped toward her now, pressing his body into her side. Taylor gripped the edge of the bar to keep her hands from clawing into him. Levi lowered his mouth to her ear and spoke slowly.

"Do you want stilted conversation and awkward moments, or do you want to skip ahead to the good stuff? If inventive is what you want, I can *show* you inventive."

Taylor sucked in a breath, and with it came Levi's scent—all manly cologne and beer. Her head was swimming, but she fought to stay strong in the role she was playing.

"I'm not sure you'd be up to the task."

"Oh, Olivia, I believe you know that I am."

She smiled now, knowing that he was going to be hers tonight. Taylor swung sideways on her stool so that Levi had to take a step back. He reached out and rested his tattooed arm on the bar. Her eyes followed the vibrant images of tropical flowers, fire, and some kind of exotic bird. Colorful feathers trailed from his elbow up to his biceps, turning into flames and smoldering ash. It was dark and beautiful.

"Prove it," she challenged.

Levi grinned. He closed the distance between them before Taylor knew what was happening. He didn't ask for permission or coax her into it slowly. He devoured her. Levi slid one hand beneath her hair and held her in place against him. His tongue dominated her mouth and she fought to keep up with him. When she felt dizzy and breathless, she pushed away from him.

"Point well proved," she said between breaths.

"I'm not done."

Levi wrapped his hand around Taylor's, dragged her toward the end of the bar and through a door beside the stage. She looked around the space. It was some sort of storage room filled with equipment and chairs. Levi gripped her hips firmly and lifted her up onto a long table. Taylor leaned back, resting against the wall behind her, feeling the pulsing bass from the house music shoot through her body. Levi rested his palms flat against her bare knees and rubbed soft circles on the insides of them. Taylor sighed deeply at the feel of his skin on hers.

She watched his hands slide farther, pushing up the hem of her dress. Levi eased her legs apart and pressed himself in between them. He ducked his head, ghosting his mouth lightly over her collarbone; his hair tickled her chin. Finally, his lips pressed down and sucked tenderly right below her earlobe. Taylor hummed, trying to maintain some control.

He pulled back a bit and whispered against her skin, "Relax, Taylor."

It wasn't until Taylor processed his words that she realized how tense her entire body was. Her fists were balled up tight at her sides, every muscle rigid and every breath shallow. So she let go. Taylor gave herself over to him.

Levi's fingers held firm to her body. His lips kissed, licked, and sucked every inch of available skin. Every place that their bodies connected was intensified by the vibration coming through the walls. Taylor couldn't will herself to hold out any longer. She ran her fingers through his hair, gripped it tightly, and brought his lips to hers.

There was an unhinged passion behind this kiss, a building

desire finally brought to reality. His lips sought hers over and over. Taylor tilted her head and allowed him to enter her mouth. She sucked on his tongue and wanted to bathe herself in his sweet taste. Taylor held firm to his hair, pulling and pushing at the same time. He kept his mouth pressed to hers, never pulling away for a breath. It didn't matter, because in that moment, Taylor needed him more than air.

His calloused hands pushed her dress up farther, finally reaching her panties. He yanked them down her legs and off of her body. Levi roughly grabbed her hips and dragged her to the edge of the table, causing her dress to slide up and expose her.

Breaths came quick and heavy as Taylor anticipated Levi touching her. He leaned in and sucked her bottom lip into his warm mouth, slowly releasing it through his teeth. Then he dropped to his knees and buried himself between her thighs. Taylor gasped loudly and her fingers gripped his messy hair once again.

Taylor lifted her legs, placing her heels on his shoulders. His hot breath and the scratch of his beard against her thighs made her forget who she was. Each time he moved his hot tongue over her, she let out a cry. He was the master of her body, teasing her to the brink and pulling her back from the edge.

Taylor felt the familiar tingle start in her toes and concentrated on the feel of it creeping up her twitching thighs. When it reached the point where Levi's lips and tongue were connected to her, Taylor surrendered to it. She leaned back on her elbows as her back arched and her hips lifted off the table. She screamed his name until she no longer had the breath to do so.

When Taylor came down from her intoxicating orgasm, she removed her feet from his shoulders and noticed where the heels of her shoes had dug into his skin. Taylor immediately sat up and ran her hands over them.

"I'm sorry," she whispered.

Levi stood up slowly, his palms still resting on the tops of her quivering thighs. "A small price to pay."

Taylor reached up, slipped her hand into the waistband of his jeans and pulled him to her. She kissed his lips greedily, sliding her tongue into his mouth, tasting herself.

"Let's get out of here," she said.

He nodded, righted her dress, and pulled her from the room.

"Wait! My panties!"

"I've got them," he said, his voice a scratchy kind of growl.

Taylor closed out her tab with Gregory, handing over a wad of cash and very generous tip. Levi was back by her side after grabbing his guitar case. She followed him out to his piece of junk truck. He opened the door for her and waited until she was in before closing the door and climbing in on his side. He placed his guitar between them.

"Anyone at the house tonight?" he asked.

"Can we go to your place?"

He hesitated, then nodded and eased the truck onto the street. The drive was quick and the silence only amped up the pulsing tension between them. Taylor could barely contain herself as Levi opened her door and ushered her up to his apartment. He unlocked and pushed the door open, placing a hand on her lower back to urge Taylor inside.

"It's not much, I know. But it's home."

Taylor looked around at the secondhand furniture and drab decor before shrugging.

Levi set his guitar down near the door. "Do you want something to drink? I have beer, water, and scotch."

"All the basics," she countered. "No. I'm fine."

Taylor was driving him crazy. She looked so shy and out of her element here in his apartment. Levi stalked forward and pinned her to his door. Her blue eyes looked up into his, and he could see that this raging lust was not just his. They were both affected. He kissed her again, because he could. She tasted like citrus and smelled like flowers. Her skin was smooth beneath his hands and he couldn't get enough of it.

Taylor's hands came between them as she pushed his T-shirt up. He helped by pulling it off and throwing it to the floor. Her fingers ran down his chest and over his abs before curling into the waistband of his jeans. His hips snapped forward, letting her feel what she'd done to him. He wrapped his hands around her waist and they stumbled to his bedroom. Levi flipped on the light and Taylor turned it off.

"I want to see you," he said, turning the light back on.

"Okay," she whispered.

Levi walked over to his bed and sat lazily on the end. He motioned for her to come closer. Taylor sauntered over, the confidence she'd displayed at the bar wavering. It felt so strange to have her here, so strange seeing Taylor in his space. She wedged her body between his open legs, wrapped her hands in his hair, and pulled his face into her cleavage.

Levi's hands were busy worshipping her body when he found the zipper on her dress. He turned her and delicately slid the metal pull down, revealing that familiar flawless skin. Taylor slid the straps down over her shoulders and pushed the dress to the floor. Levi lay back on the bed, resting on his elbows, drinking her in.

"Beautiful," he whispered, so low it was barely audible.

Taylor leaned down, resting her hands on his thighs, and attacked his lips. She sucked his bottom lip into her mouth, dragging it through her teeth and creating the most delicious bit of pain. Levi moaned into her mouth.

"You're really good at that," he said.

Levi removed the last of her clothes and pulled her into a sitting position on his lap. Taylor leaned against him and lifted her arms up to grab handfuls of his hair while Levi kissed and sucked on the tender flesh of her neck. He wrapped his arms around her, one hand massaging her breast while the other found its way down to her inner thigh, squeezing hard.

"Levi," she panted softly. "Please."

Levi flipped them over, pinning Taylor beneath him. She unfastened and pushed his jeans down as far as she could, and Levi finished, kicking them off the bed. Taylor sat up, flipping them over again, and looked down at his body like she wanted to feast on him. Straddling his waist, she placed her palms on his chest and raked them down his body. When she got to his boxer briefs, she slid her fingers under the waistband and slid them all the way down.

When she lowered herself onto him, both of them squeezed their eyes shut and let out matching moans of pleasure. Slowly, Taylor began rocking her hips, grinding down onto his body. Levi's lips trembled, his eyes rolling toward the ceiling before he forced them back down to her body. She set a frantic rhythm, one he fought hard to hold on to.

Needing to regain control, Levi turned them over and pushed into her so hard that his bed frame cried out in protest. She wrapped her hands around his strong arms and her legs around his body, leaving no space between them. The creaking of the bed and their pleasing rhythm filled the room.

"Fuck, Taylor. Give me what I want, baby."

Mixed with the feel of Levi inside her, the scent of their sex, and the taste of his salty skin, the sound of his demand brought her over the edge. Taylor screamed long and hard, her entire body tense, his name on her lips. Levi followed right behind her, closing his eyes to the blinding pleasure that ripped through him. He leaned into Taylor and covered her face, neck, and chest with small kisses until their breathing returned to normal.

Levi got rid of the condom, returned to bed, and pulled her close to his body. Taylor lay there tracing the patterns of his tattoos, moving over his shoulder and down his arm, before entwining their fingers and resting their joined hands on her stomach.

Levi woke to an empty bed and a burning smell. He threw on his jeans and raced into the kitchen, where Taylor Hudson stood wearing only his T-shirt from the night before. The vision was jarring and provocative at the same time. In his apartment, even among the low-end appliances and ugly carpet, she seemed at home.

"Good morning," she said, giving him a smile that was shy and questioning.

He stepped toward her and wrapped his arms around her waist. Levi buried his face in her hair and placed a kiss at the base of her throat. Taylor hummed in approval.

"I made breakfast. I hope that's okay."

Levi released her and gave a skeptical look. "Breakfast? That sounds promising."

"Well, I tried," she answered, giggling. Taylor waved her hand toward a plate of burnt toast triangles covered in jam.

His eyes swept across the counter to the open jar with the handwritten label. Anger ripped through him as he picked it up and peered inside.

"Shit, Taylor! Why did you open this?" he yelled.

Taylor shrank away from him, pressing herself against the refrigerator. Levi felt himself teetering on a dangerous edge and stormed into the living room to put some distance between them. He threw himself onto his sofa, resting his elbows on his knees, and stared down at the open jar. His heart drummed against his chest as he took deep breaths in search of calm.

Taylor approached him carefully, tucking herself against the opposite end of the sofa. She pulled her knees up and wrapped her arms around them.

"I'm sorry," she whispered. "Tell me how to fix it."

Levi shook his head and kept his eyes on the jar. "When I was little, my mom used to take me to this farm in Irvine. One day a year you can go and pick your own strawberries. It's one of the most vivid memories I have of her. I can picture her giant sun hat and her smiling face. I remember her letting me eat berries right off the vine, like it was the biggest secret. Every year, when we'd get home, she'd go crazy cooking and baking to use all the berries. My dad and I always complained about eating it all, but we loved it."

Taylor scooted forward, placed her hand on Levi's back, and rested her head on his shoulder.

"After she died, my dad and I would go to the farm every year, but I hated it without her. Eventually, when I was a teenager, I refused to go anymore. This jar is the last of the strawberry jam she made before she died. I found it in my father's cabinet when he passed away. It's sixteen years old, probably not even good anymore."

"I'm so sorry, Levi."

He set the jar down and leaned against the back of the sofa. Taylor wrapped her arms around his waist and laid her head on his bare chest. She placed several kisses there.

"It's fine," he said. "You didn't know. I'm not sure what I was saving it for anyway."

Taylor felt good wrapped around him. She soothed him in a way that made all his anger and dejection disappear. He was comfortable and relaxed beneath her touch. And then he remembered who she was and who he was and what they were doing. His body tensed at the realization. Every lie seemed to surface at once, propelling Levi off the sofa and away from her touch.

"Uh, I've got to be somewhere in an hour. So . . ."

Taylor looked up at him, the hurt evident in her expression before she wiped it clean.

"I'll just go, then," she said.

Levi nodded and walked to the kitchen to start a pot of coffee. A few minutes later, Taylor emerged dressed in her clothes from the night before. She eyed him leaning against the counter, sipping his morning drink. Levi returned her gaze but didn't say a word.

"You need a ride?" he asked.

"I called a cab. I'll see you Monday," she said icily.

"Monday," he agreed.

He didn't watch her leave, but the slamming of his apartment door told him all he needed to know.

15. happy birthday and good-bye

Levi woke in a cold sweat. He rolled over in bed and checked the time on his phone: nine o'clock. They had a meeting with the Boss at noon to discuss Plan B. Levi dragged a pillow over his head and held it there. He wanted to stay in the dark for just a little while longer. He didn't want to face his defeat or his growing frustration and feelings for Taylor.

A couple of hours later, he slid out of bed and into the shower, where he let the hot water wash away his self-loathing. By the time he made it to the meeting, he was fifteen minutes late.

"Nice of you to join us," the Boss said. "We're on my time now,

Levi, not yours." Levi nodded and took his seat between Kyle and Crystal. "Because you were unsuccessful in finding the safe, we're moving on to Plan B."

"But—" Levi said. The Boss raised a hand to stop him.

"You are done talking. The plan is set in motion already. Crystal, Kyle, I'll need a copy of the updated blueprints. After that, your services are no longer needed. Levi, I need you to return to work like normal on Monday morning. Taylor will be taken before noon that day. I need you in the house. Once the target is acquired, you'll be free and clear."

The trio stared at the Boss and then threw anxious looks at each other.

"Don't worry," the Boss continued, "you'll each be compensated fifty thousand dollars for your work once I receive the ransom."

Levi dropped his eyes to the table. He took slow, deep breaths, trying to hold on to the last bit of calm.

"Who are these guys?" he asked.

"The less you know, the better. They're instructed not to harm the girl. Unless I say otherwise."

That last statement was a direct jab at Levi and he knew it. It sent him over the edge. He jumped up, his chair tumbling to the floor behind him. The Boss matched his stance, their eyes held firm in a standoff.

"Is there a problem, Levi?" the Boss asked.

So many words and thoughts screamed to be set free. Fear and anger clawed at his chest, but somehow he was able to hold them at bay.

"Are we done here?" Levi asked.

The Boss nodded, and Levi stormed out of the building, slamming the door behind him. When he reached his truck, he banged his fist against the door and immediately felt splintering pain shoot up his arm. He hurled his fist at it again, screaming out when his knuckles connected with the metal.

"Fuck!" Levi swung again, and this time the skin of his knuckles split open and blood ran into his fist.

"Levi."

"No!" Levi shouted.

"Levi," he heard again.

A hand wrapped around his shoulder. Pure instinct drove him to turn and swing. Kyle caught his fist midair and lowered it. Levi fought for breath, his head swimming. He ripped his hand out of Kyle's grip and slumped against the beaten truck.

"It'll be okay," Kyle said.

"You don't know that."

"It will. They won't hurt her, Levi. They have no reason to. If they want the money, they won't hurt her."

Levi nodded. He knew these things, but he still couldn't fathom the idea of strangers taking Taylor. Thumping his head against the truck's window a few times, he looked up at the sky.

"This is such bullshit," Levi growled.

"It's not what we planned, but it's a way for us all to get paid. A much smaller payout, but still paid. I'll have enough for a year's subscription to kink.com and a bitchin' flat-screen TV."

Levi gave him a hollow laugh. "Porn and a giant TV to watch it on. The American dream."

"Go home. Get drunk and forget about it. At least you'll still be in the house when they come, right? You can make sure she's safe."

"And what about when she's gone? Who knows what kind of animals these guys will be. If they touch her . . ." Levi's voice drifted off and the rage inside built again. "I can't let that happen. I won't."

Levi shrugged Kyle's reassuring hand off his shoulder. His chest heaved as he fought to remain in control of his emotions. This job,

Taylor, the money—it all turned out to be a lot more than he bargained for. He couldn't bear being the one responsible for putting her in harm's way.

"I know you have an attachment to the girl, man, but use your head here. Don't screw up this job. It's not only your life you're fucking with."

"You think I don't know that?" Levi roared. "We're in over our heads. We fucking failed and now Taylor could get hurt. Who knows if her piece of shit father will even pay the ransom. Ever think of that?"

"Think about this, Levi. Henry Hudson is all about appearances. If he's hesitant to pay the ransom right away, we leak it to the press. What choice would he have then, huh? He'll do anything to preserve the Hudson name."

Levi exhaled and leaned against his truck. He thought about Kyle's strategy and was satisfied with the theory. It wasn't the best plan of action, but it was the best they had. He nodded at his friend.

"How'd you become the level-headed voice of reason here?"

"All part of my charm, you emo bitch."

They shared a grin and Levi climbed into his truck. "So, Monday it is," he said.

"Monday," Kyle agreed. "Good luck."

Taylor left her house after lunch to go shopping for Suzanne's birthday gift. This would be the last birthday they would celebrate together. Suzanne was all she'd ever known, and while the thought of going off to college felt liberating, Taylor was devastated to lose that bond.

In August, she would be in Massachusetts and Suzanne would be out of a job. Henry had tried to get rid of Suzanne a few times before, but Taylor had thrown fits and threatened him. When the threats didn't work, Henry told her that if she wanted to keep Suzanne around, her salary would come out of Taylor's trust fund. That was six years ago.

Taylor hadn't told Suzanne any of this and hoped Suzanne didn't find out. She had no idea where Suzanne would go or what she would do. Taylor only wanted to make sure she was happy, because all the best moments of Taylor's life had been because of that woman.

As she browsed from store to store, nothing jumped out at her. Nothing felt special enough to say good-bye to the woman who loved Taylor as her own child. Just when she'd given up, Taylor came across a pair of beautiful champagne diamond earrings at Tiffany's. She purchased them and had them wrapped before heading back home.

Taylor sat at her desk. Sheets of engraved stationery waited beneath her hovering pen, and her eyes glazed over as she stared at the blank page and wished for the right words to come to her. How could she condense eighteen years of gratitude into one small note?

Suzanne was her only example of what a caring mother should be. She was Taylor's rock, her best friend, the only person who understood the inner workings of the complicated girl. Taylor knew that her life would have been unbearable if it weren't for Suzanne. And yet, she couldn't find the right thing to say to express all of that. So she simply wrote what she felt, in the most basic terms.

For the last eighteen years you've raised me as though I were your own. You took me to the park where we played in the sand and had stick sword fights. You played house and let me be the mommy every time. You taught me how to ride a bike and kissed my scraped knees and elbows. You made peanut butter and jelly sandwiches with the crusts cut off and drove me to school in the mornings. You helped me survive the mortification of starting my period at the sixth-grade dance, while teaching me about tampons and where babies come from. At every school play, you were in the front row, cheering me on and clapping the loudest. You held me after Dylan Watts broke my ten-year-old heart and, years later, took me to the doctor for birth control when I started having sex. Through all your lessons, I've grown into a better person—someone I hope makes you proud. In all aspects, you are my real mother. I love you, Kitty. I'll miss you. Be happy.

She signed it *Boo.*

Levi parked his truck behind the garage and cut the engine. He sat in the quiet darkness for a few moments, gathering his strength for this party. He was okay with celebrating Suzanne's birthday, but he hated that he was at this house. Even the slightest chance of seeing Taylor again sent his pulse soaring. All the hurtful words and declarations between them had brought nothing but confusion. What they had was complicated, passionate, and completely frustrating. Levi knew he wouldn't trade it for anything.

He walked to the front door and paused. Levi wasn't sure if he should knock or just walk in. Before he could decide, Mandy swung the door open.

"Levi, come in," she said.

She wore a tight black dress and a smile just for him. The heels gave her normally petite body a lift. Her hair was pretty brown curls that hung around her shoulders. Her smile grew twice as wide when she caught Levi appraising her.

"Thanks," he said immediately, dropping his gaze to the guitar in his hands.

"Oh! And you brought your guitar! Sweet," she said. "You look great, by the way. That shirt makes your eyes look . . ."

Mandy never finished her sentence as she escorted him through the foyer and into the kitchen, as if he didn't know the way. Suzanne looked up and waved from across the room, seemingly surprised, when she saw him. He smiled and returned the gesture.

Levi set his guitar down and grabbed a beer from one of the ice buckets on the counter. He popped the top off and took a long pull. Mandy slid in next to him and wrapped her arm around his elbow.

"This is great, isn't it? I love parties."

"Yeah," he said, his eyes traveling across the room, through the foyer, and to the stairs.

Taylor stood there, leaning against the banister. Their eyes met and neither showed any reaction to the other. Levi turned his attention back to Mandy and her endless chattering, but he could feel Taylor's gaze on him, feel her body drawing closer.

". . . and then, I told him to get the good stuff in the back. This is a special occasion," Mandy continued. Taylor moved past them and approached Suzanne. "What is she doing here?"

"She *does* live here, Mandy," Levi answered.

"Doesn't mean she's invited."

"Suzy?" Taylor said. "Sorry for interrupting."

"Did you need something?" Suzanne asked, her full attention on Taylor now.

"No. I just wanted to give you your present." Taylor handed over a small blue box with a white bow and a note card.

"Thank you, sweetie. You didn't have to get me anything."

"Yes, I did," Taylor said. Suzanne started to open the card, and Taylor placed her hand over Suzanne's to stop her. "Please read that later."

A pink blush stippled Taylor's cheeks and Levi grinned at the sight. That was something he'd never seen before and he quite enjoyed it.

"Sure, sweetheart," Suzanne said.

She placed her hand on Taylor's shoulder and pulled her in for a tight hug. Levi was not surprised by the sweet moment between them. He knew how important Suzanne was to Taylor, and vice versa.

"Okay, everyone. Let's head into the dining room for dinner," Mandy announced.

All the guests made their way into the other room, bringing their drinks with them. "Levi, can you grab that tray and bring it with you, please?"

Levi nodded as his eyes followed Taylor to the door. "You're not joining us?" he asked.

Taylor shook her head. "I don't think anyone would have much fun with the boss's daughter around." Levi shrugged and picked up the tray of food. "I'll see you Monday," she said.

He froze, his feet rooted to the ground, his stomach flipped inside.

"Yeah, Monday," he confirmed.

Dinner was delicious, the conversation comfortable and easy. Soon after, the group moved to the back patio for cocktails. Mandy lit the fire pit while Levi took a seat near the pool, his trusted guitar in his lap.

"You guys are in for a real treat," Mandy announced.

"This evening is supposed to be about Suzanne," he said, embarrassed by Mandy's enthusiasm.

Levi plucked a few strings, trying to find the perfect song. Even though he was used to performing, for some reason it felt unnerving in such an intimate setting. He placed his fingers on the frets and strummed the opening chords of "Have You Ever Seen the Rain?"

As soon as he started singing, all conversations ceased. Every pair of eyes focused on Levi and his guitar. The words came easily as he sang his father's favorite song. And when the chorus hit, he closed his eyes and felt the music in his very soul.

I wanna know, have you ever seen the rain . . .

When the last note was plucked, Levi was met with enthusiastic applause. A couple of the ladies even jumped to their feet. He gave them a nod and quickly moved on to another song. After a few more songs, he saw Mandy leave and reappear with a cake, candles aflame.

Levi broke into a round of "Happy Birthday" and was accompanied by the other party guests. Mandy held the cake in front of Suzanne, who blew out the candles when the song was finished. The rest of the group cheered and raised their glasses into the air.

Levi ate his cake and wished everyone a good night. He placed a kiss on Suzanne's cheek and slung his guitar over his shoulder.

"You're leaving?" Mandy said, scurrying to block the door.

"Yeah, I've got to go. I'll see you on Monday."

"Well," she said, twirling a piece of hair around her finger and looking up at him. "Do you want to come back to my place? We could continue the party there."

"Uh, I've actually got somewhere to be. Maybe another time," he said.

Mandy dropped her hands to her sides and blew her bangs from her eyes.

"Yeah, okay."

She frowned at him as he waited for her to move aside. Finally free, Levi tore through the house, and before he even knew what he was doing, he was halfway up the stairs. He decided not to overthink his actions. He needed to see Taylor. He needed it like air and poetry and music.

Her door was open. Levi knocked twice and entered, finding Taylor on her bed reading.

"Hi," he said. He shuffled his feet and switched his guitar to the other shoulder.

"Hey. How'd you manage to escape Mandy?" Taylor asked.

He chuckled, propped his guitar against the wall, and closed her door. "I was about to leave for the night, but I wanted to see you first."

Taylor scowled at him and turned back to her book. "Well, you've seen me. Now you can go."

Levi exhaled and held his hands up in a gesture of surrender. "I deserve that. I do."

Taylor nodded but did not look at him. "Forget it. Apology accepted. I heard you playing. You're so talented, Levi. What are you doing at a job like this?"

"I'm earning an honest living," he defended. The guilt from that statement sat heavy on his tongue like a mouth full of lead. "Music is too sacred to me to commercialize it. It's just a passion that I don't want diluted by rich executives in suits who sit behind their desks and make educated guesses at what teen girls want to listen to."

She looked at him now, really looked. He felt as though she could see right through his skin to the underlying deceit and regret that ached with every breath, as if it was carved into his ribs. His chest heaved, expanding with all the lies he'd told to find that safe, and deflated with the despair of never seeing her again. It made Levi want to hide himself away.

"I guess I'll get going," he said.

Levi walked toward the bed and held out his hand for Taylor. Her confused gaze went from his formal and stiff outstretched hand to his face.

"It's been a pleasure, Miss Hudson."

She placed her hand in his and let his long fingers embrace hers. Taylor's eyes became slits, and he could almost see her mind working out this cold farewell.

"What happened to your knuckles?" she asked, flipping his hand over and inspecting his injuries.

"I lost a battle with a rusty 1995 Chevy."

"Wow. Your truck is older than I am."

With their joined hands still hanging between them, Levi felt like he could never let go. He didn't want to give up the feel of her soft skin beneath his calloused fingers.

"I should go," he said.

"Why does this feel like good-bye, Levi?"

He shook his head and took his hand back. Levi walked to the door and gave her one last look over his shoulder. Her pretty face held no anger or suspicion. From the hairpin line of her lips to the small indentation between her furrowed brows, she looked utterly terrified.

With that one look, he knew he'd never let those bastards kidnap her come Monday. He didn't know how he'd stop it, but in this moment, he knew he would. Even if it meant sacrificing his role in this game and his promised fortune.

"Levi," she whispered breathlessly. He turned to fully face her now, waiting for something, anything, to keep him there. "Stay," she said. "Please, stay."

Those words hung in the air as both of them held their breath. Time seemed to still and wait for a decision. Levi stalked forward, his footsteps heavy. For a moment, Taylor looked shocked. She wanted him to stay only because she had no idea how he'd failed her. Monday he would lose his mind with worry and probably betray his closest friends, but today, he would stay.

He pulled Taylor from the bed, his lips on hers before she'd even gotten her footing. The moment he touched her, he knew that he needed this one last time. Her hands wrapped around his neck and slid into his hair. Taylor kissed him back. She kissed him like she knew all his secrets and still wanted him anyway. Levi moaned when her tongue entered his mouth.

His mind was frantic with thoughts of claiming her, but his body moved slowly as he worked to retain every memory of her taste and sound, every poetic movement of this last dance. Levi felt dizzy with need, his usual guilt erased by her lips.

Taylor's shaking fingers moved to the buttons on his shirt and popped each one open. She placed her hands against the muscles of his stomach, ran them over his chest, and pushed the shirt from his shoulders. Circling him now, she placed kisses along Levi's shoulders and across his back.

He spun, needing to see her face, to commit to memory the curve of her cheek and the exact shade of blue of her eyes. There was an emotion there he recognized but vowed to deny. Instead, Levi focused on his immediate physical need for Taylor. He slid her shirt off before placing a kiss over each nipple. His hot breath soaked through the lace of her bra and she hummed at the feel.

Levi flipped the button open on her shorts and pushed on the material until it fell away. He groaned at the satisfying torture when he noticed her lace panties. Taylor fumbled with his belt buckle until he pushed her hands away and pulled it free himself. He slid out of his jeans and kicked them away.

Taylor looked crazed as she attacked his lips again, pulling him onto the bed. They fell together and rolled until she was pinned beneath Levi. Their hungry mouths devoured each other, exchanging sighs and throaty whispers.

"Romeo," Taylor whispered, *"you kiss by the book."*

He moved his mouth down to her cleavage, leaving a dark, possessive mark on the swell of her left breast. His fingers rubbed over the mark, a look of wonder on his face.

"What are you doing to me?" Levi whispered against her skin. His desperation was tangible. It was a fiery lead weight that sat heavy on his shoulders, reminding him that this would be his last touch, last taste of Taylor Hudson. *"Give me my sin again."*

He unclasped her bra and pulled it from her body. Levi's lips and hands slid over every inch, giving equal attention to all of her anatomy. He kissed Taylor's neck, her jaw, her chin, and finally her lips—lips that through all their smiles and frowns and sometimes hateful words had always been asking him to stay.

Taylor exhaled as Levi traveled down her body. He placed kisses along her ribs, the longer pieces of his hair falling forward and tickling her like feathers. His tongue trailed a path from her navel to her hip, where he let his teeth scrape against her tan line. Taylor bit down on her bottom lip when he placed soft kisses on the insides of her thighs. She couldn't help but slide her hands into his hair and look down at his face.

Levi held her gaze, the fiery look between them sending the pair farther into their desire. His tongue flicked out to taste her, and Taylor cried his name. She rocked her hips against him, the feel of his stubble against her sensitive skin driving her wild. Taylor felt like she was floating. A euphoric feeling pooled in her belly like falling over the first crest of a roller coaster. She screamed out when her orgasm hit, her fingers curling through Levi's hair. She pushed him away and pulled him closer, undecided about how much pleasure her body could endure.

When Taylor could breathe again, Levi crawled up her body, his strong arms caging her in. She took in everything that he was—his love of poetry and fools like Romeo, his colorful tattoos, his hurt and loss, his talent and soulful voice—and was overwhelmed. She brought her lips to his in a slow kiss that only stoked the fire inside her.

Taylor pushed on Levi's shoulders, having him lie back. He looked like a work of art laid out before her. She climbed on top of him, her hands resting on his hard chest. Levi's hands wrapped around her wrists like cuffs before he slid them up slowly, tracing every curve of her arms, shoulders, and neck.

"You're beautiful," he said, looking up at her. "And mine."

For how long? she thought. Taylor pushed that question from her head and gave a tiny smile, giving in to the rawness of this moment. She shifted against his hardness, and the delicate moment was lost to something more primal and necessary. When Levi slid inside her, both of them sighed at the feeling of being reconnected. *Yes,* Taylor thought. *This is perfect. He is perfect.*

Levi's hands flew to her hips when she moved over him. His fingers sank into her flesh as he helped. Her rhythm was relentless, never giving in to the desire to slow things down and make their time together last. This was Taylor taking what she needed and giving him what he craved.

They moved together, the act boiling down to their fulfilled moans and desperate, frenzied hands. When she fell over the edge again, she brought Levi with her. He whispered her name as every muscle in his body pulled tight with satisfying pleasure.

Taylor collapsed onto his chest, not bothered by the thin sheen of sweat that painted her cheek. She rose and fell with each breath he took. Levi's arms wrapped around her, and she reveled in the feel of his hard calloused hands against her skin. Taylor closed her eyes and placed a kiss on his chest before sliding off him.

She threw one arm and one leg across his body, anchoring him as if she thought he'd disappear during the night. *My only love sprung from my only hate.*

16. balconies and prison

Sunday morning, Taylor woke up in the most wonderful, warm co-coon. Her first reaction had been panic, but that melted away when she opened her eyes to find Levi's vibrant inked arm wrapped around her. She slid onto her back and took in his beautiful sleeping face. He looked so peaceful, his expression free from that usual contemplative frown he wore. His thick black lashes rested on his cheeks, fluttering slightly from whatever visions danced in his head. The pout of his pink lips begged to be kissed awake.

She couldn't help herself as she kissed his shoulder, then his neck, and finally his jaw. His breathing changed and his arm pulled her closer. Finally, she kissed his waiting lips, feeling them tighten into a smile beneath hers.

"Good morning, Romeo," she said.

"Yes, it is," he said, his voice rougher than normal.

Taylor shifted her body on top of his and continued placing kisses on his neck. She traced the lines of his tattoo with her lips before he rolled her over. Pinned beneath his naked body, Taylor felt every inch of his need for her.

"Can I please be woken up like this every fucking day?" he mumbled, still half asleep.

She laughed and ran her hands through his hair. They floated on the air of their pleasured afterglow with no worries to weigh them down.

"Surely you'd like to get some rest, Virginia!" Suzanne's voice shouted from out in the hall. "You must be tired from your long trip."

Taylor's eyes grew wide, and the breath left her body in one swift whoosh.

"Oh, don't be silly, Suzanne. And why are you shouting? Taylor will be thrilled that I'm home early!"

The sound of her mother's voice sent Taylor into a tailspin. "Fuck," she whispered, pushing Levi off her.

They both flew out of the bed, slipping on clothes as fast as possible.

"Taylor! Sweetheart!" Virginia sang from the other side of the door.

"Hide," she whispered at Levi.

"Where?"

Her eyes darted around the room and she pointed to the floor. "Uh, under the bed. I'll distract her while you get out!"

Levi had his jeans on and nothing else when he nodded and dropped to the floor just as the bedroom door swung open. He slid under the bed, pulling his shirt with him, and saw two pairs of feet come barreling in.

"Taylor, wake up. Mommy's home," Virginia said.

Taylor faked a yawn and spoke in a slow, sleepy voice. "I thought you wouldn't be back until August."

Levi slid to the middle of the bed, making sure he was perfectly hidden as he listened.

"I didn't want to miss my baby going off to college," she gushed. "Besides, my passport expires next week. I forgot to renew it before I left."

"Excellent," Taylor said.

Suzanne remained quiet, but Levi could see her feet pacing near the door.

"Now, get up and get dressed so we can go to lunch. You can tell me all about your summer. Have you met any boys?"

"Not really," Taylor answered. "But let me show you the new samples I got from Gucci. They're in my closet."

Taylor jumped out of bed and hurried toward her closet. Levi watched the pair of shiny black high heels follow. He slid toward the edge of the bed and heard a click. He scooted farther and turned to look back to where he'd been. A large panel on the floor had sunk in about an inch.

His pulse spiked, and the sound of Taylor and her mother disappeared as it pounded in his ears. Levi slid the panel back, knowing exactly what he'd find. *The safe.*

Levi took a quick glance at the model. Then his shaking fingers pulled the panel closed and it popped up level with the floor again, seamless and completely hidden. His head was swimming, a voice inside screaming for him to get out.

"Levi!" Suzanne hissed, her face appearing below the bed. "Come on!" He crawled out and ran for the door. "Not that way! Mandy is here helping Vanessa clean up from the party," she whispered.

Levi changed directions and slipped out onto the balcony just as Taylor and her mother returned to the room. Suzanne pushed him out of sight and leaned against the doorframe, blocking the view. Checking the ivy next to her balcony, he slid his arms into his shirt and threw himself over the railing. Climbing down the trellis was easier than he expected, and his feet hit the ground with a soft thud. He darted across the lawn and behind the garage, all the while high on the knowledge of the safe's location. Once in the safety of the cab, he dug his phone out and called Kyle.

"It's too fucking early, Levi."

"Kyle! I found it! I found the safe! Call the Boss. Call off Plan B. We're in!"

Levi tore down the driveway, tapping on his steering wheel as he waited for the slow-moving gate to let him out.

"Are you serious?" Kyle screamed.

"I would not fucking joke about this!"

"Okay, okay. I'll make the call."

Levi hung up and called Crystal next.

"What?" Crystal grumbled into the phone.

"Don't 'What?' me. I found the safe!"

"No shit? When? I thought we were no-go on Friday."

"This morning," Levi admitted. "Kyle is calling the Boss to scrub Plan B."

"Sweet. See, I told you it would be fine. Wait. What were you doing at work this early? And on a Sunday?"

"I wasn't working."

"Oh," Crystal said. There were three seconds of silence and then, "Ooooooooh."

"I'll call you back when I know more," Levi said, smiling out at the empty road before him.

He ended the call and threw his phone in the cup holder. By the time he was entering his apartment, Kyle was calling him back.

"I talked to the Boss. Plan B has officially been put on hold. Did you get a look at what kind of safe it was?"

"Yeah. It's a Gardall G3600, but custom-made. Looks like it's narrow and deep."

"Nice, Levi. The Boss wants to meet tonight to discuss our next move. Six o'clock."

"I'll be there," Levi said.

After another call to Crystal, Levi hopped in the shower, still pumped full of adrenaline. All of their man-hours, everything they had worked so hard for, had been under Taylor Hudson's bed the whole time. He couldn't help but smile when he thought of the irony of it all. Levi wondered if Taylor even knew the safe existed.

He grabbed his guitar and walked the three blocks down to the neighborhood park. It was a beautiful sunny day and the park was full of people milling about. Levi picked a bench in the shade of a large palm tree, left his guitar case open at his feet, and began to play. Being here brought up memories of sitting beside his father, doing the same thing, when he was a kid. Once Levi learned to play, they would often take turns, showing off for whoever stopped long enough to listen.

Like the dinner party, playing here was so different from playing at Mavericks. Here, children stopped to dance to the more up-beat songs. Toddlers, with their chubby little legs, teetered and bounced to the sound of "Brown Eyed Girl" before being dragged off by their mothers. Some people gathered around and stayed for a while, some just passed by and offered a tip and a smile for the little bit of joy.

Levi sang and gladly nodded at the applause between songs. And even when no one was around, he still smiled down at his strumming fingers, feeling free and hopeful and back in the game.

———

The four of them sat around the table. The air felt electric with the promise of Henry Hudson's fortune awaiting them. Now that they'd located the safe, they had to work out a way to get in and get the money out undetected. The safe would be hard to crack, but that's where Kyle came in. He'd been studying up on this for months.

"Levi, you said the safe is a Gardell G3600?" the Boss asked.

"Yeah. Hidden by a sliding panel beneath Taylor's bed," he replied.

"I'm not going to inquire about how you located this." Levi nodded, appreciating the pass. "How did we miss this in our layout?"

"Taylor's room is directly above the study," Crystal said. "The safe is nestled right behind one of the bookcases there with the opening at the top beneath Taylor's bed."

"The Gardell is a tough one," Kyle said. "I've done my research, though. I'm pretty sure I can crack it."

"I need you positive you can crack it. I'll have the same model delivered to your house. From here on out, your only focus is getting into that safe in less than three minutes."

Kyle nodded.

"Crystal, I need you to work on logistics. Find a way for us to get in and out."

"Us?" Crystal asked.

"I'll be there for the extraction," the Boss said. "I wouldn't miss this for the world."

"That's a little risky, isn't it" Levi asked.

The Boss huffed, blue eyes and an angry expression cutting through him. "Now is not the time to start questioning me, Levi. I suggest you worry about your place in the Hudson household and let me worry about mine."

Levi swallowed and dropped his gaze to the table.

"We'll be ready by Saturday, Boss," Kyle said, breaking the hostile tension in the room.

"I'll see you then."

The Boss left the room and the three of them sat exchanging hopeful looks.

"Congrats, man," Kyle said, pounding Levi on the back. "Talk about finding that safe at the last minute."

"I know, I know," Levi replied.

"So this could really happen now," Crystal said. "I always had faith that we would pull it off, but now it seems really real."

"Crystal, you work on getting us in and out. Kyle, you work on the safe. I'll get us a window of opportunity. We haven't pulled it off yet."

"That's what she said," Kyle answered, a smug smile on his face.

Levi and Crystal looked at their friend and then at each other before laughing.

"What?" Kyle asked.

"Nothing," Crystal said. "Go home and celebrate, guys."

"Try not to pull it off," Levi said, slapping Kyle on the back.

As Levi lay in bed that night with his half-empty glass of scotch, he thought about the highs and lows of his time at the Hudson house. He knew he shouldn't have stayed with Taylor last night, but he had no power against her anymore. He hated to admit it, but she possessed him in a way that was undeniable.

When her mother had shown up, he'd almost had a heart attack. He knew that if it had been any other guy in Taylor's bed, she wouldn't have thought twice about letting Virginia find them together. But to save his job or whatever connection they shared, she begged him to hide. And thank God for that.

Levi sipped the alcohol, letting it warm him from the inside out. Finding the safe validated all of his work and his worth on this team. It righted everything Levi had ever failed at. He felt whole and in control of his life, while another part of him felt traitorous. Practically torn in two directions by his warring emotions, joy and guilt, accomplishment and shame, he wasn't sure which feelings were justified. On one side, a pile of money and freedom called to him, on the other, a beautiful girl who owned him. Levi felt anger boil over at the thought of finally having things go right and still feeling empty inside. He drained the last of his scotch and hurled the glass across the room, satisfied when it shattered against the wall and fell to the carpet.

Levi had faith in Kyle. He knew Kyle would find a way to get into that safe, and when he did, they would be ready to put their plan into action. Until then, Levi was to keep his job at the Hudson house and lay low. As easy as that sounded, he knew his time there would grow more and more complicated. He knew he'd soon have to make the decision—the girl or the money? In his heart, Levi knew he'd already made it. It would be difficult, but necessary to protect everyone.

Taylor sighed as something stirred her from sleep. She hummed and started to drift off when she felt it again. Her hand flew up to swat the annoyance away, but she found nothing.

"Suzanne, stop. I'm not ready to get up."

A deep laugh vibrated against her neck, making her realize that Levi was in her bed. Taylor opened her eyes and blinked away her sleep. She grinned and covered her mouth when a yawn tried to escape.

"Does Suzanne wake you up with kisses?" he asked, covering her body with his own, only the duvet between them.

Levi kissed her temple, then her jaw, and finally her neck. His breath was warm against her skin. It smelled like mint and coffee.

"No, but it's Monday. She wakes me up for yoga on Mondays."

"Yoga?" Levi asked. He raised his head and looked down at her.

Taylor nodded. "I don't know yoga, but I could certainly help you get all bendy."

"You are such a cheese ball," she said, pushing on his shoulders. "Let me up. I need to pee."

Levi rolled over and Taylor made a show of climbing over him and out of bed. The feel of his gaze encouraged her to exaggerate the swing of her hips.

"Stop staring at my ass," she shouted over her shoulder.

When Taylor had emptied her bladder and taken care of her morning breath, she entered her room to find Levi all too comfortable on her bed. He had his hands clasped behind his head, the muscles of his biceps bulging against her pillows, one side a beautiful pattern of lines and colors, the other smooth canvas.

From halfway across the room, Taylor started running. She leaped onto her bed and straddled his hips, immediately greeting Levi with a proper kiss. It grew needy and desperate and naturally slowed down before ending with three sweet chaste pecks on the lips. She lay herself on his chest, her head tucked beneath Levi's chin.

One of his hands stayed put while the other traced the line of her spine from the nape of her neck down to her waist and back up again.

"And the sunlight clasps the earth and the moonbeams kiss the sea: what is all this sweet work worth if thou kiss not me?"

The sound of his reciting was intensified with her ear pressed to his chest. The timbre and sweet rough edge of his voice, along with the words themselves, sent Taylor falling into her own piece of heaven.

"What was that?" she asked. Her fingers rested on his chest and traced the white stitching along his pocket.

"'Love's Philosophy' by Percy Shelley."

"How do you remember them all?"

"The same way musicians remember lyrics. I set them to a melody in my head. Been doing it since I was twelve."

"Hmmm. Give me another," Taylor begged.

Levi buried his hand in her long blond hair, his fingers massaging her scalp.

"If I profane with my unworthiest hand this holy shrine, the gentle fine is this: my lips, two blushing pilgrims, ready stand to smooth that rough touch with a tender kiss."

Taylor lifted her head and hovered her mouth above his, their lips a hair's breadth apart.

"Good pilgrim, you do wrong your hand too much, which mannerly devotion shows in this; for saints have hands that pilgrims' hands do touch, and palm to palm is holy palmers' kiss," she quoted. Levi's eyes widened, and Taylor smiled proudly. "Did I mention that I was Juliet in last year's school production? That was my favorite scene."

Levi shook his head and closed the distance between them. The two devoured each other again, a mess of roaming hands. Finally, Taylor had to pull back from Levi for fear that she'd lose herself completely.

"Did you and your mother have a nice day?" he asked as she slid beside him, her head on his shoulder.

"Virginia is just down the hall. Shall we go ask her?"

"Nope. I'm good, thanks."

"Can I just keep you here, locked up in my room all day?" she asked.

"That's not in my job contract; you'd have to take it up with my employer. Besides, I don't do well with confinement."

"Really? Have you never been to prison?"

Levi looked down at her and laughed. "What? No. What the hell do you think of me? Well, I have been to jail."

Taylor shot up in bed, her face scrunched up in confusion. "What's the difference?"

"Jail means I was arrested for a minor infraction and served one night before being bailed out. It's not even on my record. Prison is long-term. It implies becoming someone's bitch and trading sexual favors for cigarettes."

She laughed and threw herself back onto a pillow. "What did you go to jail for?"

"Fighting," Levi answered.

"Hmm, that's not surprising. Did you win?"

"I won the fight. He won the girl."

"Romeo lost the girl? What did he have that you didn't?" she asked.

Levi exhaled, pressed his lips into a thin line, and then popped them out into a pout. "Money."

"Oh."

Silence.

"Have you ever eaten brunch at a country club?" he asked, teasing.

"Too many times to count."

"Did you have lobster and crab cakes and bite-sized quiches?"

"Is that all you imagine wealthy people doing?" Taylor asked.

"Answer the question," Levi pushed.

"Yes." Levi's fingers dug into her ribs, and she yelped. "Stop!"

Levi hopped up and sat on top of her legs while he continued his ticklish torture. Taylor screamed and slapped him away, but he didn't give up until she was gasping for air. He grinned down at her red face and teary eyes and, for once, she didn't care that she was vulnerable.

"I've got to get to work," he said as he hopped out of bed.

"Are you sure?" Taylor whined. She rolled onto her stomach and hugged her pillow.

"Yes, I'm sure. I don't get paid to stand around all day and flirt with the boss's daughter."

He reached back and landed a hard smack on her left butt cheek.

"Ouch! Get out of here. And take your smart mouth with you," she said half laughing while massaging her butt.

He left her there, and Taylor sat in the silence for a few moments before making her way to the shower. As she soaked in the steam and warm spray, she thought about how their relationship had seemed to change overnight. There was no longer a need to fight each other, only a desire to learn and explore in this new light.

Something had shifted between them this weekend, something that felt more real and fulfilling than anything Taylor had ever known. She could easily envision waking up to Levi every day and kissing away his worries. She could see them traveling the world. He'd recite poetry to her on every continent. She imagined all of these adventures that would never exist. As much as Taylor wanted him, wanted to be with him, she knew they had no future.

Her thoughts shifted to their affair coming to an end. Would it just be over when she left for Harvard? Would her father find out the truth and fire Levi? Would he disappear back into his own life, leaving nothing behind but her memories?

The thought was too sad to dwell on, so instead she found herself wondering what-if. What if she tried to hold on to Levi? Sure, it was crazy, but she'd spent the past eighteen years being sane.

17. googlin' and good-bye again

"Okay, I want you to write six sentences about your favorite basketball player or team," Taylor instructed.

"I need to learn to read better, not write," Dee insisted, pouting at Taylor.

"Stop fighting me on everything, Dee. I'm trying to help you."

"Maybe I don't need no help."

"Without a good education, you'll never get a good job. Without a good job, life will be much harder. Reading makes learning easier. If school is easier, you're more likely to stay there."

"What for?" Dee asked. "I'm good at math. I can make change

and stuff. I could get a job right now if I wanted. I don't need to write no sentences."

"Writing is the first step to being a better reader. That's what I found while doing research online," Taylor argued.

"Pssh, just 'cause you been Googlin' stuff don't make it right."

Taylor leaned back in her chair and crossed her arms. She'd grown accustomed to this sparring with Dee. She'd even learned to like it.

"So, if the Internet said that Peyton Manning scored the most home runs from behind the three-point line, that would be wrong?"

Dee let out a loud roar of laughter before dropping her head to the table. She continued to silently giggle, with her shoulders shaking and her hand slapped over her mouth.

"What?" Taylor asked, a sly grin pulling her lips sideways.

"I can't even deal with you right now."

Dee was still chuckling when she started writing her sentences. Taylor watched her with a sense of pride. She had been doing research on how to help teens become better readers. Not that the Internet is to be trusted for all things, but she felt confident in the information she'd found.

When Dee was finished, Taylor had her read them aloud. Her enthusiasm was evident as she read facts and opinions about LeBron James. She didn't trip or stutter over any words. When their eyes met over the table, the girls wore matching grins. Though Taylor's methods may not have been standard practice, they were working.

"How did it go?" Adrienne asked on the drive home.

"Today was great," Taylor said. "We're finally getting somewhere."

"See? I told you."

"It feels really good, you know? Of course you know, you're like Miss Volunteer of America or something. I just had no idea."

"My mom says that's called maturity, realizing that being selfless is rewarding."

"Well, your mom has always been good at life lessons. Remember when she took us on that so-called field trip to East L.A.?" Taylor asked.

"'See, girls? Not everyone has sprawling mansions and a staff to wait on them. Appreciate what you have, because I guarantee these people do,'" Adrienne said, imitating her mother's voice. "Yeah, I'll never forget that."

"It was all fun and games until someone tried to sell us weed at that intersection. I thought she was going to have a heart attack. Those electronic locks in her Range Rover seemed to come in handy real quick, huh?"

"Her face was priceless," Adrienne agreed.

The two girls fell into a fit of giggles. They laughed until Taylor's side cramped and Adrienne had to pull over and wipe the tears from her eyes. When they were back on the road, Adrienne reached over and turned the radio up. They rolled down their windows and let the wind cool their heated faces as they sang their hearts out all the way home.

The days flew by fairly quickly. Levi tried to keep to himself and his duties for the most part. Now that Virginia was home, he was even more paranoid about being caught sleeping with his employer's daughter. Though Taylor didn't make it easy on him.

She loved to sneak up on him in the house. She pulled him into closets and behind furniture while kissing him breathless. A kiss here, a grope there left him wound up and teetering on the edge of restraint. He'd almost crushed his foot when he dropped the treadmill he'd been working on after Taylor started yoga in front of him in the gym. The poetic words meant to calm him—*lady, i will touch you* by E. E. Cummings—held no power once she bent over, folding herself in half.

lady,i will touch you with my mind.
touch you and touch and touch
until you give
me suddenly a smile,shyly obscene

To say he was wound up tightly was an understatement.

Kyle and Crystal worked on cracking the safe every day while Levi maintained his role in the house. They were all excited with their progress and had no doubt they would complete the job soon. It was a bittersweet feeling for Levi, knowing that he'd finally get what he came for but also realizing that life as he knew it would be irrevocably changed. That thought tore at him, but he pushed it down, happy to live in denial for a bit longer.

Wednesday afternoon, Levi found Taylor swimming laps in the pool. She wore the tiny white bikini that was nearly sheer when wet. The material clung to her body and he found it hard to see anything else. When she climbed the steps out of the pool, Levi stood aside. He didn't even try to hide his wild, hungry gaze.

He practically chased her into to the pool house, slamming and locking the door behind them. There were no poetic words or declarations this time, only unadulterated lust. Levi pushed Taylor against the wall, assaulting her mouth with his own. His tongue stroked hers, mirroring what he wanted to do with other parts of his anatomy. She gave as good as she got. Her hands clawed at the stiff material of his uniform when he shifted his hardness against her stomach.

"You're driving me fucking crazy, Taylor. I think you like teasing me, making me lose control. You wore this on purpose, didn't you?"

She kept quiet and continued to pull his clothes off. Levi grabbed her chin and raised her face, forcing her eyes to meet his.

"Didn't you?"

It was a silent standoff, one that she would never win.

"Yes," Taylor whispered.

Levi ripped her bikini bottom off and bent her over the arm of a large, overstuffed chair. He entered her hard and fast, his most basic instinct to claim and conquer taking over. Taylor's breath was forced out each time his body connected to hers. She rested on her forearms, her fingers gripping at the soft material beneath them.

He felt wild, but in the most delicious way possible. When being inside her wasn't enough, he slid his hands beneath the cold wet material of her bikini top and palmed her perfect breasts. Taylor whimpered when his rough fingers curled into her skin.

"Oh, God," she said. "Yes."

Her breathy voice sent Levi spiraling out of control. His rhythm increased, grunts leaving his parted lips in an effort to communicate his need. When Taylor dropped down on her chest, creating a new angle, Levi broke. Dancing white lights moved beneath his eyelids as every muscle in his body pulled tight from the strain. The feeling was euphoric and so satisfying.

When he caught his breath again, Levi softened his grip on her. He leaned over and placed feather-light kisses on her back and shoulders.

"I'm sorry," he whispered into her hair. "Fuck. I'm so sorry."

"Don't be sorry. That was so hot," Taylor answered.

Levi removed himself from her and zipped back up. Taylor cleaned up in the bathroom before retrieving her bikini bottom from the floor.

"You're lucky I'm not keeping those as a souvenir," he said, watching her slide them up her endless legs.

Taylor stepped forward. She hesitated a few inches from his lips, looking into his eyes.

"You don't need a souvenir, Romeo. You can visit anytime you want."

He frowned, knowing that her words weren't true. Soon he'd be gone and she'd be gone and all that would be left were their daydreams of each other. Levi pulled her into a tight hug, crushing her body into his. She fit so well, felt so perfect, he never wanted to let go.

"I really am sorry," Levi repeated.

Taylor placed a kiss on his chin. "Stop apologizing. I told you it was amazing and I meant it. When it comes to me and my body, you can do no wrong."

Another pang of guilt stabbed at Levi. He closed his eyes.

"I wish I was a better man."

She rubbed circles on his back. "Levi, you're perfect. You're so comfortable with who you are, no apologies. You're honest about it. I love that."

The word "honest" felt like a punch to the gut, and he squeezed her tighter. "I'm just a man, Taylor. I'm not perfect. Soon . . ."

"You're perfect for me. And right now, you are mine. We'll worry about soon later."

Thursday morning, Levi showed up early at the house. He woke Taylor up with kisses and promises of coffee. She groaned and begged him to let her sleep, but Levi was persistent. After twenty minutes, she was dressed and sliding into his truck. His guitar was on the seat between them.

"Where are we going?" she asked, stifling a yawn.

"You'll see."

A half hour later, they turned onto a dirt road. A large sign welcomed them to Mamber Farms.

"Mamber Farms?" Taylor asked.

Levi gave her a wide smile and nodded. "It's strawberry day."

Taylor turned toward him, delighted at this sweet gesture. She loved that Levi was willing to share something so personal with her. She loved seeing this side of him, something beyond the sharp words and possessive man.

"Why are you looking at me like that?" he asked, parking the truck.

Taylor shook her head. "I'm just surprised, that's all."

The two walked side by side toward the main gate. They were greeted and ushered to the waiting wagon ride. Levi climbed up and helped Taylor onto the wagon. There were a few people on board already, but none of them paid attention to the couple.

During the tour, they were shown fields of lettuce, tomatoes, watermelon, and carrots. Their driver explained the history of Mamber Farms and entertained them with random facts about the family and trivia questions for the kids. Taylor loved watching Levi during the tour. He smiled and laughed so easily, seeming relaxed in this familiar place with her by his side.

When they reached the strawberry patch, Levi and Taylor hopped down with the rest of the guests. They were each given a basket and instructed on how to pick the berries and how to tell which berries were ripe. Taylor listened closely while Levi wrapped his arms around her waist and rested his chin on her shoulder.

"Ready?" he asked, when they were dismissed.

"Yep."

He led her across the field, past all the others who were already filling their baskets. In the far back corner, he bent down and inspected some strawberries.

"These will be good," he said.

Taylor bent next to him. "How can you tell?"

"My mom always said to check to make sure they are red on all sides, no green showing. You can also squeeze it gently. Ripe berries will be softer than others. If all else fails, just taste it."

"Right off the vine?" Taylor asked.

Levi shrugged, plucked a berry, and bit into it. Taylor was horrified that it hadn't been washed first, but the satisfied grin on his face and the juice coating his lips in a red glossy mess made her forget her squeamishness. Levi picked another berry and offered it to her. Taylor hesitated and he raised his eyebrows in question. Without overthinking it, she leaned forward and bit into the strawberry. It was sweet and tart and delicious.

"Mmm," she hummed. "That's so good."

He leaned forward and kissed her. It was just a quick peck on the lips, but it was enough to taste the sweet berry mixed with Levi, and it made her crave more.

They worked their way through the patch, filling their baskets. Taylor concentrated hard on following the instructions they had been given. Every now and then, Levi would throw a berry at Taylor to get her attention. He didn't need to, though. He was all she could see here in this field of red and green. His brown hair was a mess today, and in the sun, there were hints of red and gold highlights. He wore an old Red Hot Chili Peppers T-shirt that was soft and a little tight across his chest. Taylor loved the way it hugged his shoulders and biceps. His jeans were much more flattering than the Hudson uniform pants. She wanted to run her fingers through that hole ripped in the knee.

Sometimes when she looked up to find him, he was already looking at her. Though she couldn't see his eyes behind his sunglasses, she could feel his gaze burning into her. It made her skin prickle, even beneath the warm summer sun.

When they were finished, they were brought back to the main gate, where Levi paid for their baskets of strawberries. He placed them on the floorboard of the truck and held the door open for Taylor. She stopped and leaned against the open door.

"Thanks for bringing me here today," she said.

"Thanks for coming with me. It's been so long since I've been."

"What are we going to do with all these strawberries?"

Levi stepped forward, trapping her against the truck. Taylor ran her hands up the hard planes of his chest and held on to his shoulders.

"I could think of a few things," he whispered against her neck before placing a kiss there.

She ran her hands up into his hair, pulling him closer. "Oh, yeah? Like what?"

Levi moved his mouth to hers and kissed her breathless. He shifted his hips against her body, and she pushed right back. This hunger for him only grew stronger every day. Today she felt completely overwhelmed.

He gave her a crooked grin and helped her into the truck.

"I think we should make jam in honor of your mom. We can try a bunch of recipes until we find one that tastes just like hers."

"I think that's a great idea," he answered, staring at her with a new appreciation before starting the truck.

"Are you playing hooky today?" she asked. Levi smiled and nodded as they headed toward the Hudson house. "Can we go somewhere else?"

"Where?"

"I don't care. I'm just not ready to go home yet."

Levi stared out at the road. "Yeah, I know a place."

She drifted off into a trance, closing her eyes and enjoying the sun on her skin, the wind whipping her hair around. When the truck stopped, Taylor looked out the windshield and realized they were on a cliff overlooking the beach. The ocean looked like glossy blue ink spilling out onto the sand.

"This is beautiful," she said.

"I come here to think sometimes," Levi said.

"I had fun today."

"Me too," he said, but his tone was tinged with darkness. Then he stared out at the water. His beautiful face seemed troubled, an expression that was becoming more and more familiar.

"Are you okay?"

"Yeah, I'm fine," he said. "Just . . . distracted. Worried about something that I seem to have no control over."

"Do you want to talk about it?"

"No," he replied.

"You can talk to me, you know." Taylor picked up his guitar, slid to the middle of the bench seat, and placed it near the door. With nothing between them, she could feel the warmth of his body. She let her fingers trace the patterns on his skin from his elbow to his shoulder. "I won't judge you, whatever it is."

When he didn't respond, Taylor got up on her knees and turned sideways on the seat. She placed a hand on each of his cheeks and turned him toward her. The evidence of his internal turmoil was written so plainly on his face. Taylor pulled his sunglasses off so she could look into his eyes.

"What is it, Levi?"

He shook his head. "You don't know everything about me, Taylor."

"Thick and thin, tried and true. Against the world, it's just us two."

He opened his mouth to speak, then closed it and shook his head again.

Unwilling to let this mysterious darkness overtake him, she tried to distract him. "Play something for me," she begged.

Levi didn't respond. Instead, his hands turned and he threaded his fingers through hers, bringing each to his lips and kissing her knuckles tenderly.

"Come on," he said.

Levi opened the door and gestured for Taylor to get out. She climbed over him as Levi grabbed his guitar and hopped out of the truck. He walked her to the back of the truck and lowered the tail-gate. Levi took a seat. She smiled and hopped up beside him.

"What do you want to hear?" he asked, as he strummed the guitar.

"Your favorite song," she said, swinging her legs back and forth.

He grinned and shook his head. "Don't think I could ever commit to one song as my favorite. I'll sing you my mom's favorite. My dad played it all the time."

She smiled and nodded for him to continue. Levi looked sinful perched on the back of his old truck with that guitar so perfect in his lap. Taylor couldn't imagine anything more beautiful than this moment. His random strumming turned into a melody that she recognized but couldn't place. She watched his fingers move over the guitar, mesmerized by his skill and comfort with the instrument. When he started to sing, Taylor felt the breath pulled from her lungs.

Something in the way she moves attracts me like no other lover.

Taylor was in awe as his deep, raspy voice washed over her. She recognized the Beatles song but didn't know the lyrics. She didn't need to. She felt them in every part of her. She felt overwhelmed and hypnotized as he continued. Her insides were like liquid fire, her hands trembled. When his words finished and the last note hung in the air, Taylor felt like she would burst. She threw herself at him, the guitar crushed between them.

Her lips found his and she greedily took everything he gave. Levi slid the guitar out of the way and leaned into her kiss. Taylor's hands found purchase in his hair, pulling him closer until there wasn't an inch of space between them. She straddled his hips, Levi holding her against his chest.

"I want you," she said against his lips.

"Here?" Levi asked as he shifted his hips against her.

"No. Levi, I want *you*," Taylor breathed against his neck. "Come to Harvard with me in the fall."

His shoulders stiffened and his arms pushed her away, sliding her off his lap. He jumped up and paced in front of her as his hands pulled at his hair. They laced behind his neck, flexing biceps framing his worried face.

"I can't," Levi finally said.

Taylor looked down at her feet and tucked her hands beneath her thighs.

"Can't or won't?"

"Doesn't matter," Levi said.

He grabbed his guitar and got back in the truck, slamming the door behind him. Rejected and unable to face Levi, Taylor climbed in and stared out her window. The drive home was silent and unbearable. Taylor thought she would scream if she didn't escape soon. When he pulled up to the gate, she hopped out, practically running from the truck.

"I can bring you to the house," he called out.

"I'll walk," Taylor said over her shoulder.

She stumbled across the lawn, moving as fast as her shoes would let her. When she reached the front door, Taylor threw herself inside and slid down to the floor. Her chest heaved from the run and from the rejection. She felt on the edge of panic. Taylor leaned her head back against the wooden door and thought about her outburst. She hated Levi for saying no, but more than that, she hated herself for even asking.

18. cougar bait and the laundry chute

By Friday afternoon, Virginia had been hanging around the house more, and Taylor prayed it wasn't in hopes of seducing Levi. Taylor could tell that he'd caught her mother's eye, and the woman was unstoppable when it came to something—or someone—she wanted.

After searching the second floor, Taylor set out toward the kitchen. She was so desperate to find Levi that she was considering asking Mandy if she'd seen him. Taylor would have to make up some maintenance issue so that the girl wouldn't suspect anything. Maybe she could say her bed was broken. She smiled and shook her head. A problem in the shower?

On her way to the kitchen, Taylor passed the study and froze at the sight before her. Virginia had Levi pinned against one of the bookshelves. Her arms were on each side of him, gripping the shelves, trapping him. She wore a ridiculously short pair of shorts and a tiny tank top. As summer attire goes, it was certainly appropriate. For a ten-year-old.

"Mrs. Hudson, I should get going."

Taylor could see his panicked expression, his eyes searching for an escape.

"Ah, ah, ah. I told you to call me Virginia. Do you want me to punish you for your slipup?"

"I thought you needed me to get that book for you." His voice was firm.

"That's not *all* I need," Virginia purred.

"Mom!" Taylor yelled, stomping into the room. "What are you doing?"

Virginia immediately straightened her posture and dropped her arms, freeing Levi.

"Levi was just helping me reach a book. Weren't you, dear?"

"Yeah. A book," he said.

He shot Taylor a grateful look and quickly left the room.

"Can you please control your cougar tendencies for five minutes?"

Virginia strolled over and took a seat in one of the chairs, picking up a book that lay open there.

"I'm sure I don't know what you are talking about, Taylor."

"I'm sure you do," Taylor seethed.

Virginia put down the book and crossed her legs. "Listen, I had to come back to this hellhole a lot sooner than planned. I'm not happy about it and I'm lonely." She tucked her hair behind her ear and looked up at Taylor. "Stay out of my way, little girl."

Taylor couldn't help but feel a stab of pain at her mother's warning. She should be used to this kind of behavior, but it still hurt to be viewed as an obstacle instead of a loved one. She crossed her arms and glanced up at the stupid family portrait that hung over the fireplace. It concealed the lies with fake smiles. Henry and Virginia still kept up the charade, convincing everyone that their marriage was as strong as ever.

Storming from the study, Taylor turned the corner to find Suzanne standing there wearing that familiar pitying expression.

"What's wrong with her?" Taylor asked quietly. "What is wrong with this family?"

"I wish I had an answer for you, sweetheart. Her priorities are more mixed up than a manatee at a fashion show."

Taylor chuckled and took a deep calming breath. Suzanne grabbed one of her hands and squeezed it. "Thick and thin, tried and true. Against the world, it's just us two. Love you, Boo."

"Love you, Kitty."

Suzanne nodded and released her grip. The gentle smile she held for Taylor disappeared as she set her sights on the study.

Taylor huffed and made her way back to her room. She found Levi waiting for her and gave a sigh of relief.

"Crazy bitch," she said.

"You okay?" Levi asked, pulling her in for a hug.

"Yes. I should be asking you that. You were the one subjected to the claws of Virginia Hudson."

"I'll live."

"I've survived her for eighteen years, so your chances are pretty good. Thank God she's leaving for La Jolla tomorrow."

Levi took a seat on the edge of her bed. He pulled Taylor into his lap.

"What are you doing this weekend?" he asked.

He realized the heavy intention of his words as soon as they left his lips. Taylor would assume that he wanted to see her or keep tabs on her. While that was true, he also needed a schedule for planning the heist. Kyle and Crystal were ready to go and the Boss had given the green light.

Levi felt torn in half by this job and his feelings for Taylor. He questioned his ability to remain professional when the time came. Could he betray her? Could he leave? Even though the answer felt questionable, he knew what he had to do. He was unworthy of someone like Taylor. He would only corrupt her life. She was better off without him.

"I promised Reese that I'd hang out with her this weekend. Seems I've been neglecting my friends. She's picking me up tomorrow morning, and we're heading up to see her brother again."

"What does Suzanne do when you're gone?" he asked.

"I think she's spending the day at the spa tomorrow. The staff gave her a gift certificate for her birthday." Taylor hopped up and pulled Levi with her. "Well, I guess I won't see you until Monday," she said.

But she wouldn't see him Monday. With Virginia, Taylor, and Suzanne out of the house, the job would get done this weekend. By Monday, Levi would be a much richer man and halfway around the world.

He pulled Taylor against him, squeezing so hard he felt every place where her body connected with his. His hands held on to her like his most valued possession. Levi leaned down and inhaled her scent, burying his face in her hair. He closed his eyes and committed all of this to memory.

"Levi, I can't breathe," Taylor said against his chest.

He immediately released her, trying to mold his face into something neutral and indifferent.

"What's wrong?" she asked. "Whatever it is, just tell me. I'll understand."

He shook his head, suddenly unable to speak. Levi wove his

fingers into her hair and urged her forward. He pulled Taylor's lips to his and gently sucked her top lip between his. He breathed her in and slid his tongue against hers.

Levi slipped his hands down to her shoulders, skimming the soft skin of her arms, until he laced their fingers together. He poured all that he possessed into that kiss. Images of their times together flashed before his closed eyes, each one another wound. He memorized the taste of her and the tiny whimpering sounds from the back of her throat. He pictured the way her honey blond hair fell around her face, the feel of her soft, delicate hands, and the way her eyelashes fluttered against her cheeks. He recounted every word between them, the good and the bad. It brought to mind "Farewell" by Anne Brontë. Though he knew the poem well, the words were lost to him, as he was lost to Taylor.

> Farewell to thee! but not farewell
> To all my fondest thoughts of thee:
> Within my heart they still shall dwell;
> And they shall cheer and comfort me.

Taylor pulled away for a breath, releasing one of his hands and clutching at her chest. "Wow," she whispered, looking up into his troubled face.

Levi placed one more kiss on her forehead. "Good-bye, Taylor." He turned to go and forced himself not to look back.

"See you later," she said.

Levi didn't answer. He just couldn't lie to her anymore.

Before leaving the Hudson house, he placed a call to Kyle, letting him know the house would be empty on Saturday. A few minutes later, Kyle sent a text confirming that they were go for tomorrow.

Levi went to the laundry room and unplugged and removed the back panel of the washing machine. He reached in, grabbed a handful of wires, and yanked them out, rendering the machine in-operable.

Even though he didn't work weekends, he was on call for any major problems. Levi knew from the work chart posted next to his that laundry was done on Saturdays. He had no doubt they'd be calling him when the machine didn't work.

With everything back in place, Levi stepped outside and glanced up at Taylor's balcony only to find her doors closed. He walked backward for a few steps, willing her to come out so he could see her one last time. Unfortunately, it didn't happen. He went to his truck and climbed inside. *A thousand times the worse, to want thy light.*

That night, the four members of the team sat around a table at their usual location, the last meeting before it all went down.

"Levi, you took care of the washing machine?" the Boss asked.

"It will definitely be out of order."

"Good. Kyle, what's your time with the safe?"

"Two minutes forty-one seconds," he answered, puffing out his chest.

"Excellent. Do you have all your affairs in order? As you know, disappearing is part of the deal. You'll all leave and not come back. I don't need anyone around to point fingers once it's done."

Everyone nodded, confirming their plans to abandon this place and leave no trace behind. Each of them was heading in a different direction, so not only was Levi going to lose Taylor, but he was also losing his best friends. As he contemplated that, it again felt like all this money wasn't worth it.

"Crystal, give us a rundown," the Boss ordered.

"First, we wait for the housekeeper to call Levi. He'll go in and confirm that the machine needs to be replaced. He'll place the call to one of us, in front of the housekeeper, and arrange the delivery of the new machine. There is only one person on staff on the weekends, so navigating around her will not be difficult. While Levi waits for us to arrive, he will gather as many bedsheets as possible and place them in Taylor's room."

"Do you want them on or under the bed?" Levi asked.

"Under," Crystal said. "Kyle and I will sneak into the house and get upstairs to Taylor's room, where Kyle will get us into that safe. We'll empty the cash, place it in sheets, and tie them up."

"Then we'll drop them down the laundry chute." Kyle continued the explanation. "Levi will be waiting to place them in the broken washer. We'll sneak back out and arrive as the delivery guys with the new machine. The new machine will be installed and we'll kindly haul away the old one."

When he was finished, all of them leaned back in their chairs, smiling. *This will work,* Levi thought. There wasn't a doubt in his mind.

"I'll wait in the delivery van," the Boss said. "We'll come back here, divvy up the cash, and part ways for the last time."

The team nodded and said their good-byes to the Boss. Then there were three. Three longtime friends left to contemplate never seeing each other again.

"I can't believe we're finally doing this," Crystal said.

"I know. Seems like only a few days ago when Levi came to us with this plan. I thought you had lost your mind."

"That's still to be determined," Levi said.

After a beat of silence, Kyle spoke up again. "I don't suppose anyone knows the current conversion rate of U.S. dollars to Aruban florin?"

Crystal laughed and shook her head. "Can't help you there, mate. I'll be trading mine in down under."

"Subtle," Levi said with a grin.

"And what about you?" she asked.

"The mighty euro. What I lose in conversion, I'll make up for in scenery."

"Nice," Kyle said. "I'm going to miss you fuckers."

"Me, too," Levi said.

"Me, three," Crystal agreed.

"If I forget to tell you later, thanks for pulling us in for this job. I know I should feel guilty, but with people like Henry Hudson III, it's too easy to justify," Kyle said.

"Yeah. And I bet we don't know the half of it," Crystal replied. "Thanks, Levi, for changing our lives."

"I wouldn't have it any other way," he answered.

As Levi lay in bed that evening, he tried to compartmentalize the swirling mess of thoughts in his head. He struggled to avoid his fear of losing Taylor and focus on the job. This was no longer an easy task. She had saturated every part of him. When he finally fell asleep, his dreams were filled with her pretty blue eyes and airy laughter.

Taylor sat in the kitchen Saturday morning, waiting for Reese to arrive. She ate a banana and thought about the day before with Levi. Something had felt strange between them, unfamiliar and tense.

Taylor had been kissed hundreds of times before, but never like that. The way he held her and pulled her close, the way his lips devoured her and his fingers folded between hers left a burning ache inside her body. That kiss said things that they'd never spoken out loud. It felt like promises and declarations. She had lost herself to Levi in those moments.

When Reese honked from the driveway, Taylor threw her bag over her shoulder and practically skipped down the front path. She gave Reese a wide grin and slid into the car. Reese immediately noticed Taylor's cheerful mood.

"Well, hello, sunshine. Someone finally woke up on the right side of the bed today," she teased. Taylor smiled and nodded as she applied her raspberry-lemonade lip balm. "I talked to my brother this morning and he said the party isn't until late. We're going to hang out by the pool and grill. That cool?"

"Sure," Taylor answered, feeling up for anything.

As they made their way up the highway, Taylor let herself relax completely. Her body sank into the leather seats as she closed her eyes and let the sun warm her skin. With the top down, the wind whipped her ponytail around. She felt weightless and peaceful, like a drifting cloud.

A few minutes later, Taylor noticed a couple in the car next to them fighting. The guy driving was waving one hand around and yelling while the other hand stayed on the wheel. The woman in the passenger seat yelled right back, throwing a finger in his face to emphasize her point.

Outside the city, Reese floored it and the couple disappeared behind them. Ten minutes later, they reappeared next to the car. Their fight was still going strong, seeming to have escalated. They went back and forth, sometimes not paying any attention to the road. It made Taylor nervous.

"Check them out," she said.

Reese looked over and grinned at the fighting couple. "Wow. They're really going at it."

"Yeah."

Suddenly, the woman in the car reached over and slapped the driver. Before the girls could react, the couple's car was drifting into their lane. Reese slammed on the brakes, but it wasn't enough. The other car clipped her front fender with just enough force to send them spinning. Taylor's fingers clawed into the door as they swung around, and by the time the car came to a stop, they were facing the wrong direction on the highway.

Both girls screamed when they noticed oncoming traffic hurtling toward them. Despite a loud grinding sound, Reese pulled the car over onto the shoulder and parked it.

"Holy shit!" she shouted. "What the hell?"

"They didn't even stop," Taylor pointed out, one hand resting over her furious heart. "Are you okay?"

"Yeah, I think so. You?"

Taylor nodded. Reese climbed out of the car, and Taylor followed. They both stood assessing the damage. Part of the front fender was bent in so much that it was rubbing against the front tire. There was no way they could drive it.

Reese called the police before calling her brother to let him know they weren't going to make it. He offered to come help, but she insisted that they had it under control. Both girls climbed back into the car to wait.

"This sucks," Reese said.

"It's okay. We can get some sun while we wait."

"Who are you? And what have you done with the real Taylor Hudson?"

"Ha ha. I'm just happy, Reese. I know it's a strange concept."

"I don't know what got you to this blissful place, but you better hold on to it," she said.

"I intend to."

"I saw Beau at the Boulevard yesterday. He's a mess, Tay. He said you gave him the boot. Said you picked the maintenance guy over him."

Reese turned to Taylor and waited.

"It's not like that. I finally decided that we both deserved more than meaningless sex. I want something real."

"I'm pretty sure Beau was willing to give you more. He's a great guy."

Taylor sighed and finally faced her friend. "I don't love him. Not that way. It would have been really easy with Beau, but it would have been boring. Why are you suddenly Team Beau?"

"Because I'm a big fan of his father," Reese answered simply as she tapped on her diamond earrings.

"What?" Taylor yelled. "The guy you've been seeing is George Upton? Are you kidding me?"

Reese nodded and chewed on her bottom lip. "He's great, Taylor. He's so good to me. It's not all crazy monkey sex. He actually listens when I talk. He's so inquisitive and wants to know everything about me."

Taylor couldn't believe what she was hearing. Her hands fluttered in front of her chest as she tried to comprehend what this meant. But when she looked at Reese, all of that disappeared. The look on her face was sublimely happy. It was a look that Taylor recognized.

"I guess we all have our secrets, don't we?" Taylor asked.

Reese didn't respond. She just leaned back in her seat and stared out at the road ahead of them as traffic whizzed by. Taylor thought their conversation was over, but after a few minutes Reese spoke again.

"So, you were never going to tell me—your best friend, by the way—that you're fucking the maintenance guy?"

"Why? So you could pass judgment on me? Or him? No, thanks."

"Come on, Tay. Don't underestimate me like that."

"And we're not just sleeping together. There's something else there, Reese. I don't know what it is, but it's amazing."

"Do you love him?" Reese asked.

"Maybe. How on earth would I know what real love looks like? Or feels like?"

Taylor pulled down the visor and studied herself in the mirror. Did she look like a girl in love? She didn't know. All she knew was that Levi invigorated her. He made her feel transformed and like anything was possible. He ruled her thoughts and her body in a way that made her question if she could ever belong to anyone else.

Reese shrugged. "I know I said some terrible things before, but if he's what you want, I can accept that."

"I'm not looking for your acceptance," Taylor snapped, flipping the visor up and folding her arms across her chest.

"Sorry, that came out wrong." Reese offered an apologetic smile. "If that guy is responsible for all this ooey gooey goodness coming out of you, then please keep him around."

They both laughed and it felt like they were kids again, making up after a silly fight over who got to play with Malibu Barbie and who had to play with Ken.

The cops took almost forty-five minutes to arrive, wrote the report, and told Reese where she could get a copy of it.

"What about my car?" she asked the officer.

"That's your responsibility, ma'am. You can't leave it here."

Reese huffed. "I guess I can call AA or something," she said.

"Your car is not an alcoholic. You mean Triple A," Taylor corrected.

"Whatever, smart-ass."

Reese was on the phone for a while, pacing the shoulder of the highway and kicking rocks into traffic. Taylor leaned against the hood, checking her phone. Triple A confirmed the girls' location and promised to be there within the hour.

19. stacks on stacks and retribution

Levi woke early on Saturday morning, full of nervous energy. He spent his time packing up the last of his apartment. He made two trips to different Goodwill stores to drop off his furniture and other belongings. When all was said and done, the only thing left was one large suitcase and his father's guitar.

He sat on the floor in the empty space and looked around at the almost white walls and beige floor. He rubbed at the indentations where his old couch had been for the last three years. Levi lay back on the carpet and stared up at the ceiling. He closed his eyes and mouthed the words of T. S. Eliot's *The Hollow Men*, each line a metered measure of his departure from this life.

We are the hollow men
We are the stuffed men
Leaning together
Headpiece filled with straw. Alas!
Our dried voices, when
We whisper together
Are quiet and meaningless
As wind in dry grass

All these things would soon be gone and he would be homeless—wealthy and homeless. Countless poems floated through his head, followed by songs he knew by heart. None of them seemed to make a difference. None of them soothed his aching heart.

Around eleven, Vanessa, the weekend Hudson housekeeper, called. She was in a panic because the washer wouldn't start. Levi smiled into the phone and promised that he'd be there as soon as possible. His adrenaline kicked in as he sent a text to Kyle indicating their game had begun.

As he drove across the city toward the Hudson home, Levi's anxiety seemed to grow exponentially. By the time he was sitting before the pretentious iron gate, his insides were practically vibrating. After parking behind the garage, Levi sat quietly for a few minutes, trying to calm himself and his thunderous pulse. He cleared his head and focused on his objective.

Wearing the uniform he'd never have to wear again, Levi found Vanessa in the kitchen.

"Hi, you must be Levi," she said. She held her hand out and Levi shook it once. "I'm Vanessa."

"Nice to meet you. Well, let me have a look at the washer for you," he said.

"Thanks. I didn't know what to do when the damn machine wouldn't even power on. So I called Mandy and she said to call you because you were on call for weekends. Sorry to bother you on your day off."

"No problem. All part of the job," Levi said.

"I'm the only one here today, so I'll be busy doing other stuff. If you need something, just page me," Vanessa said, pointing to the panel on the far wall.

"Will do."

He went into the laundry room, pulled out the washer, and tinkered around a bit. When twenty minutes had passed, he stepped back into the kitchen. Levi spied Vanessa moving around in the foyer, so he headed toward that side of the room to place his call.

"Hello."

"Hi. This is Levi Russo, head of maintenance at the Hudson residence." Kyle laughed on the other end of the line. "The washing machine has completely gone out. We'll need a replacement. Maytag Commercial Energy Advantage, eighty pound, soft-mount, front load."

"Blah blah blah," Kyle said.

"Can we get that today?" Levi paused. "Great. By two o'clock will be fine. Thanks."

Vanessa stepped into the kitchen, a duster in her hands. "It can't be repaired?" she asked.

"No, sorry. The replacement should be here in a few hours, though. I'll wait and make sure it's installed correctly."

"Oh, you don't have to stick around on your day off, Levi. I'm sure the delivery guy can do it."

"I don't mind." He gave her a smile and she seemed to relax.

"Okay."

Vanessa left the room and disappeared into the basement. Levi crept to the linen closet on the second floor and pulled down as many sheets as he could find and slid them under Taylor's bed. He pulled his earpiece out of his pocket, turned it on, and placed it in his ear. His mic was already turned on.

"Are you guys getting me?" he asked.

"Loud and clear," Crystal answered. "I've rerouted all cameras during the heist. They are looping a few seconds of video while we're there. We're approaching the south side of the house now. What's our entry point?"

"Taylor's balcony. There is latticework beneath all that ivy."

"Copy that."

Levi made sure the balcony doors were open before heading back downstairs. He entered the kitchen and got a bottle of water from the fridge, swallowing most of it down in one pull. Vanessa flitted in and out of the room while he nervously waited to hear from his friends. The seconds ticked by, each one matching his pulse.

"We're in," Crystal said. "Moving the bed now." He exhaled and threw his water bottle away. "Sliding the panel away. Kyle's getting to work."

Levi stepped into the laundry room and propped open the chute door. He sat on top of the broken washer and waited. After three minutes of silence he heard a muffled sound in his earpiece. He pressed it harder into his ear.

"What's that?" he asked.

"The damn housekeeper is upstairs, Levi. I can hear her in the hall."

"Shit."

He hopped down and ran to the intercom panel in the kitchen. "Vanessa, could you come to the kitchen please?" Levi asked.

Everything in the house was quiet. His gaze stayed glued to the kitchen's entryway. Levi pressed the button again. "Vanessa?" His voice echoed through the empty rooms.

A short scream sounded out.

"Fuck!"

Levi sprang into action. He took off running, across the kitchen, through the foyer, and up the stairs, preparing to do whatever it took to handle the situation. His friends were quiet in his ear, and he knew that wasn't a good sign.

"Vanessa?" he called out at the top landing.

"In here," she answered from Taylor's room.

Levi rushed inside, his eyes searching the room. Everything seemed to be back in place. It all looked normal. Vanessa was coming in from the balcony.

"Are you okay?" he asked, trying to slow his labored breathing.

"Yeah, I'm fine. There was a damn pigeon in here. Scared the shit out of me, and him." She pointed to two spots of bird poo on the floor. "Taylor must have left her balcony doors open."

"Oh."

She bent down and wiped up the mess with a rag from the pocket of her apron. "Stupid bird."

"Could you come downstairs for a minute? I need your help with something."

"Sure."

"Where are you guys?" he whispered halfway down the stairs.

"Pardon me?" Vanessa asked.

"What was the size?" Levi replied quickly. "Was it a big bird?"

She answered him, but he couldn't hear a thing with Crystal laughing in his ear.

"We were under the bed," she said. "Back to work now."

When they were in the kitchen, Vanessa turned to him and waited expectantly. Levi searched his mind for some way to keep her busy. He rubbed at the back of his neck and shuffled his feet.

"I feel embarrassed now, but I was just wondering if you could make me some lunch? I was about to eat when you called and now I'm starving. Mandy always does it for me during the week and I don't feel comfortable going through the fridge." He punctuated his request with his signature crooked smile. It worked like a charm.

"Oh, Levi, that's no problem. Don't feel embarrassed. I'd love to."

He sat at the bar, his knee bouncing up and down with nervous energy.

"Stacks on stacks, baby," Crystal said excitedly. "We're in."

Levi exhaled and smiled up at the ceiling. After all their hard work, their efforts had paid off. The safe was real, the money was real, and they'd be rich.

"Coming your way," Kyle said in his ear.

A soft thud was heard and Vanessa's head popped up. "What was that?"

"Just me," Levi replied. "I kicked the cabinet."

He connected his shoe with the wood in front of him and was relieved when it sounded similar. Satisfied, Vanessa continued to make his lunch. She slid the sandwich in front of him and dusted off her hands.

"Well, it's not a Mandy original, but it'll do," she said.

"Aren't you going to eat with me?" he asked.

"No, hon. I need to go dust Taylor's room while she's out."

Levi choked on his sandwich.

"Are you okay? Can I get you some water?"

He nodded emphatically, his mind struggling to come up with a way to stall her.

"Last one," Crystal said through the earpiece. "We're closing up and heading out."

Vanessa set a glass of water in front of him. "Well, I've got to get back to work. Did you need anything else?"

"No, I'm good. But you might want to start with the gym in the basement. I heard Mrs. Hudson complaining about it yesterday afternoon."

She nodded and left the kitchen. As soon as she was out of sight, Levi hurried to the laundry room.

A soft yellow sheet sat at Levi's feet, its corners tied up like a sack. He could barely see the bricks of cash through the material. The sight made a grin spread over his face. He closed the chute door and leaned against it, imagining how this money, these kind of resources would change his life.

After a few minutes, he had to ask. "How much?"

"A little over twenty million," Crystal answered, out of breath.

"Holy shit."

"Yeah, I know. We're down the trellis now. Prepare for phase two."

Levi waited a few minutes and snuck back up to Taylor's room. He told himself it was to make sure everything was back in place. But in all honesty, he just needed to see the space one more time.

The bed was returned to the middle of the room and everything looked normal. The smell of the room was way off, though. Levi couldn't smell Taylor's shampoo or perfume anymore. It was the stench of metal and money. He ran his fingers over the white fluff of her bed, remembering exactly what her skin looked like against it. He glanced at the double doors and remembered their open conversations and the way the sunset painted her face.

"Levi, we're at the gate." He blinked out of his memories.

"Buzz the house. The housekeeper will let you in."

Levi headed downstairs, where he found Vanessa watching the delivery truck through the front window.

"Hi," he said, startling her. She spun to face him. "I'll take care of the installation and let you know when it's ready."

"Thanks," Vanessa said. "The gym looked clean to me. Maybe Mandy got to it before she left yesterday. I'm so behind on my work. I'll be upstairs if you need anything."

Levi nodded and she left the room. He entered the laundry room and opened both doors, creating a wide enough entry for the new machine. He watched as the team used a pallet jack to move it onto the lift gate and lowered it down to the driveway. They worked together and wheeled it to the back door and into the laundry room.

Levi detached the old machine and, with their help, slid it away from the wall. Crystal and Kyle cut out one side of the huge box and then the three of them moved the new machine into place. They loaded the old one onto the pallet jack and started filling it with the bags of money.

"It's not all going to fit in here," Crystal said.

"We'll load the rest into the empty cardboard box. Let's bring this to the truck," Kyle replied.

While they hauled the full broken machine away, Levi worked to install the new machine to the wall connections. It had a special kind of hose attachment and he would need a different wrench to connect it.

When Crystal and Kyle returned, they loaded the empty box onto the pallet jack, pulled the remaining sacks of money from the laundry chute, and started placing them inside.

"Is the Boss really in the truck?" Levi whispered. Kyle and Crystal both nodded silently. "I need a different wrench from the garage. I'll be right back."

"Okay, we're almost done here," Crystal answered.

Levi walked out the door and got only about six steps before he heard something that made his stomach drop.

"What the fuck is going on here?"

Taylor, his brain screamed.

After taking a taxi home from the dealership where Reese's car was towed, Taylor had been exhausted. Walking up the driveway, she'd seen a large delivery truck parked near the house. She entered the kitchen and heard voices coming from the laundry room. When she'd peeked in, she'd found a guy and a girl pulling sacks from the laundry chute and loading them into a huge cardboard box.

Her stomach had dropped as she watched the guy open one of the sacks and pull out a stack of cash. He fanned it over his face and smiled. That's when her mouth acted before her brain.

"Oh, shit," the guy said.

He rushed toward her and covered her mouth before she could scream again. She fought against him, kicking and yelling behind his hand, but it was no use.

"Shh," he whispered in her ear. "We're not here to hurt you."

Taylor's body shook, but she opened her eyes to face them anyway. That's when she saw Levi come running into the room. She squinted at his form silhouetted by the bright midday sun in the doorway. Her pleas grew quiet.

"Taylor," he breathed. She blinked a few times, trying to clear her eyes. He walked past the girl, past the box, and approached her carefully. "He's going to let you go now, don't scream, okay?"

Kyle's hand loosened from her mouth and dropped away, but his other arm still held her hands down. Taylor's mind raced with possible explanations, but none of them made any sense. She looked to Levi, who wouldn't meet her gaze

"Who is that?" she asked. "And that? And what is this?" Taylor nodded to the sacks of money.

Levi stood there silently. His mouth dropped open a few times but nothing came out. The other two just stood there silently, obviously waiting to take their cue from Levi. Taylor tried to shake out of the guy's hold, but it was no use. Over the sound of their heavy breathing and chirping birds outside, came a *click-clack* noise that drew closer. Someone was coming.

Taylor's eyes darted around the room to each of them before settling on the open doorway.

"Whoa! What's all this?" Mandy asked.

"The washing machine broke," Levi almost shouted. "I had to order a new one."

He waved toward the new machine against the wall, his eyes pleading with Taylor to play along. The guy that held her dropped his hands but still stood too close. She was so confused, but something in her wanted to help. Mandy's eyes glided over the room before coming back to Levi.

"I was just keeping Levi company while these guys delivered the new machine," she said. "They were showing me their tools."

Mandy looked at her, really looked at her. Taylor felt like the lie was a neon sign blinking over her head. She wasn't sure why she was lying for Levi, but she felt compelled to do so. Mandy looked leery, but she shrugged and turned toward Levi.

"Well, okay. When Vanessa called me this morning, I knew you'd be here," she said, trailing her fingertips along his shoulder. "While I was out running errands, I just wanted to make sure everything was under control."

"It is," Levi said, stepping away from her.

"And I was hoping we could grab lunch or something when you're done. I'd really like to talk to you about"—her eyes nervously scanned the group before finishing—"something."

Before Levi could answer, Taylor blurted, "You were running errands dressed like that?" The skin-tight dress and three-inch heels hardly looked like errand clothes. This girl looked like she was headed to a nightclub or out to seduce a man. The latter being abundantly clear.

Mandy looked shocked and frowned at Taylor. "Yes, well, I have a social engagement in a few hours. I won't get a chance to go home before."

"Of course," Taylor answered.

"Well, I really need to get this installation done," Levi insisted. "I've got somewhere to be as well."

Mandy huffed. "Okay, then. Seems like you've got it taken care of. See you on Monday. We'll talk then."

Mandy gave a wave and scurried away as fast as her imitation heels could carry her. When they heard the sound of her car starting, Levi stepped toward Taylor. He gave her a weak smile.

"Thanks for that," he said.

"It still doesn't explain what's going on here!" Taylor whispered through gritted teeth.

"What's going on here, is retribution," a familiar voice said.

"Boss?" the tall guy said, turning toward the sound. "What are you doing in here?"

Taylor sucked in a breath, though the oxygen did nothing to help her spinning head.

"Nadine?"

20. julia hudson and banished

"Hello, Taylor."

As hard as she tried, Taylor could not work out the scene unfolding before her. Nadine, Levi, two other people, and box full of cash just didn't make sense.

"I don't understand. Will someone please tell me what's going on?" The silence hung in the air and no one moved. It felt surreal and, at the same time, like the most real nightmare she'd ever had. "Levi?" she asked, looking to him for an answer.

"Taylor, I—" He stopped and ran his fingers through his hair. She could see the muscles in his jaw twitch as he ground his teeth together. "I can't," he started and stopped again.

"I got this, Levi," Nadine said, pushing past him and standing before Taylor.

"Boss, I can—"

"Obviously, you can't," Nadine interrupted. Gone was the cheery assistant that Taylor knew. This woman held authority here.

"Why do you keep calling her Boss?" Taylor asked.

"Because that's who I am, Taylor. I'm his boss. Levi doesn't just work for your father, he also works for me."

"What? I don't—"

"Enough," Nadine said, stepping toward Taylor. Taylor shrank back into the man behind her, trying to escape the woman's threatening gaze.

"I've been planning this for a year now. Had these guys with me for six months. Your dear Levi is what we like to call 'the inside man.' He was here for one reason only, to find your father's safe."

Taylor looked at Levi, who looked at the ground. He leaned back against the wall and banged his head against it. When he finally raised his eyes to meet hers, they were flooded with guilt.

"This is Henry's money?" she asked.

"Not anymore," Nadine answered. "Now it's mine."

"Ours," the guy behind Taylor corrected.

"Yes, ours," Nadine said.

"But you said it was retribution. For what? What the hell has my father ever done that you didn't beg for?"

Nadine threw back her head and laughed, her voice returning to its usual light and sweet tone. "I never slept with your father, Taylor. I couldn't sleep with him. That would be incest."

"What?" Levi said, pushing off of the wall.

Taylor watched the guys look at each other and back to Nadine. It seemed they were in the dark as far as this was concerned.

"Boys, go ahead while I handle this situation," Nadine said. "Kyle, you can go. She's not going anywhere. Crystal, help Levi get this to the truck."

Levi stepped next to her and crossed his arms over his chest. "Nah, I think we'd all like to hear this."

"Actually, we don't have time," Nadine pointed out. "There is another person in this house. We've got to get moving."

"She's right," Crystal said.

"What do we do with her?" Kyle asked, gesturing to Taylor.

Nadine looked at her watch and sighed. "Take her with us."

"What? No," Levi said. "No way."

Nadine turned to Levi, her expression irritated. "We can't leave her here to call the police before we're even gone. Stop thinking with your dick and get her in the damn truck," she said.

Levi pulled his lips into his mouth and bit down as Taylor watched Nadine stare him down. He finally nodded and grabbed Taylor by the elbow.

"Let go of me," Taylor growled.

"Just cooperate, Taylor," he begged. "Please."

But she didn't cooperate. He dragged her out the door and toward the truck, where he forced her to crawl inside. Levi hopped up after her and leaned against the broken washing machine. Taylor looked at him, and suddenly all the fear fell away. She became enraged. He was a lying, manipulative asshole. No better than her parents. He'd once passed judgment on her and only now did she see the irony.

"So you were just using me to get the money, right?" she blurted out. Levi's eyes met her watery ones, but he didn't say a word. "Just keep the dumb Hudson girl busy while you find the safe, huh?" His brow furrowed, heavy over his blue-green eyes. She couldn't stop the tears that left trails down her cheeks. "Were you getting paid extra to screw me too? Or was that just a bonus?"

Taylor twisted her shaking hands together before wiping the tears from her face.

"It wasn't like that, Taylor."

"It wasn't like what? It wasn't like you were planning to rob my father blind while sleeping with his daughter? Man up and be honest with me. You know what?" she yelled, her arms crossing over her stomach, fingers clawing into her ribs. "I don't even care about the money. Henry deserves that and worse. But you? You were supposed to be different."

Taylor broke down, sobbing into her hands, as she realized it had all been a lie. Her heart went from sharp stuttered beats to a dull ache inside her chest. Her knees felt weak and she slid down the truck wall, sitting on the floor. Taylor cursed her body's reaction to heartbreak. The way his hands held her, the secret kisses and deep connection had all been an illusion. Levi had played her like a fool, and she'd fallen hard and completely.

"I never meant for this to happen. I never meant for things to get so . . . complicated."

"Complicated? Levi, I fell in love with you!" she admitted, the words spilling from her lips before she could stop them. Instantly, Taylor wanted to take them back, no matter how true they were. She had made herself vulnerable and now it was out there, declared in front of the one person who didn't deserve to hear it.

Levi frowned at her and rubbed the back of his neck, his eyes shifting from her face to the ground. Taylor sniffled and pulled her knees up to her chest. She felt suffocated, as if the walls of the truck were closing in on her.

Kyle and Crystal loaded the box onto the lift gate and pushed it into the truck.

"We've got to go, Levi," Crystal said. "I'll ride back here with Taylor. Kyle, you and the Boss are up front."

Kyle nodded and hopped down out of the truck. Levi turned

his back to Taylor and jumped out as well. He closed one door and looked up at her, his eyes not giving anything away. With a heavy arm and a cold shoulder, he slammed the second door shut, severing their gaze and what was left of her heart.

Crystal took a seat across from Taylor in the dark and leaned against the wall.

"Just cooperate and all this will be easy, okay? We're not going to hurt you."

"Too late," she whispered to no one but herself.

When Levi finished installing the new washer, he cleaned up the space and took a look around. He wandered from room to room in search of Vanessa, meanwhile saying good-bye to the house that had proved to be quite an adversary. In the study, he took his time looking over the books and running his fingers along the leather chair Taylor had occupied while he recited Whitman.

Not finding anyone downstairs, Levi used the panel in the kitchen to page the entire house.

"Vanessa, the new machine is installed. I'm heading out."

He let go of the button and waited for a reply. When it beeped, loud music played and she shouted over it.

"Thanks, Levi! Have a good weekend. Sorry I messed up your day off. See you around."

Levi didn't reply. In a daze, he walked to his truck and climbed inside. The drive to the Boss's place was a mindless blur. He robotically made each turn, stopped at each light, and merged in and out of traffic, never thinking about his destination until he arrived. The sight of the delivery truck seemed to shock him out of his stupor. *Taylor is here.* She'd better be safe, or everyone else in that building would be sorry.

Levi grabbed two empty suitcases from his truck and carried

them inside. In the main room, he found Nadine, Kyle, and Crystal dividing the money.

"Where's Taylor?" he asked, searching the room. Kyle nodded toward the bathroom. "What are you going to do with her, Boss?"

"We'll just keep her here until we're ready to go," Nadine answered, tucking stacks of cash into shipping boxes. "I have a feeling after she knows the truth, she won't be telling anyone anything."

"What about this retribution talk? Do you have some kind of connection to this family?" Crystal asked.

"I'd like to know that too." Everyone spun to find Taylor standing in the bathroom doorway. Her arms were wrapped around her body, armor between her and them. Her blue eyes were red, and they watched Levi closely.

Nadine took a seat and gestured for Taylor to sit. She shuffled toward the table, pulled a chair away from Nadine, and sat down. Distracted from their money, Kyle and Crystal took seats as well. Levi remained standing, his nerves making it impossible to sit. Nadine turned toward Taylor and casually crossed her legs, her expression softened.

"Have you ever heard of Julia Hudson?"

Taylor shook her head. Even though she now remembered the name Julia from her grandmother, she wasn't sure how much she should share.

"That name was on the folder you took from Henry's office."

Nadine nodded. "She is Henry's older sister."

"My father doesn't have a sister. He's an only child," Taylor argued.

"That's not true. She was born with Down syndrome. Because of that, your grandfather placed her in a shoddy mental care facility at the age of five. Since then, she's never spent one day away from that place. She was never cared for or educated, never treated with respect or dignity. She was locked up and hidden away, because she represented a flaw in the pristine Hudson family."

Taylor shook her head in disbelief. "Why would he do that?"

"You know that this family is all about appearances, Taylor. All about the illusion of the prestigious Hudson name.

"When Julia was nineteen, she became pregnant. The administrators didn't know who the father was. It could have been another patient or someone on the staff. The facility was afraid of backlash from the wealthy family and never notified anyone. Instead of investigating, they covered it up and pretended it never happened. They didn't even know she was pregnant until she was six months along."

Taylor covered her mouth with her hand.

"You're her daughter," Levi said.

"I am," Nadine answered. "I was put into state custody and adopted out. They were so desperate that no one ever be able to trace my existence back to the Hudson family that they listed my last name as Smith."

"I didn't know," Taylor said.

"How could you? When our grandfather died, Julia's care passed to your father. In true Hudson fashion, he didn't want anything to do with her either. He moved her to a shit hole worse than the first one to save money." There was fire in Nadine's voice now, a fiery sadness. "I'm here to take what's hers, so I can provide her with a better life for whatever time she's got left."

"How did you find all this out?" Levi asked.

"I hired a private investigator to find my birth parents when I discovered I was adopted. He was very thorough. Once he connected me to Julia, the rest was easy. You have no idea how many disgruntled employees will spill information with hardly any coercion."

"I'm sorry, Nadine. I'm so sorry."

"It's not your fault, Taylor. But what you can do now is not be like them. Be different . . . better. Return some kind of honor to this family."

"Well, I sure didn't see that coming," Kyle said.

He and Crystal resumed packing up their money, leaving the women at the table. Levi unzipped his suitcases and began loading his share.

"You're my cousin," Taylor said.

"Yes. I'm sorry I couldn't tell you and that I can't stick around. I just need this money to get my mom somewhere safe and then I'll disappear. Are you going to be a problem?" Nadine asked, one eyebrow raised over blue eyes that matched Taylor's.

"No," Taylor answered, her voice barely audible.

"Okay, we're done here," Crystal announced.

Nadine stood and held her hand out toward Crystal. "It's been a pleasure working with you. Good luck," she offered.

Crystal and Kyle shook her hand. She approached Levi and held out her hand again. He grabbed it and shook twice before pulling away.

"Levi," she said, "thanks for all your work and putting together this team."

He nodded and that was it. Nadine taped up her boxes, slapped shipping labels on them, and left them stacked by the front door.

"I'm having a courier service pick these up. As soon as you are ready to go, she's free to leave."

With that, Nadine was out the door and gone from their lives forever. Taylor stared at the door, looking so young and frail. Levi wanted to go to her, to hold her and whisper promises in her ear. But he couldn't. He shouldn't.

"Well," Kyle said. "It's been real, you fuckers. Maybe we'll run into each other one day."

"Try not to spend it all on beer and hookers," Crystal teased. They hugged and patted each other on the back.

"Levi, take care of yourself," Kyle said. The two embraced, and Kyle disappeared through the door without looking back.

"I'm out too," Crystal said. "I've got a hot boyfriend to pick up before splitting town."

Levi smiled, surprised at Crystal's admission. "You're taking Gregory with you?"

Crystal nodded and grabbed her bags. "I'll see you around," she said before the door closed between them.

"No, you won't," Levi answered.

He turned to find Taylor watching him. The despair and anger were no longer a mask on her face. She stood and walked toward him. Each footstep seemed harder than the one before. Levi balled his hands into fists and crossed his arms to keep himself from reaching for her.

"So, Saturday? That kiss? That was good-bye, wasn't it?" she asked.

"Romeo is banished, there is no end, no limit, measure, bound, in that word's death."

She took another step toward him, and Levi retreated. He felt his willpower growing weaker by the second, her mere presence his kryptonite. He steeled his resolve and knew that he needed to make her see that he wasn't worth her tears.

"I'm sorry, Taylor. I'm so damn sorry I dragged you into this. When we started this job, I didn't know you. I had no idea this would happen. I never meant to hurt you."

Taylor nodded and shifted from foot to foot. "Was it real? Was any of it real?" she asked.

Levi turned away. He drew in a deep breath and released it slowly, trying to clear his head. He couldn't do it. He couldn't deny her this.

"It was real, Taylor. Everything. Every word. Every touch. But if it makes it easier for you to hate me, remember the con man, the one who lied. Because I don't want to be the cause of any more hurt for you. You're the best thing that ever happened to me, but I can't keep you." He zipped up both his suitcases and pulled the handles out.

"I've got to leave," he said, his eyes darting toward the door.

"Where will you go?"

"I can't tell you that. Thanks for not calling the cops. It'll give us enough time to disappear."

"Levi."

He shook his head and rolled his bags toward the door. "Goodbye, Taylor."

Levi concentrated on putting one foot in front of the other. Taylor's sniffling was the only sound in the room, and it killed him to leave this way. He pushed on the door and let it slam behind him, cutting all ties.

He lifted each bag into his truck and climbed inside. He started the engine, soothed just a bit by the familiar rumble and his father's guitar sitting shotgun. A loud bang on his window made him jump. Levi looked up to find Taylor looking back at him, her fist resting on the glass. He reluctantly rolled the window down and waited.

"Take me with you," she begged, her fingers gripping the door of his truck.

"You have a life here, Taylor."

"I don't want it. Levi, I want you. Please, take me with you."

His grip tightened around the steering wheel as he forced himself to make the best decision for them both.

"I'm sorry," he said.

Levi threw the truck in drive and floored it, leaving her standing in a cloud of dust. As he drove away, he dared to look in his rearview mirror and was crushed by the sight of Taylor screaming, tears soaking her face. "The Road Not Taken" flashed through his mind, though Robert Frost's poem did nothing to soothe the searing pain he felt.

> *Two roads diverged in a yellow wood,*
> *And sorry I could not travel both*

Instead, each word seemed to get stuck in his throat and strangle the air from his lungs.

The odds had always been stacked against them. Mistake after mistake, Levi and Taylor's passion had not been enough to save them. Instead, fate had delivered them to suffer in their own isolated hells. He looked out at the road ahead of him and vowed to never criticize Romeo again.

21. bergamo and robbery

The days following the heist were mostly a blur. No one suspected anything, and Taylor certainly wasn't going to confess. She felt terrible for what her family had done to Julia, her aunt. How could her grandfather have been so cruel? Why had her sweet grandmother let him do it? She was ashamed of her family, more so than ever.

Taylor lived in her bed, getting up only to use the bathroom or when Suzanne forced her to eat. Of course the woman connected the dots with Levi gone and Taylor's foul mood. But she didn't ask questions. Suzanne checked on Taylor often and left her to sulk.

She even missed her appointment with Dee on Tuesday, asking

Adrienne to apologize for her. On the fourth day, in the late after-noon, Suzanne turned down the covers and crawled into bed with Taylor. She pulled the girl into her arms and rubbed soothing circles on her back. Taylor tried to hold herself together but failed miserably. She cried until all her tears were gone. Suzanne held her and promised that she'd be okay.

"I know that my pay comes out of your trust fund," Suzanne admitted. "Thank you for that, Taylor. Thanks for keeping me around even after you didn't need me."

"It wasn't completely selfless, Suzanne. I do need you."

Suzanne ran her fingers along Taylor's hairline and gently pushed back the blond tendrils from her face.

"When you were four years old, I took you and Beau to the park to play. You were fearless—climbing over everything, jumping off swings—but Beau wouldn't leave my side. When you saw that he was nervous, you came and sat next to us for a while. Eventually, you coaxed Beau onto the slide and walked him up the ladder."

Taylor smiled and tucked her hands beneath her pillow. "I never liked to play by myself," she said.

"It was more than that, Taylor. You couldn't stand to see him alone. You have a big heart, sweetie. Along the way, you learned to turn it off so that no one could hurt you, but it's always been there. You finally opened yourself up to love."

"And look where it got me," Taylor said.

"I know it hurts now. There's nothing like your first heartbreak, kid. You feel like your heart got put in a blender with some ice and Bloody Mary mix, pulverized, and served to you with a celery stalk." Taylor gave her a strange look, trying to make sense of another Suzanneism. "I know it feels like it won't get better. But it will. And when it does, you'll be stronger because of it."

"It felt real, Suzanne," Taylor said as yet another tear fell and soaked into her pillow.

"It was real. Anyone could see the way he looked at you. Men are stupid when it comes to love, baby girl. I don't know what happened or why he left, but I don't doubt that it was the hardest thing he's ever done."

Taylor closed her eyes and took a few deep breaths. "I think I'm ready to get up now."

"Good. You grab a shower and I'll have Mandy make you some lunch."

"Okay."

Suzanne placed a kiss on Taylor's forehead and crawled out of bed. She grabbed some clothes for Taylor and laid them out on the bathroom counter. Taylor stripped and stepped into the shower. The steam filled her lungs and surrounded her in a soft embrace.

As she dried off and slid into her clean clothes, Taylor wondered where Levi had gone. She wondered where on earth he fled to before feeling safe enough to stop running. She also wondered if he was running from his crime or from her.

Sitting at the counter in the kitchen, Taylor traced the granite pattern with her fingertip while Mandy made her a sandwich. Her eyes would drift to the seat next to her, Levi's seat, and she would quickly correct herself.

"Here you go," Mandy said, pushing a plate in front of her. "It's your favorite, peanut butter and banana."

Taylor managed a small smile before taking a couple of bites. Suzanne's gaze shifted to Taylor's plate, and her expression hardened. "If you don't finish that, I'll just make you another one and have you start over."

Taylor groaned but took another bite to satisfy Suzanne. After she finished her sandwich, she was allowed to return to her room. Taylor checked her phone and sent Reese and Adrienne a text letting them know that she was still alive. Everyone else, she ignored.

"This finally came back from the cleaners," Suzanne said, bringing her blue ball gown in and hanging it in her closet.

The sight of that gown reminded Taylor of her grandmother, and guilt took hold of her again. But then she remembered something else. Taylor walked to her jewelry box and opened it. She pulled out the bottom drawer, and tucked behind it was her grandmother's locket. The one she'd given her in secret.

Taylor pulled the chain out and opened the locket. Inside was the same photo she remembered, an adorable toddler with big curls and a toothy smile, a toddler with Down syndrome.

"Julia," Taylor said.

"Taylor?" Suzanne asked.

Taylor dropped the locket in the drawer and turned to face the door. "Yeah?"

"I've got some errands to run. I'll be back in a couple of hours. Call me if you need anything. Okay?"

"Okay," Taylor answered.

When Suzanne was gone, Taylor retrieved the locket and looked at the photo again. This poor woman had been abandoned by her family, neglected and abused by people meant to help her, and until Nadine found her, no one knew and no one cared. The anger took over Taylor's heart and made the pain of losing Levi a little easier to bear. So she held on to that feeling. She nailed it down and let the anger take root.

Taylor slid the locket around her neck and tucked it beneath her shirt. The cool metal against her chest helped remind her to stay angry, to be different . . . better.

Leaving Taylor behind had been the hardest thing Levi had ever done, especially after she'd begged to go with him. As much as he wanted her, he refused to be responsible for ruining her future. She had so many opportunities and so much freedom. She didn't deserve the kind of aimless life he would give her.

The first few days, Levi was consumed with paranoia. He tried to place as much distance as possible between himself and the Hudson house. He had no idea if any of them were suspects, but he knew sooner or later his name would top the list.

He flew to Mexico first. There he used a fake passport to purchase a ticket to Brazil. From Brazil, he went to New Zealand, then Hong Kong, and finally Italy. Levi had shipped his luggage from Mexico to Italy, but he kept his guitar with him. Through the exhaustion of traveling and the constant worry, he used the guitar to soothe the ache and anxiety. He would play anywhere, sometimes to the delight of fellow travelers.

Once in Italy, he made his way to Bergamo. His father used to talk about that small town when Levi was a child, telling tales of their enormous extended family. It had always been a foreign concept to Levi, having a large family. For so long, it had just been him, his father, and his uncle Zach.

When he checked in to Hotel San Lorenzo, Levi found his bags waiting in his room. He unlocked them and checked inside, still awed by the stacks of hundred-dollar bills. He sat on the edge of the small bed and stared at those open suitcases: $5 million stared back.

For the first time since they'd pulled off the heist, Levi realized that he was now a millionaire. He lay back on the bed and stared at the plaster ceiling. He should be elated, he'd gotten exactly what he wanted. Then Taylor's face flashed before him, and he realized that what he wanted most probably hated him and was halfway around the world.

He already missed Taylor. It was a horrible feeling and one that he felt he'd never escape. So he didn't even try. He stayed in bed and let the suffering and self-pity consume him. He felt like he deserved it. Levi told himself that he just needed rest and all would be right in the morning. But when the morning came, there was still that agonizing emptiness and a recollection of blond-haired, blue-eyed dreams.

Tired of looking at the four walls of her room, Taylor had ventured down to the study. She sat sideways in the large chair and laid her head back on the plush arm. On her lap sat a collection of poetry, open to Sonnet 140 by William Shakespeare. Taylor grew frustrated that in her own home, she could not escape Levi. He was everywhere, he'd tainted everything.

"Your father called," Suzanne said as she entered the study. "Said he was on his way home and asked me to make sure you stayed here."

Taylor swallowed and looked to Suzanne. "What's going on?" she asked.

"I don't know. He did say his assistant quit and her replacement was not doing so well. That's why he had to call me himself."

"Can you imagine the horror of having to place a phone call all by yourself?" Taylor deadpanned.

Suzanne smiled and patted Taylor's shoulder. "There's my girl."

The front door opened and slammed closed.

"Taylor!" Henry shouted. "Taylor Hudson!" Taylor sighed and pulled herself from the chair. "Taylor!"

"What?"

She found her father in the foyer, his face red, his tie hanging loose around his unbuttoned collar. Just the sight of him made her nauseated and resentful all over again. Her hand came up and pressed the locket against her skin, letting it anchor her to that anger.

Henry stomped toward her, like a freight train out of control.

She slumped back against the wall, unsure of what he would do. Taylor had never been afraid of her father before, but in this moment, she knew exactly what he was capable of.

"Has Beau Upton been in this house?" he said, stopping just short of her. Taylor stood there, wide-eyed and not sure how to answer. "Well? And don't even think about lying. I'll check the video footage for the last six months if I need to."

"Yes," she answered.

Henry's hands flew to his salt-and-pepper hair. He looked crazed.

"George Upton had the audacity to come by my office today. He said that he was coming after me and the contracts I stole from him. Threatened that he was working on something big to take me down. He said he had eyes everywhere, even in my home!"

"Beau wasn't spying for his father. He's my friend. We were just hanging out!" Taylor defended.

"You ignorant, naïve little girl. He was just using you! I warned you to stay away from him and his whole thieving family. If he touched anything . . ."

Henry's eyes glanced upstairs. In an instant, he took off toward the second floor. Taylor was on his heels. She tripped up the stairs and followed him down the hall. He punched in the four-digit code to his private office and swung the door open.

"Son of a bitch!"

Taylor followed him inside and found him hunched over his desk. Papers and books lay scattered around the room, the antique Tiffany lamp was overturned. She smiled at his back, knowing that she and Levi were responsible for this mess.

"Beau didn't do this," Taylor said.

"Who else, then, Taylor?" He spun on her. Again his face displayed rage, and she shrank away from him. She couldn't tell him the truth. "Who else would have come in here? They were looking for something. For what?"

Henry's chest heaved with shallow breaths. Taylor kept the satisfied smile off her face. She'd never seen him so out of control, so rattled.

"My safe!" he shouted.

Again Henry took off down the hall, this time toward Taylor's room. She was right behind him. She watched him throw open her door and scramble inside. He pushed on her bed until it slid against the farthest wall.

"What are you doing?" she shouted.

Henry stepped to the middle of the room and a panel sunk in. Taylor gasped and covered her mouth with her hands. Henry dropped to his knees and slid the panel back. Taylor moved forward, wanting to see for herself. All the color drained from his face as his eyes landed on the perfectly round hole drilled into the face of his safe. Henry gripped the handle and pulled the door open to find nothing inside.

"Empty," he whispered, falling back into a seated position. "Fucking empty."

Suddenly, his head whipped toward her. He jumped to his feet, grabbed Taylor by the shoulders, and shoved her against the wall.

"How did this happen, Taylor?" he yelled as he shook her violently. "How? No one knew that safe was there. No one would ever think to look under my daughter's bed. It was the perfect hiding place! Are you a part of this?"

"I didn't even know that thing was down there," she answered with tears in her eyes.

"You know something, you little bitch. Now tell me!"

Henry wrapped his hand around Taylor's throat. She clawed at his large hand, trying to pull it off of her, trying to take a breath.

"Henry!"

They both turned to see Suzanne standing there, her expression full of rage. He let go of Taylor, and she slumped to the floor, gasping for air. Suzanne knelt down and took Taylor into her arms.

"Are you okay?" she asked, swiping at her wet cheeks.

Taylor nodded and looked on as Henry paced in front of them, his phone pressed to his ear. Suzanne continued to rub circles on Taylor's back as Taylor sucked in shuddering breaths and bit down on her bottom lip. She could hear the ringing on the other end of the phone and then someone pick up. Henry's eyes met hers, a silent stare of rage and mistrust, until he spoke.

"I need to report a robbery."

22. lebron james and postcards

Disgusted with himself and his self-pity, Levi eventually left his hotel to explore the city. It was a beautiful place with Old World charm and interesting locals. The buildings and architecture were stunning. He was impressed with the simpler way of life here, the slower pace. It was refreshing and just what he needed.

Over the next few weeks, Levi began the search for his distant relatives. They weren't hard to find in a town this size, and soon he was observing them from a distance. They owned a cozy little restaurant on the Via Colleoni. As he dined there one evening, charmed by the ambiance and rustic feel of the place, he tried to embrace his connection to these people. Besides the resemblance of the Russo men to his father, Levi felt no attachment.

Sure, they shared the same blood, but that was all. Seeing them did not bring his father back and it didn't provide the kind of resolution he always thought it would. He didn't know these people and these people did not know his father. They didn't know that he loved to play music and sing in their living room. They didn't know that despite his Italian roots, he was a terrible cook. They didn't know of his love for a woman he'd lost too soon or the heartbreak he lived with for the rest of his life.

Soon, Levi abandoned the idea of connecting with this family. He explored the city and found that his favorite place was in the Palazzo Nuovo, the Angelo Mai Library. He spent some time there, flipping through books in a language he didn't understand. His fingers trailed over yellowed pages and foreign words with a reverence to their beginnings.

No matter how he tried to distract himself, his thoughts always returned to Taylor. Every head of blond hair sent him reeling back into memories of her. It was a torture that he felt he deserved. No poem could soothe his pain, no music brought comfort. His poetic crutch was completely useless now. One night he got drunk in a pub and ended up fighting some guy in a back alley. When they were done, an observer offered him a place in an underground fight club. Though the idea of fighting for money did appeal to his darker side, Levi declined. He liked living life on his own terms, by his own rules.

Levi left the city and traveled through northern Italy. Whether it was by coincidence or a subconscious decision, he ended up in Verona, the setting for Shakespeare's *Romeo and Juliet*. He settled in there, renting a small apartment above a family-owned bakery. Every morning, he was woken up by the smell of freshly baked breads and pastries. Levi had become acquainted with the owner, Augusto, and often stopped in for breakfast and late-night snacks.

"*Buongiorno*, Levi. Still alone in our fair city?"

"*Ciao*, Gus," he answered. The man smiled, tickled with the American nickname Levi had given him.

"Verona is for lovers, no? Why not let me introduce you to my niece? She's a fine girl, so beautiful. And her cooking? *Fantastico*."

"Just breakfast today," Levi said, shaking his head in amusement.

"What can I tempt you with?"

Levi smiled across the glass case. "*Cannoli, per favore*."

"*Sì, sì*. You remind me of my grandson," Augusto said, his accent thick. "Always the same thing, every time."

"I know what I like," Levi said.

"Ah, but how do you know you don't like something else better if you never try?"

Levi handed over two euros in exchange for his breakfast. "*Addio*, Gus."

Since arriving in Verona, Levi had explored the many cafés, bookstores, novelty shops, and even tourist attractions. Sometimes he would find a park or plaza to sit and play his guitar, singing whatever songs came to him. People were impressed with his talent here. Some of them would sit and listen to him for hours. Many days, he took home handfuls of euros collected in his open guitar case. Though he didn't need the money, it was nice feeling appreciated.

There would be no playing today. Today he was going to take the popular Romeo and Juliet tour of the city. The first stop was the Capulet house in the Via Cappello. It was a tall building with a large central courtyard. From the courtyard, you could see Juliet's famous balcony. New growths of ivy climbed the walls like green curtains against crumbling brick. Above the chatter of tourists, he could barely hear the sweet chirping of birds.

A bronze statue of Juliet stood alone in thoughtful contemplation. The tour guide explained that it was good luck to rub her right breast. Levi meandered around as tourists lined up to take photos with her.

He found himself standing before the wall where modern lovers left messages and letters. What some would call graffiti or defacement, he considered a beautiful gallery. There were simple notes consisting of two names surrounded by hearts, declarations for lost lovers, prayers to Juliet, and full pages of verse.

Levi watched a young girl step to the wall, a purple marker in hand. She searched for an empty space to write but settled for layering her statement over someone else's. She smiled when she was done and leaned forward to blow on the ink. He grinned at the look on her face, the complete belief that love would always prevail. He wished he still had that.

When the group was ready, they were ushered to the next stop on the tour, the Montague house. The medieval building was in such poor condition that they weren't allowed inside. They had to be satisfied with plaques posted out front. Levi stepped up to read one and felt stifled by it: "Tut, I have lost myself, I am not here. This is not Romeo, he's some other where."

I have lost myself, he thought. He endured the rest of the tour, making an effort to pay attention when each new place was pointed out. He knew there was no proof that any of these things were accurate. They were simply used to bait tourists.

The tour ended at Juliet's tomb. Levi expected it to be a somber place, quiet and filled with people paying respect. He was surprised to find that the locals actually used this place for weddings. He watched a couple pose for photos after exchanging vows. Not long after, they were cleared, and another couple was ushered in to start the process again. Confetti and flowers littered the area. Levi frowned at the celebration of a love that ended so tragically.

———

After Henry discovered his money was gone, the house had been a whirlwind of police asking questions and taking evidence. Henry claimed that he thought to check his safe because his office had been vandalized. Taylor knew that if she'd just cleaned up her and Levi's mess, none of this would be happening.

After George Upton, the number-one suspect had been Levi, mainly because of his timely disappearance and evidence that the video feed in the house had been tampered with. No one knew of his and Taylor's relationship, except Suzanne, and she never mentioned it to the authorities. Weeks went by and they were unable to come up with any solid evidence against Levi, but he was still wanted for questioning.

Though Nadine, Levi, and his friends had made off with Henry's money, the Hudsons were still financially okay. Most of the family's money was invested in the market or tucked away in foreign banks. Taylor loved the notion of her father's paranoia being the key to his losing $20 million.

On her last tutoring session with Dee, Taylor had a present hidden away in her bag. Today was a big day. Dee was being retested to see if her reading level had improved since their sessions began. Taylor nervously paced the hall for an hour, waiting for the results.

When the door opened, Dee came out, a disgusted look on the fifteen-year-old's face.

"What? Is it bad? Tell me!"

Dee's frown transformed into a grin and she threw herself at Taylor. Shocked at first, Taylor stood there dumbly until finally wrapping her friend in a hug. The director of the program stepped into the hall, wearing her own smile.

"Dee has moved from a third-grade reading level to a sixth-grade level. That's a huge improvement. Way to go, ladies!"

She offered each of them a high five before disappearing into her office.

"Well, let's start our last session," Taylor offered.

"Let's do this, Clueless." That was the nickname Dee had branded her with since their talk of basketball began.

They took their usual seats and wordlessly stared at each other across the table. There was a feeling of accomplishment in the air. Both of them felt untouchable.

"I don't feel like workin' today."

"I think you've probably earned a day off," Taylor answered.

"I can't believe it's our last session. I'm gonna miss your silly ass," Dee said, chuckling.

"Hey, just because I don't know anything about sports doesn't make me silly. Maybe I'll learn more once I get to college."

"You going to college?" Taylor nodded. "Where at? Around here?"

"No, Massachusetts. I'm off to Harvard."

"What? Yo, guys," Dee announced with pride, "my tutor is going to Harvard." No one responded, but Taylor blushed anyway. Dee lowered her voice. "That makes me Ivy League by one degree of separation."

Taylor laughed and nodded, knowing she would miss Dee once she was on the East Coast.

"Oh. I brought a present for you."

"What? A gift me for? You shouldn't have," Dee teased.

"Well, I could just keep it."

"Nah, girl, you know I'm playin'. Gimme."

Dee held her hands out and made a grabbing motion. Taylor dropped the gift into her hands. Dee tore at the paper, and when it was laid out on the table in front of her, she didn't say a word. Her face was expressionless, her mouth silent. Taylor thought she'd failed.

"You don't like it?"

"You got me a signed, number six, Miami Heat, LeBron James jersey with the MVP patch? Are you for real?"

"I thought you'd like it. My friend knew someone who knew someone. It's not a big deal."

"Like it? I *love* it. I want to marry it. I want to make sweet love to it and have jersey babies. Not a big deal? Oh, my God!"

Dee hugged the jersey to her chest and rocked back and forth. She pressed it to her face and inhaled deeply while Taylor watched, fascinated.

"Believe me, Clueless. It's a big deal."

The girls stood and fell into an awkward hug with nothing but the table and LeBron's jersey between them. Taylor held her tears in for the ride home.

Taylor filled her days getting ready for Harvard. Her dorm assignment was a double with Adrienne on the fourth floor of Apley. Reese would be just an hour away at Brown, and they already had plans to see each other often. As ecstatic as she was to get away from everything familiar, Taylor was glad to have her friends along for the ride.

"Do you want to bring this?" Adrienne asked, holding up a framed photo of Taylor and Suzanne from when she was ten years old.

"Yeah," Taylor answered. "Just add it to that box." Reese lay across Taylor's bed, flipping through their senior yearbook. "You're supposed to be helping me pack."

Reese folded her arms on top of the book and laid her head down. "I know. I'm sorry," she said huffing.

Taylor caught her eyes, they looked like a reflection of her own. "Do you want to talk about it?" she asked.

"No."

Reese had suffered heartbreak at the hands of George Upton. He'd broken off their scandalous relationship after the robbery. He admitted that he'd only been using her because she could give him inside details on the Hudson family. George had been pulling information from her the whole time.

Adrienne hopped onto the bed and lay down next to Reese. "Can I join this pity party, or was I supposed to RSVP?"

The girls laughed. Taylor threw a pillow at her before making them all get back up and finish packing. With each girl assigned to a designated area, they finished in no time.

When they were gone, she stepped onto her balcony and looked over the lawn. She slid the locket back and forth on the chain around her neck and thought about Julia. Taylor had so badly wanted to confront Henry about her but didn't want to answer questions about how she'd found out. She feared throwing unnecessary attention toward Nadine, since no one had ever suspected her involvement. Even though her departure from her assistant position had been sudden, it had also been accompanied by a letter threatening to come after Henry for sexual harassment. Of course, he'd swept it all under the rug and hired a replacement the next day.

Each day that passed, Taylor went through the motions. She ate, she slept, she showered. On her last night at home, Taylor climbed onto a stack of boxes and retrieved the shirt tucked all the way at the top of her closet. She slipped the green uniform shirt on and pulled it closed before crawling into bed. Burying her face in the fabric, she inhaled deeply. Tears blurred her eyes when she realized that it didn't smell like him anymore. She held it tight against her skin anyway and fell asleep, dreaming of Levi's melodic voice and the warmth of his skin.

Suzanne put one foot on the top of the suitcase and yanked at the zipper. It wouldn't budge.

"Taylor, did you pack every piece of clothing you own? Geez!"

Taylor sat on her bed and watched Suzanne struggle, "No. Just the necessities."

"Well," Suzanne said, plopping down on the suitcase and bouncing a few times, "I hope nothing is breakable." She pulled on the zipper and it slid around the track, sealing the contents inside. Suzanne stood and raised her arms in victory. "Yes!"

Taylor gave her a smile and swallowed down the sentiment that tried to choke her. She didn't want to cry. She was not successful. Tears raced down her cheeks and Suzanne dropped her arms.

"Oh, sweetheart. It'll be okay." She took a seat beside Taylor, rubbing calming circles on the girl's back.

"No it won't," Taylor insisted. "I'll be all the way across the country. We'll never see each other anymore. I'll promise to call, but I won't. You'll promise to visit, but you won't. I'll be alone."

"You'll have Adrienne and Reese. They love you. Don't think of it as the end of something. Think of it as the beginning of something new. And don't worry, my love will reach you way over on the East Coast."

"Will it stretch that far?"

"Honey, my love stretches farther than Lycra yoga pants over a Kardashian ass."

Taylor let out a chuckle and wiped her tears away with the back of her hand. Suzanne turned Taylor's face toward her and pressed their foreheads together.

"Thick and thin, tried and true. Against the world, it's just us two. Love you, Boo."

"Love you, Kitty."

Suzanne promised to visit soon and Taylor promised to hold her to it.

The next morning, Reese, Taylor, and Adrienne flew into Boston together. Of course, Henry and Virginia weren't even present to see her off. While starting this new phase of life was exciting,

Taylor felt like there was always the dark cloud looming over her head. She wondered if she would ever feel normal again.

Outwardly, she was almost back to normal. Taylor smiled at the appropriate times and actively participated in conversations. It was only instinctual reactions so that no one would worry, a mask she wore all the time. The good-bye with Suzanne had been so difficult it had only added to Taylor's misery.

Taylor stood in her dorm room, looking around and taking in everything. She was in a new place, with new things, and somehow the only thing that felt new was her. Taylor eyed herself in the full-length mirror on the back of her door. All summer she'd been searching for some kind of metamorphosis, some way to leave behind the girl she was and become a woman.

Looking at her reflection, she realized it wasn't graduating high school or moving across the country that had reshaped her. It was falling in love. Loving Levi had molded and changed her in ways that seemed impossible. It had broken her and forced her to reconstruct who she was and what she believed. A broken heart had given her what she thought she desperately wanted. But seeing the empty shell of a woman now, she knew all she really wanted was Levi.

Time passed quickly as she began her freshman year and attended classes. Before she knew it, Thanksgiving was approaching. Adrienne knew Taylor wouldn't want to return home, so they decided to stay and organize a holiday dinner in the dorm. Reese agreed to come up and join them. Only Adrienne knew how to cook, but Reese and Taylor promised to be helpful assistants.

Each day, it seemed easier to get out of bed, to breathe in and out, to resemble her old self. There was still a hollowness inside Taylor, but she fought it, not willing to let it conquer her again. She still thought of Levi often, and sometimes she'd pull out his shirt, thinking about their progression from hateful words to claim-staking declarations to complete and utter betrayal. Many nights, Taylor lay awake and wondered where he was in the world and if he ever thought of her too.

If she had judged Levi by his actions alone, it might have been easier to let him go. He had dismissed her so easily, pretended she meant nothing. But thanks to his friend, Taylor knew better. On that ride from her house, in the back of the delivery truck, she had confessed Levi's secret.

"He loves you, you know," Crystal said.

Taylor turned to glare at her, lifting a challenging eyebrow in the girl's direction.

"Please don't fuck with me anymore. I don't think I can handle it."

"I'm not. I swear. Look, I've been his best friend for almost ten years. I know he's hard to figure out and I know he doesn't open up, but I also know that he's completely, stupidly in love with you."

"How do you know?" she asked.

"Because I know him better than he knows himself, and I'm willing to admit things that he won't."

Taylor blew her hair from her eyes and dropped her head into her hands. She hated to entertain this possibility if it meant nothing would change.

"Why did he do this?" she asked.

"Look, when we started this, we didn't know you. We had a job to do and that was our only goal. I don't think you realize how completely owned he is by you. But Levi is stubborn. He's going to make decisions he feels are best for both of you. It's going to hurt like hell."

Taylor nodded. "It's not fair."

"Maybe if you're meant to be, you'll cross paths again some-day."

"I don't believe in all that. We make our own destiny," she said, ending the conversation.

On his way home from the park one day, Levi came to the Ponte Pietra. It was an old Roman stone bridge, open only to foot traffic, crossing the Adige River. It was almost sunset, so he walked to the center and leaned over the side, waiting for the gold and pink hues to light up the sky over Verona.

"*Che bello!*" he heard a deep voice exclaim.

Levi turned to find an elderly man, his knotted fingers gripping a cane as he leaned against the side of the bridge. His eyes were turned up toward the sky in amazement.

"*Sì,*" Levi responded.

"American?" the man asked, his voice thick and slow. Levi nodded and turned to look out over the city again. "What brings you to *la città dell'amore?*"

Levi shook his head at the question before answering. What did bring him to the city of love?

"A lost love," he answered. "Separated by impossible circumstance."

"For true love, one should move heaven and earth."

"We can't be together," Levi said, trying to convince himself.

"*L'amore domina senza regole.*"

Levi raised his eyebrows in question.

"Eh . . . love rules without rules," he clarified. "If she is yours, you must send for her."

Both men looked out on the city now, the old stone buildings bathed in a golden glow. The reflection of the sky made the river appear to be on fire. *Maybe the old man was right,* Levi thought, *maybe we could make our own rules.*

Levi left his new friend there on the bridge and found his way to a nearby tourist cart. He purchased a simple postcard with the bridge on the front and headed back to his apartment. After extensive research, Levi found Taylor's name on Harvard's housing roster. He scratched a few simple words onto the postcard and prayed that she would understand his message.

23. juliet and happy christmas

"I'm back!" Adrienne called out, slamming the door behind her. "Can I get some help in here?"

Taylor hopped up from her desk and met Adrienne in the common room. There were bags of groceries piled on the futon.

"What's all this?" Taylor asked.

"This," Adrienne said, waving her hand across the clutter, "is Thanksgiving dinner. I've already unloaded all the cold stuff in the fridge downstairs. Hopefully nobody eats it before tomorrow."

Taylor started looking through the bags, amazed at all the ingredients it took to make one meal.

"I need to take this to Michelle next door," Adrienne said, producing a box of condoms. "And collect my money because I refuse to fund someone else's good time when I'm not getting laid."

Taylor laughed as her friend disappeared through the door. Once Adrienne returned, Taylor helped her finish unpacking the food, taking inventory as she went.

"Wow, I may have gone overboard," Adrienne said, looking over her stock. "When will Reese be here?"

"In the next hour or so," Taylor replied.

"Oh! I almost forgot. The girl at the front desk gave me this. It didn't have a room number on it, but she said it's for you."

Adrienne reached in her back pocket and pulled out a postcard, handing it over to Taylor. Taylor studied the photo on the front. It was an old bridge somewhere in Europe as far as she could tell. She flipped it over and didn't recognize the handwriting, but the words made the breath leave her body.

I am fortune's fool.
Romeo

"I'll be right back," Taylor said.

She stumbled to her room and closed the door behind her, leaning against it. Even though she'd been furious with Levi for making decisions that affected both of them, she couldn't deny that she still loved him. He'd seen the real Taylor, the pretty girl who said ugly things to push people away. He'd changed her and made her better.

Taylor read the words on the back of the postcard a hundred times. She memorized the way her name and address were casually written, but the five words on the opposite side were more harsh, each stroke sinking into the thickness of the paper. She ran her fingers over the words, feeling the texture. Taylor closed her eyes and tried to picture Levi's face as he wrote them. *I am fortune's fool.* Did he regret his lies and want her with him? Or was he simply letting her know that he was alive and okay?

It took her only one day to decide the answer.

Finding someone to help put her plan into action was easier than she'd thought at a school like this. Harvard was full of the brightest minds in the world, and thankfully not all of them had the morals and values of a saint. For the right amount of money, you could buy someone's secrecy and a new identity.

Jenni was a tiny brunette that lived on the third floor of Hall F. She had the sweet face of a child and the talent of an evil genius. She used her seemingly innocent charms to acquire anything she wanted, and Taylor was eager to put that to use. It took exactly three weeks for Jenni and Taylor to finish all the preparations. Meanwhile, Taylor continued life as usual, not wanting to raise suspicion.

She sat through classes, studied for finals, met her friends for dinner, and even attended a Semester End party. It was all a ruse, though, a way to pass the time before she disappeared from their lives. Taylor checked in with Suzanne regularly and, out of everyone, it proved to be most difficult to keep the secret from her.

It was the last day of the semester. Finals were over and everyone was abandoning the dorms like they were sinking ships. While Adrienne packed her bags to head home for the holidays, Taylor packed for a completely different reason. She tucked her warmest clothes, toiletries, and two pairs of shoes into her bag. Sitting on her bed, she reached out and ran her fingers over the photo of her and her two best friends.

It was easy imagining Reese's future. She'd be married, part of a wealthy East Coast family, by the time she graduated. She'd start her own business or run a nonprofit and be wildly successful. Adrienne would finish med school and become a successful doctor and volunteer. She'd meet her future husband out in a village somewhere, where they'd share childhood stories until he worked up the nerve to ask her out. These visions made it easier to leave them behind. Taylor would miss them so much, but she knew they'd be okay without her.

She placed the photo inside her bag and zipped it up before shoving it to the back of her closet and arranging boxes in front of it. She took a look around the small room and smiled at the simple and uncomplicated life she was leaving behind.

Taylor had gone back and forth a million times. She didn't know if she was doing the smart thing, going to Levi, but it certainly felt like the right thing. Her family meant nothing to her, and she was sure they'd barely notice when she disappeared. Her friends had become more important than ever. For the first time, Taylor truly felt like she had people who cared about her. Leaving them behind was a sacrifice she was willing to make.

Many students were already gone, so Taylor and Adrienne sat on their sofa, discussing the events of their first semester at Harvard.

"American lit was, by far, the hardest class," Adrienne complained.

"Only because you were too busy lusting after the TA to pay attention," Taylor said, giggling.

"Yeah, I guess so. This is the longest I've ever gone without having sex. I'm frustrated. Simon asked about you again today," Adrienne said, nudging her. "He mentioned that he's not going home for the holidays either."

Taylor rolled her eyes.

"You want me to tell him that you're a lesbian? No, that won't work. He'll probably be more interested. I'll tell him you're dating that big beefy guy on the rugby team. The one that looks like he has more muscles than brains."

"Don't tell him anything," Taylor begged. The two laughed and eventually fell silent again. "I'm going to miss you. Reese too."

"Aww, Tay. We'll miss you, sweetie. I'm meeting Reese at the airport in the morning. We'll be back in a few weeks," Adrienne said, squeezing Taylor's hand.

Taylor laid her head on Adrienne's shoulder and sighed. She wanted a proper good-bye, one filled with long hugs and silly tears.

"Come on," Ade said. "You'll have the whole place to yourself. You can walk around naked and eat all the disgusting pizza rolls you love with no judgment from me."

"As if I care about your judgment. Pizza rolls are the most amazing junk food ever invented. Seriously, they're even better than cheesy puffs and Twinkies."

"Ugh, stop. You're making me nauseated," Adrienne said. "Well, I'm off to bed. We have an early flight." She gave Taylor a tight hug before looking her up and down. "Are you sure you don't want to come home? You wouldn't have to see your parents. You could stay with one of us."

"No. I'll be fine by myself."

"Okay. But try not to do any laundry until I get back," Adrienne said, giving Taylor a motherly look.

"I promise. Hey, I only ruined one shirt last week."

"Yeah, you're getting better. I guess we won't see you until next year," Adrienne said. Taylor nodded and avoided her friend's gaze. "Don't throw any wild parties. Avoid dark alleys. And look both ways before crossing the street."

Adrienne ruffled Taylor's blond hair. Taylor gave her a guilty smile and offered a wave as Adrienne closed her door. She let herself mourn the loss of these girls. Reese and Taylor had helped each other through heartbreak, while Adrienne had always been the voice of reason. She'd taken Taylor under her wing and taught her how to do laundry and cook healthy meals, while other girls in the dorm had introduced them to the joys of frozen junk food.

Taylor didn't know how much that mattered now. She had no idea what kind of life, if any, awaited her in Verona. Levi could have moved on, or she could have misinterpreted his message. She'd be stuck in Italy, chasing down someone who didn't want to be found.

She had never taken a chance on anything. Taylor had never made herself vulnerable enough to step into a situation that she didn't have control over. So as she handed her new passport to the security guard at Newark Airport, she squared her shoulders and held her breath.

The man looked it over, matched it to her boarding pass, and handed it back without question.

"Enjoy your trip, Juliet."

Taylor smiled and exhaled before heading to her gate. After three cups of coffee and two trips to the bathroom, it was finally time. Every step toward the plane felt heavier than the one before. Her heart pounded against her chest. Her fingers wrapped around the handle of her carry-on so tightly her knuckles turned white. This was it. There was no turning back.

Love give me strength, and strength shall help afford. Farewell, dear father.

After dropping that postcard in the mail, Levi held onto the hope that Taylor would come. He knew it was a long shot and that the odds were against him, but some tiny spark kept him returning to that bridge every day. He'd lean against the stones, always accompanied by his nameless friend clutching his cane, and wait for her to appear. And each day he was disappointed when the sun was gone and he was still alone.

Levi wasn't sure how long he would stay in Verona, but the possibility that she would show up kept him firmly in place for now. His days were filled with explorations of the city and impromptu concerts, but he felt like he was just treading water. He visited libraries and ducked into bars, trying to find someplace that felt like home.

Italian bar life was the one thing that resembled American culture. Pretty girls were always present, in their best outfits, trying to play coy while also making sure they appeared available. He was sometimes approached by women wanting to show the American a good time. They were nice girls and often beautiful, but never who he wanted.

His nights were spent alone in his apartment, accompanied only by his trusty guitar and an expensive bottle of rum. He penned lyrics and melodies to go with them and drank until the pain in his chest was down to a dull throbbing sensation.

After a few weeks, Levi began to lose faith that Taylor would come. Maybe he'd been too brazen in assuming that she would give up her privileged life and forgive him for his sins. Maybe she'd already moved on.

Eventually, he began exploring outside the city. He took day trips to small villages, visited vineyards, and even toured Venice. No matter where he traveled, Levi was always sure to get back to Verona by sunset. Every day, his elderly friend greeted him. He didn't offer much in the way of conversation, but Levi could tell the man was waiting for something as well.

"Why do you come here?" Levi finally asked.

"To feel closer to heaven. This was *mio amore's* favorite place in Verona."

Levi nodded, understanding that while he waited for his improbable love, this man had already lived, loved, and lost.

"*E voi?*"

"I sent her a message. I'm hoping she'll come," Levi answered.

"Ahh, your Juliet?" The man smiled and placed a gentle hand over Levi's. "We are not so different. We both wait to be reunited."

"What if she doesn't come?" Levi asked, barely able to say those words out loud.

The man's tired eyes looked out over the river. *"Some shall be pardoned, and some punished."*

As much as Levi wanted to dismiss Shakespeare's words, he felt the truth in them. If Taylor never showed, she'd be pardoned from this life with him, and he'd be punished to live with regret. At the age of twenty-two, Levi had experienced love and heartbreak. It had changed him, he could see that now. For some reason, Taylor had been the one to push past his anger and resentment and find the man beneath that mess.

They weren't a perfect match, both of them had faults. And their relationship was far from traditional, but it worked. Beneath the deception and physical connection, they'd discovered a passion that bound them together.

As usual, when the sun was gone, Levi's friend left the bridge without a word.

Christmas Day, Levi woke to no gifts, no well-wishes, and no expectations. Augusto's bakery was closed, so there was no breakfast either. With the large amounts of rum he'd consumed the night before, there was plenty of hurt.

He pried himself out of bed, only to use the bathroom and check on the radiator. Levi winced as the cold air hit him. He turned up the heat and crawled back into bed. When he woke again, the light was low. It seemed as if he'd been asleep for only a few minutes. With one look at the clock across the room, he was sent into a panic.

Levi flew from the bed, tripping over the sheets wrapped around his legs. He hurried through his shower, dressed quickly, and pulled on his coat and scarf before heading out. The streets were mostly quiet, with families tucked into their homes in celebration. Levi glanced at the sky as he moved toward the bridge. It was purple and amber, beautiful and completely cloudless.

When he saw his friend leaning on the bridge wall, his cane clutched in one hand, Levi breathed a sigh of relief. He made his way next to the man and leaned there.

"*Si è quasi troppo tardi,*" he said, his eyes meeting Levi's briefly.

"I know," Levi answered. "I slept in today."

"*Buon Natale.*"

"*Buon Natale,*" Levi repeated. "Happy Christmas."

The two men stood in silence, as always. When there was only the slightest tinge of pink left in the sky, the man turned to Levi and smiled.

"*Addio, amico.*"

Levi watched him wobble away and wondered why he'd actually said good-bye today. Maybe he had no plans of coming back, or maybe he'd grown tired of waiting. Maybe the man had lost hope. Maybe Levi had too.

"What if I told you I took that whole 'deny thy father and refuse thy name' thing seriously?"

Levi spun to find Taylor standing a few feet from him, backlit by the pink sky. Her cheeks were red from the cold, her hair a mess. She was bundled tightly in her coat, waiting for his reaction. He stepped toward her, his hand reaching out to make sure she wasn't a hallucination. His fingers ran over the wool of her coat before fisting the material and pulling her into his arms.

24. suspects and declarations

Levi crushed Taylor in his embrace. She inhaled deeply and wrapped her arms around his waist. Her fingers clawed into his coat, hating the material between them. Levi rocked them back and forth a few times before loosening his grip and tilting his face down to hers. It wasn't the fevered, frantic kiss that she'd imagined a hundred times before. It was soft and slow, a perfect kiss. Their cold lips warmed immediately, their tongues so eager to consume. They kissed until they were too warm in their coats, dizzy and breathless.

He grabbed Taylor's bag and slung it over his shoulder.

"I can't believe you're here," he said, kissing her again.

Taylor smiled at him, unable to find the words to express herself. Levi took her hand and led her from the bridge. They walked for a while, passing closed storefronts and navigating narrow streets. Taylor wanted to take in the sights of the city since her journey had been so rushed to get here, but her eyes never left Levi. Every few minutes, he would stop and turn to kiss her again—sometimes just a peck on the lips, and other times he'd press her against the nearest building until she felt completely overwhelmed. Being back in his presence, she felt claimed and wholly his.

Levi led them up a flight up stairs next to a bakery and unlocked the door. He dropped her bag inside the space and pulled her in. It was a small, simple place with decor that Taylor assumed was left by the last tenants. She spotted his guitar in the corner and smiled, remembering how much she loved to hear him play.

Levi stepped into her line of sight and kissed her again, this time pouring all of his passion and need into it. Taylor worked the buttons of her own coat and slid it from her shoulders before doing the same to Levi's. They were lips and hands and moaning desire as they clawed at each other so desperately.

He led them to the bedroom, where he slowly, reverently peeled Taylor's clothes from her body. His eyes found hers and they gazed at each other with renewed adoration. Taylor's hands gripped the edge of his shirt and she pulled it over his head. Then they were just familiar inked skin and electricity.

Taylor slid her hands into his overgrown hair and urged him down to her. They tumbled onto the bed and she gasped at the sheer pleasure of the heat and weight of his body holding her down. His lips pressed to her skin as he worshipped every part of her anatomy.

When they finally came together, their breaths were stolen by ecstasy. It was heaven and bliss and home. Levi's body trembled against hers, and she wanted to tell him she felt it too. Instead, Taylor placed light kisses over his face as he moved against her, above her, inside her.

"I thought I'd lost you," Levi whispered against her lips. "I was so stupid."

"I'm here," Taylor said. "I'm here."

Levi lowered his forehead to her shoulder. He rested on his elbows and slid his forearms beneath her back. Everything that needed to be said, every bit of pain that lived in their hearts, was burned away by the love that ignited between them.

"Please stay, Taylor," he pleaded.

Taylor wrapped her hands around his shoulders and dug in. Her nails scratched over his skin as she fought to pull him impossibly closer. She chanted his name, realizing that she'd missed the sound of it. The swirl and heat of her release tickled her fingers and toes before plummeting to her center and throwing her off the edge. Levi stilled, his own climax ripping through his body.

There was no sound, no movement, no breaths for those few moments of euphoria. Finally freed from their torturous separation, they held on to each other until their heartbeats returned to resting. Though there was much to be said, they were both exhausted and content, so they surrendered and let sleep take them under.

Taylor woke to the smell of baking bread, sunlight filtering in through gauzy curtains, and the sound of church bells ringing in the distance. It took a moment for her to remember where she was, but when she did, she couldn't help but smile.

She turned to find Levi still asleep. He was lying on his stomach, his tattooed arm disappeared beneath his pillow. The sheets were pushed down low. Taylor's eyes traveled up his frame, taking in all of the skin and muscle that she wanted to taste. His lashes fluttered and she wondered what he dreamt about. The brown-and-red-tinted stubble on his face was about three days' worth. It framed his pouting lips perfectly.

Taylor brushed a lock of hair from his forehead and he stirred, blinking rapidly. The blue-green of his eyes and his bright smile stunned her.

"You're really here," he said. "I thought it was a dream."

Taylor bit her lip and nodded. After five days of traveling on trains and planes, months of heartache, and a long good-bye to her former life, in every possible way, she was really here.

"I'm sorry," he said.

"I know," she answered.

He rolled onto his side and pulled her closer. "How did you get away?"

"You'd be surprised by what you can buy from the geeks at Harvard."

Levi's eyebrows shot up toward his hairline and he smiled at her. "Does your father know about the money?"

"Yeah, he found out a few days after you left. He thinks it was Beau's father, but you're on the list of suspects because of your disappearance. I didn't tell them anything."

Levi leaned over and kissed her forehead. He stared into her blue eyes and felt as though there was something deeper there, something new.

"Are you sure about this? Are you sure you want to leave that life behind?"

Taylor sat up, holding the sheet over her naked body. "I'm sure, Levi. I don't need any of that. I need you."

"What are we going to do with ourselves here?"

"Whatever we want. I could teach English. I'd really like that. You could play gigs. We could travel. Would you want to travel?"

"I'd follow you to hell and back." He ran his fingers up the soft skin of her arm and back down again, still in disbelief. "It won't be easy, Taylor. The money won't last forever and—"

"We were never easy, Levi," Taylor interrupted. "But we're worth it."

Levi pulled her down into his arms and buried his face in her hair.

"God, I missed you," he admitted.

They made love again, feeling as if they'd never be able to get enough, never be satisfied. When they were feeling starved, they shared a shower and got dressed. Levi took her downstairs and introduced her to Gus and his love of pastries. Taylor tasted a sampling of the bakery's best as Levi watched her with adoring eyes. He escorted her around Verona, sharing his most frequented spots and favorite foods with her. He took her to the park where he played and showed her the maze of hedges and pointed out the many sculptures. Just before sunset, he pulled her toward Ponte Pietra.

"Come on, I want you to meet someone," he said.

Levi was excited to introduce them and thank his old friend for the advice that had brought them back together. They leaned against the bridge and awaited his arrival, content to be in each other's arms again. Taylor wrapped herself inside his coat and buried her face in Levi's sweater to escape the cold air.

When the sky turned into its mixed palette of colors, he turned her around and let her look out over the city. She smiled and leaned into his embrace.

"*Juliet is the sun.*"

"It's beautiful."

"I've done some research and I've been thinking. How would you feel about donating some money to the Global Down Syndrome Foundation?"

Taylor looked over her shoulder at him and beamed. "I think you are the sweetest man and I would love if you did that."

"It doesn't make everything right, but it could make a big difference in someone's life. Maybe prevent what happened to Julia from happening again."

He wrapped his arms around her waist and pulled her tight against his chest. He rested his chin on her shoulder and sighed in contentment. From the moment they'd met, there had been an undeniable energy between them. There was no first date, no meeting the parents or dinner at his place. There had been only lust and passion and tempers flaring. Somewhere in the middle of all that, they'd found something so true and unexpected.

"I love you," he said, his breathy words creating a swirl of white vapor that disappeared up into the air above them.

"I love you, too," she answered.

He kissed her neck and smiled down at the water below them.

"I don't know what I'm doing. I might screw up."

Taylor turned her face to his and kissed his lips. "Don't worry, New Guy, you'll get it."

Levi chuckled and then checked the bridge for his friend. Not finding the man, Levi huffed in frustration.

"What's wrong?" Taylor asked.

"I wanted you to meet someone, but he's not here."

"Maybe he just stayed home today," she offered.

"Yeah, maybe," Levi answered, knowing better.

A grateful sadness crept into his chest as he remembered the man's company and kind words. Levi had a feeling that, just like him, the old man had finally been reunited with his Juliet.

My bounty is as boundless as the sea, my love as deep: the more I give to thee the more I have, for both are infinite.